SCOUNDRELS' BARGAIN

Peggy Fielding

For Karen.
Hope you enjoy my naughty story.
Best wishes
Peggy Fielding

Diva—Denton, Texas

COPYRIGHT © 2007 Peggy Fielding
All Rights Reserved

Published by Diva, an imprint of AWOC.COM Publishing, P.O. Box 2819, Denton, TX 76202, USA. No part of this publication may be reproduced, stored in a retrieval system, or transmitted in any form or by any means, electronic, mechanical, recording or otherwise, without the prior written permission of the author(s).

Manufactured in the United States of America

ISBN 13: 978-0-937660-30-0
ISBN-10: 0-937660-30-2

PROLOGUE

Van Buren, Arkansas December 1888

"If it hadn't been for old Lucifer..." That's what Annie always said about the run but she left the rest of it unsaid. She never admitted she had Lucifer only because no one else had wanted him, the same way she'd gotten everything they had in their wagon then. What little they'd had. Nearly everything that the Twigs said was theirs, was something that no one else had wanted.

All the tears, the old man's tears of guilt and drunkeness, her thirteen year old sister's tears of pain and shock, had filled Annie's ears for the first few miles of the long trip. Annie had cried, too, but finally she'd decided she had had her fill of tears. She kept her face turned toward the place where the sun set... to the West. Her felt her vision brighten. She planned to laugh, or at the very least, to smile from now on.

On their journey toward the West, she and her little sister had both laughed when Uncle George had toppled off the wagon seat and sprawled out in a big pile of oak leaves looking for all the world as if he were sleeping in a bed he'd purposely made amongst the brown leftovers from summer.

Annie had put his filled jug of homemade lightning into her yarb sack. With a little piece of rope hitched through the belt loops on his trousers, then tied to the back of the wagon seat, they'd continued their trip and kept him riding along safely until he'd sobered up some.

"Tears never helped nothing," Annie told Ary and George, her own face dry-eyed and determined. "We're going to the Territory. Oklahoma Territory. We ain't never farming for nobody else again. We're gonna have us our own place."

She'd had to roust the two of them into action to get the rickety farm wagon loaded. Looked like the whole thing depended on her. She'd put her medicines in first, and her yarb sack, then she'd had to force Uncle George to help her put the bodies in the back behind the sack of chickens and their other meagre belongings.

That's probably what had gotten him started on the drink that morning... not that he wasn't pretty well sotted out from the early evening before. She'd taken Fleurey's other old mule, too. For the wagon. Had to.

She'd never felt guilty about that. Middle of the night and all. Cousin Fleury, the mule's owner, had long ago had more than his pound of flesh out of the Twig family. No sir, they were deserving of that mule and more.

They'd buried Pap's body several miles outside Van Buren, just before first light. Annie didn't say anything over the body. Didn't want to.

The others couldn't say a word, either. Poor old bastard. So they sang a song, "I'm Bound For The Promised Land," Pap's favorite, and buried him.

Annie reckoned she owed him less than nothing.

He'd been a pretty good father until mama had died but after that, the only thing he had ever given her was her name. Annie Lee Twig. And she'd gotten her name 20 years ago. All she could do was see that the name never dishonored him.

They buried him before he began to smell too much and they left him. A couple of miles down the road they did the same with the other one except they didn't sing any songs. A few hours later they were in Indian Territory and heading for what later became Guthrie, capitol of Oklahoma Territory.

"Gonna make the run, I am," Annie told the others. "I'll let Lucifer do the running with me up on top of him, and the two of you can come trundling along behind in the wagon." She knew getting themselves set in their new life would take awhile but when they opened the run she wanted to be there. When she flew off from the starting line on Lucifer's back, Aramantha and George in the farm wagon could just catch up with her whensoever they could.

At least on the trip to the run area they'd eat. Uncle George had stripped the Fleury's henhouse as best he could, all the while the snot and tears were just pouring out of him.

They'd survive, she knew, what with the bags of cornmeal and flour in the wagon and a few other things she'd put by. Maybe catch some fish. Find some nuts in the woods. Trap some rabbits. Uncle George might even sell a little moonshine along the way... soon as they were far enough away from Van Buren. They had all his crocks and the stuff for the still in the back.

They'd just make out somehow until spring came when she could finally get them a place of their own. A place where they'd be safe.

When they left Arkansas, Annie saw to it that Uncle George and her little sister Aramantha were settled onto the wagon seat and the "borrowed" mule whipped into motion before she finally swung up onto her own spotted mule's back. She set old Lucifer's head toward the new land, then kicked him into racing ahead of the two in the slower mule powered wagon. *She* wanted to be the one who led their tattered parade toward tomorrow.

After they said their goodbyes to Mama up in the Fleury family graveyard, Annie never looked back at the Twig's fallen down cabin nor at the Fleury place nor at any other thing that they were leaving in Arkansas. The *Territory* was her new home and she couldn't wait to get there.

Chapter 1

Oklahoma Territory Summer 1889

"You looking for work?" Annie bent once more to her task while she waited for the man to answer. She lifted the post hole digger, then let it drop, just as she had been doing for the last three hours. As if she were a machine of some kind. She couldn't let a minute of daylight go to waste. Even so, she could talk and work at the same time. This stray drifter just might be the answer to her prayers.

"Maybe." His voice sounded husky, a bit rasping. Probably thirsty, Annie decided. "You hiring, lady?"

"Maybe." Annie looked up at him through her lashes then raised her head to stare openly. She wasn't going to make the same mistake with this one as she had with that old man, Calvin. She'd been so desperate for help that she'd hired the man without really looking at him and then after a couple of days he'd just up and died on her. Annie was still mad as hell about that. Just up and died. Right when she needed him most. And the others she'd "hired" had been all but useless. Nope. She was going to look this one over right and proper.

He was tall, she reckoned. She couldn't remember ever seeing many six footers but he looked to be all of that. Sat his horse easy like. Broad shoulders. No fat on him. In fact his high cheekbones looked as if they were pressing out of his skin. He was probably hungry as well as thirsty but he did have a little meat on his bones. Enough. Not like that scrawny old Calvin.

She pushed an errant strand of blonde hair out of her eyes so she could look up at his face. He stared back with a kind of insolent mischief peering from behind those amber colored eyes.

Might be trouble something whispered inside her head.

The man's skin was dark, leathered by the wind and weathered by the sun. He was pretty old, probably in his thirties, but he didn't look over-the-hill. Maybe thirty-five or so. She was nearly twenty-one, which was plenty old enough, but he was a deal older than she was, she figured. Looked like he had all of his teeth. Probably black hair, his cheeks and his chin were covered with a black stubble.

His clothes were kinda beat up looking but this old boy was no hangdog. He sat in that saddle as if he were sitting in an easy chair, shoulders straight, bony jaw square to the world. The saddle had cost someone a pretty penny once upon a time, too.

"Yeah. I'm looking for a hand." She pushed the strand of cornsilk colored hair back up under Uncle George's old campaign hat which she'd made her own.

"How much you paying?"

"Twenty-one dollars and found."

"Hell. I might as well be back in the army." He jerked the big roan's reins as if to move on.

"I'll give you twenty-one fifty and I'm a good cook." She let her blue eyes make the survey over him and his horse once more. What'd it matter what she promised him? He wasn't going to get any money out of it anyway. "You and your animal will both get fed pretty good here on the Circle Twig."

"Circle what?"

"Circle Twig. I'm Annie Twig. This here is my ranch."

He took off his stained felt hat.

"Pleased to meet you ma'am."

"Call me Annie. If you'll get down and help me finish this last post we'll ride on in together." She watched him slide from the saddle and stride toward the post she'd already had laid out. He smelled some like he needed a bath but nothing really bad. Just man smell. You could tell he wasn't one of those filthy bastards that didn't scrub the nastiness off themselves from one year's end to the next.

Yes. He looked okay. Picked that post right up like it was nothing at all. Deep voice. Kinda good on the ears. Kinda fancy talking too, but what the hell? Maybe he'd do.

He'd have to do. Not many cowpokes drifting way off out here in the Oklahoma Territory looking for work these days. At least none had been trying to hire on to the small spreads like hers.

It was like all the working men had been killed off in the war with the damned Yankees or they were out looking for gold or they'd hired on with Henry Trent's big outfit or something. She brushed aside thoughts of the greedy rancher who was her nearest neighbor. Some said Trent was a *Sooner* but nobody said it in the wealthy man's presence. She'd learned early on that *Sooner* was a fighting word in Oklahoma Territory. No one wanted to be known as a cheat who had slipped across the line into the territory before the starting gun sounded.

Workers sure weren't beating down the doors at the Circle Twig... and she had to have some kind of help, what with Aramantha almost due and with Uncle George acting up and all.

She looked at the cowboy's hands. Good, square, long fingered hands that looked like they knew how to work. He really might do. She hoped so.

When she stood behind him she could see his back muscles bunch and move easily. He had a narrow little rear. Uncle George had once told her he'd never seen a good working man who had a big butt.

"What's your name, cowboy?"

He turned to give her a long slant eyed amber look before he answered.

"They call me Matlock, ma'am. John Wesley Matlock."

"Oh, John Wesley, huh? Your folks was religious?" He settled the post into a more secure position before he answered.

"My mama was." His smile didn't reach the watchful golden eyes. The smile said, "I'm being polite" but the eyes said, "No more questions."

Annie nodded. Fair enough. Out here plenty of people had come to this very spot just to get away from something back East. Things they didn't want to think about or remember. Things they didn't want anyone else to know. In Oklahoma Territory it wasn't polite to question a body too much.

She pulled out a red bandana from the back pocket of Uncle George's old trousers, trousers which she'd adapted to her own use. She wiped her hand before extending it.

"We got us a deal, then, John Wesley?"

"Just plain John or Matt or even Matlock's okay, ma'am. Your choice." His hand clasped hers. "If you cook as well as you say, ma'am, we do indeed have us a deal."

Suddenly Annie was aware that she was a woman. She looked down. Her hand had almost completely disappeared within his big paw. His handshake was a good one. His hand around hers felt warm, strong, honest. What did it matter that he was hiding something? Who wasn't? Shoot, she certainly was.

"If I don't cook, Aramantha will."

"Who's Aramantha?"

"She's my younger sister. Turns fourteen pretty soon. She's a pretty fair cook herself."

A picture of Aramantha's sweet smile rose behind her eyes. *I'll do anything I have to do to keep our little family together,* Annie promised herself for the hundredth time and she looked again at the mental picture of the young girl with the smile, *I'll take care of you, Aramantha, even if that includes lying to this stranger.*

Aramantha's not cooking much these days, she continued the conversation inwardly, but she'll feel better in a month or so and then she can take over the kitchen duty again. Then things'll get easier. Maybe Uncle George can help her. He was always fair-to-middling around a stove when he wasn't so drunk he was falling into the fire.

"Ride on in to the house with me, John. Get you settled. Then we'll get some supper started." She pushed the windblown hair up under the old hat once again as she loosened the hobbles on Lucifer. The wind whipped the hair right back down across her eyes. She smiled up at the stranger. "One thing about this Oklahoma wind... it sure helps build up your appetite. Clean air sweeps out the cobwebs, Uncle George says, makes you listen to your belly. You ready to eat?"

"Yes ma'am." He nodded unsmilingly.

"Call me Annie."

He moved toward her as if to take hold of the mule while she mounted. The animal's ears flattened back against his head. Annie raised one hand in warning.

"Better stay back." She pointed to the laid back ears and the bared yellow teeth behind the animal's snarling black lips. "He don't take to folks much. Likes to bite." She swung onto the mule's back and leaned to pat him on the neck. "'Cept for me. He thinks I belong to him. Don't you, Lucifer?" The bared teeth and rolling eyeballs now seemed to be smiling at all the pats and attention. The ears rolled forward to twitch back and forth with mule-sized happiness.

"I don't believe I've ever seen a spotted mule before, ma'am."

"Yeah, I know. He's kinda special. I got him when my pap's boss told him to take the animal to the knackers." She patted the mule's neck once again. "I saved him from the glue factory and he ran like the very devil that he can be, to get us our place here." She put her heels into the animal's sides. "Old Lucifer, he likes the Oklahoma Territory as good as I do."

John Matlock nodded and pulled his roan into line behind her black and white mount. When they'd ridden a short distance she pointed toward the stand of cottonwoods where the part dugout, part log ranch house sat nestled in amongst the trees just below the rise. Smoke rose from the stone chimney of the portion of the house which was built of logs.

Further up a stand of pin oak trees ambled across a slightly steeper ridge. "We got us a real good place here during the run. 160 acres. Water and trees and a protected spot for the house and everything. On up and over the ridge there, close on to Henry Trent's place, we got us a big cedar break. That's where Uncle George keeps his squeezings." She stared at the trees that embraced the house. "But them cottonwoods is my favorites. I like the sound their leaves make in the wind. And they're pretty trees, too." She nodded as if agreeing with herself.

"I like cottonwoods myself," the man added, "Though some say they're messy when they spread their cotton."

"I even like the cotton." She pointed to the substantial double line of bright leaved trees. "Uncle George always said iffen you see a line of cottonwoods it means a vein of water is running through there and sure enough ... we found good water." The drifter just nodded.

Annie nodded back to show she was polite. "Lucifer and I did the run by ourselves but we can't do everything." For a moment the creak of their mounts' leather fittings and the wind in the brush was all that could be heard. "It's just that I need a little help around the place now and again." She tossed the words into the wind but he heard her.

"I can see that you would." He looked across to the setting sun on the western horizon, a half smile on his lips. "A ranch takes a good deal of work."

"Yeah. A heap of it. Gotta prove it up within five years. Government orders. Either do that or move on, they say."

The reminder that she had to get this place up to snuff or get out made Annie shiver slightly. Five years was a pretty long time. Look what they'd done in a few months! Not even a year yet. With this new man on the job she just might be able to get on into Guthrie and traipse right into that land office. Let them know what she'd been doing. Make sure she and her family could plant their roots permanently, right here. Hadn't Henry Trent's boy, Henry Junior, told her the land office had been painted and finished? Almost the only building in town which wasn't a tent.

Permanent like. That's how the land office looked and that's what she was looking for too. If *they* were staying *she* was staying. Might even have herself a brick house someday.

This was her place. Her's and Aramantha's. And Uncle George, of course. They were putting down roots. Family roots. Oklahoma Territory was their home now and forever. They'd have security here. Never mind what they'd left behind.

"You can put your stuff out in the shed there, John Matlock. There's a pile of hay in the corner." She pointed toward the small pole barn. "We'll get us some quilts and stuff to spread you up a bed out there for the time being. See iffen we can't get you a straw tick made up later. A working man needs a good bed, my Uncle George says."

He nodded silently and turned his horse to follow her signaled directions. She called to him again. He slowed his animal and looked back.

"You can wash up at the water trough out under the trees and then come on inside. We'll eat right soon." He nodded again.

With her chin she indicated the opened leather-hinged door of the log structure. Just outside the door on the sandstone step, a big eyed child stood looking down at them, one hand on the door, one hand on the rounded mound of her stomach. A very pregnant girl child.

"That there's Aramantha," she murmured, "My little sister."

Chapter 2

Annie searched through the small amount of foodstuffs stored on the shelves that she and George had built. Probably enough flour for biscuits, plenty of beans on the stove left over from noon dinner. She picked up a scrawny looking onion. I'll slice it up and put it on the plate with the tomatoes. One thing they had in plenty and that was tomatoes, thank the good Lord... tomatoes and the okra that was coming on real strong. She'd boil up a little okra with a clove of garlic and a dollop of bacon grease.

"You find any melons, Aramantha? We got to feed this fellow up good or he might take it into his mind to just run off 'fore we get any work out of him." She turned and looked questioningly at the younger woman. "We don't want him to disappoint us like old Calvin did. 'Course this one ain't a gonna die on us. But he could run off."

"No melons ripe yet." The younger woman shook her head. "Uncle George said it'd be a day or two more 'fore we'd want to pick any of them." Aramantha walked to the makeshift storage shelves. "He brought in a couple ears of corn." She lifted a flat black metal pan. "We could make up a little corn pudding pretty easy." She tipped the pan to let her older sister see the fresh corn that lay in the pan, newly sliced off the cob.

"Yeah," Annie peered into the offered vessel. "A little flour and sugar and say, ain't we got one egg left from what the Broughtons brung us for getting Grandma Broughton up on her feet again?"

At her sister's nod, Annie tore into the supper preparations. Aramantha adjusted the woodstove to cook the biscuits Annie hadn't yet started and the pudding she herself was making. Annie watched her sister lift the hem of her apron and pat the sweat from her forehead.

"One thing I'm going to get this old boy to do, Aramantha." She kneaded the biscuit dough with both hands buried in the battered dough pan. "I'm going to get him to help us move this stove outside. No reason why we Twigs can't have us a summer kitchen just like rich folks." She grinned at her sweating sister. "Build us an arbor and a table. Place like that'd be handy even in the winter." She looked at the log wall in front of her face as if she could see the projected convenience. "What do you think? Maybe we could even close in the space 'fore winter blows up. Make this here room into a parlor." She nudged the younger girl with her elbow. "Wouldn't it be nice to have us a parlor?"

Aramantha smiled and nodded silently then turned her attention back to the corn pudding. Annie saw her sister wince as she worked.

"Baby kicking you?"

Aramantha nodded again.

"You going to be feeling your old self real soon." Annie slapped the ball of dough out onto the slab of floured marble that had belonged to their mother. Mama's dough slab was the first thing they'd put into the wagon to bring along from Arkansas. "And then we'll both have us a sweet baby to play with." Annie watched her sister anxiously. Aramantha didn't much like to talk about the baby but Annie thought they might as well face the facts. The baby was coming and they were going to have it in their family to care for. Might as well be happy about it.

Aramantha shifted an inch or so away from Annie, as if she didn't want to be touched. She wants me to shut up about the baby, Annie surmised.

"Where's Uncle George?" Annie knew, but she had to ask. "Where is that old coot, now?" Aramantha indicated the side yard with one shoulder. "We better get the old bastard up before the new hand comes in to supper."

Aramantha nodded agreement.

"New man's named John Wesley Matlock," Annie twisted and pressed the glass jar she had saved to use as a biscuit cutter. The lip of the jar sank into the smoothed out dough. "Looks pretty healthy, For sure he ain't going to up and die on us like old Calvin." Each time she pressed the mouth of the jar into the soft white surface she made a quick turn to the left as the jar cut into the dough. Deftly she lifted the uniform cutout rounds of dough to swish them on one side through the lard that Aramantha had ready melted and waiting for her.

"But we gotta keep him happy, Ary. Keep him fed up good... so's he'll stay." She turned the greased side of each biscuit face up in the greased pan and patted the rounds close together until two flat pans were filled.

"John Wesley was a famous man among the religious folks," she said, "Methodist, I think."

She darted another look at her sister who was pouring the mixed pudding into a black iron skillet.

"He don't want to be called John Wesley, though, Sis. Just John... or maybe Matlock."

Aramantha nodded.

Annie searched for something to say.

"Hell, Aramantha. We might start us a Sunday School. Mama was a Baptist, Pap too, while mama was still alive, I guess. Yeah, she was a good Baptist but I bet she wouldn't mind was we to let a Methodist do a little preaching and singing, I reckon." She placed her flat biscuit pans into the oven next to Aramantha's pudding. "Kind of nice to have the neighbors coming in once a month or so. And probably good for baby."

She put one arm across the shorter girl's shoulder. "I bet I could remember some of them Sunday School stories. About Noah and his ark and Jonah and the whale. You remember any, Ary?"

Aramantha shook her head and her eyes filled with tears.

"Why girl, maybe we need to have us a Sunday School just for the baby's mother's benefit. Teach you some of them old stories about Moses in the bulrushes or that there coat of many colors." She pressed her lips gently against Aramantha's sweaty temple. "No need to tear up now. Tell you what I'll do. After supper I'll fix you a New York ladies hairdo. Real grown up. Would you like that, girl?"

She waited for the girl's nod. "That red gold hair of yourn would build up real good into one of them there new pompadours." She pulled at her own cornsilk blonde hair. "I'll cut off some of this stuff and make you a rat, little sister. You'll be right stylish and grown up."

The younger woman's blue eyes changed from fright to worry. "You surely ain't going to cut your hair, Annie."

"I got to honey," Annie explained. "Part of it anyways. It's driving me crazy. Always in my eyes. All I do with it now is just knot it up on top of my head." She pulled long platinum strands forward between them. "I'm just gonna cut off a lot of it here in front and then that old wind can't catch it and blow it in my eyes every second of the day." She nodded her satisfaction with the idea before she bent and looked into her sister's blue eyes. "Everything gonna be all right, little sister. You'll see. I'll fix you a little soursop tea when we're working on your hair. That'll perk you up."

Aramantha's voice choked on her murmured words.

"I'm afraid, Annie. I'm real afraid." She pressed both hands against her swelling front.

Standing at the water trough set under the largest of the pin oak trees, John Wesley Matlock could see the whole of the tiny house below. The wind slowed and the smoke from the chimmney drifted in a lazy spiral toward the sky. He could feel his mouth begin to water from the fragrance of cooking that wafted from below. He hadn't eaten since yesterday sometime. He swallowed and tried to ignore the rumbling from his stomach that disturbed the quiet of the little pole barn.

From the looks of things this was what you might call a "poor boy" operation all the way... except it looked like it was "poor girl" rather than boy. Kind of strange to figure. Looked like sweat and spit and a coil of baling wire was what was holding the little spread together. Probably mostly her sweat. If there was money here they weren't letting it show.

When Annie Twig strode from the backdoor and marched briskly toward the well to pull up the long cylinder of water to release into a wooden bucket, he narrowed his eyes.

Beautiful woman. The tattered pants and shirt couldn't hide the lush curves of her rounded breasts and her tiny waist. Hair like pale golden silk. Eyes as blue as the Caribbean slanted into a high cheekboned face. She looked to be a blue blooded aristocrat down to her long, slim feet and hands. She was burned by the sun more than "ladies" were supposed to be but he liked the rosy gold color of her flawless skin and the tiny dotting of freckles that crossed her uptilted nose.

He shrugged. She was a woman who had everything God intended a woman to have. Good teeth, natural grace, and beauty aplenty. Probably smart as a whip even if she hadn't any education. All in all, a very attractive female package... until she opened her mouth.

"Too bad." He spoke aloud and startled himself. "Just remember," he muttered. "This particular woman is off limits." He finished washing his face and hands and arms. He was tempted to take off all his clothes and flop himself into the horse trough to get the trail grime off every part of him. Later, he thought, maybe after dark.

He strode to the tiny shed and placed his saddle across the center rail. He nodded at the ordinary looking mule in the other side of the barn but he kept well away from the spotted devil she'd called Lucifer.

Both animals munched on grain he'd thrown in to them at the same time he'd fed his own mare. The two mules didn't seem to mind his mare sharing their quarters. He remembered that his old sergeant had once told him that mules would willingly follow horses because all horses seemed to them to be the "mothers" they remembered.

He hung his saddle bags on a protruding wooden peg. His hand dipped into the nearest bag and he felt for the metal edge. Yes. It was still there, all right. The other necessaries as well.

He turned and looked again at the scene below him with narrowed eyes. He was pretty sure he was in the right place and that he probably had the right people. No hurry though. He'd make sure. He'd already made sure this woman wanted his help, whoever she was, and he'd have plenty of time to look things over. He didn't mind working while he did it.

What he couldn't figure was the child. Pregnant and still a kid herself. And he hadn't yet seen the man Miss Annie Twig had called "Uncle George." Hadn't heard about him from any one of the Little Rock people. Might be some complications there right enough. Time would tell. No need to worry about that for awhile, anyway. Just now he felt like he could eat a cow who was still walking.

He ran his fingers through his dampened black hair to push it back off his face then ambled down the path toward the little log structure. As he walked the pushed back curls tumbled once again into their usual wild disarray. Something smelled bad about this whole operation but it sure wasn't the food.

Just as she had promised, Miss Annie's cooking smelled mighty tasty.

Chapter 3

"Oh, yeah, me and Ary and Uncle George here," At Annie's mention of his name the slim gray haired man seated across from John stretched a smile across his toothless mouth, his eyes so unfocused they almost seemed to roll in their sockets. "We all come to the territory from Arkansas. And glad to be here."

Annie reached to break a biscuit open and lay the two steaming halves flat on her uncle's plate. Afterward Ary dipped several spoons of the gravy over the hot bread. Annie shook a few fragments of black pepper onto the gravy before she put a knife into the old man's hand.

"Eat up, Uncle George, else I'm gonna hide your jug." She raised her voice as if speaking to a person who couldn't hear well or perhaps as if to a recalcitrant child. John studied the old man who, at the mention of the jug looked around the room as if to find the beloved object. Nothing threatening from this poor old soul, John thought. Old Uncle here didn't even know where he was.

He watched Ary direct the old man's attention to the bread and gravy once again. She whispered something to him and he began to cut the bread to lift a piece to his mouth. The pregnant youngster nodded and put three pods of the boiled okra onto the plate beside the gravy laden biscuit. As the old man gummed his supper John turned his attention to the shelves on the wall next to the stove. Everything seemed neatly and carefully placed for use. He could identify the old man's shaving utensils, a bowl of nails, *a row* of homemade candles, a few pots and pans and a chipped blue platter and a graniteware bowl as well as tin pans and cups. One quart jar seemed to hold either sugar or salt. Crockery jars and several jugs seemed to hold the place of honor on the highest shelf. There were several bulky cloth bags and two closed wooden boxes. A string of garlic and a net bag almost empty of potatoes hung on the wall next to the shelves. He didn't see much that looked like food but obviously this was the pantry area as well as storage.

He looked up in surprise to see Annie Twig's bright blue gaze studying him in turn.

"I may take it away from him, anyway."

She made the announcement to John as if he'd asked her something. "Take what away?" The crisp outside, flaky inside, biscuits were so good that John found himself holding one in each hand. He had to smile at his own greed. He put one of the heavenly buttered circles back onto his plate. "Miss Twig, you were most assuredly right when you said you would feed me well. These are the best biscuits I've ever eaten in my whole life."

"Call me Annie." She twisted her chair around and used a flour sack dish towel to reach the second pan of biscuits so she could turn them out onto the almost empty bread platter. "I was talking about Uncle George's jug of fermented flame. I may pour it out even if he does eat. He done had enough to drink for now, I reckon."

At that threat the old man whined like a pup who wanted to come in from the cold.

"I didn't say I was gonna do it, Uncle George, just *thinking* about it. Now you eat ever bite, you crazy old bastard." John could hear real affection in her voice.

Ary placed her hand on the old man's hand and patted it as if to reassure him in his distress.

"Does he drink all the time?"

Annie's glance was cool. She didn't answer his question but she gave him a searching look, as if to say, "What makes you think you can ask questions about my family?"

John nodded understanding and took another hot biscuit. He tried to make the gravy and the bread come out even but the new biscuit forced him to take another spoonful of the gravy. He sighed with satisfaction.

"Glad you like the food, John Wesley Matlock." She looked at her little sister. "I'll just dish out the pudding onto our plates from here so you don't have to get up." The younger girl nodded without answering.

"Just call me John."

"Just call me Annie."

The blue gaze again locked with his own. He could count the tiny freckles the sun had laid across her nose and cheeks. Her upper lip made a softly lifted pink vee above the slightly darker-rose of her sensuously pouty lower lip. He wondered how it would feel to put his own mouth against hers. He scraped his chair back suddenly.

"Something wrong, John? Don't you want some of this here pudding?"

Get hold of yourself boy, he warned inwardly. You aren't here for your own pleasure. How her mouth looks when she smiles is none of your affair.

He nodded and pulled his chair back to the table. "I believe I would like some of that corn pudding. It looks as delicious as the rest of the meal was."

"Our little Ary made it herself." He could hear the pride in Annie's voice. "She's a right good cook."

"Good supper." The old man spoke for the first time. Both young women turned their smiling faces toward him as if he were a child who had just done something very intelligent.

"That's good, Uncle George." Annie plopped a small spoonful of the pudding onto the old man's plate. "Try some of Ary's pudding. I'll pour you a cup of tea." She rose and lifted tin cups from the wall shelf and placed them on the stove to pour the fragrant liquid into each one. She looked apologetically at John when she handed him his cup. "Not real tea, of course. Just something I made up myself from a few yarbs, but we like it with our supper anyways." The blue eyes looked anxious.

John sipped the hot brew.

"I don't know what it is but it's the perfect ending to a perfect meal, Annie." She lowered her gaze.

"Thank you, John."

Lord above, what was wrong with her? Letting this drifter get under her skin. Hell, he wasn't no different than the rest of them dadburned cowpokes. 'Cept he wasn't dying. What did she care what he thought about her, Uncle George or her "made-up" tea? He was lucky to be putting some kind of food, any kind of food, into that there flat stomach of his.

She smiled as she sipped the tea. He sure did put them biscuits and gravy away... after he got through eating almost a whole pan of biscuits and butter. Ate the last of the butter the Broughtons had left. Maybe some of the other neighbors would need her help so's she could take in some more eggs and milk and butter.

She looked down at the hand in her lap. It still felt as though bolts of lightning had touched her in just that spot where her hand had brushed his. Dang. What was wrong with her? She rubbed one hand over the other to erase the memory of the man's touch.

She stared into the middle distance. She had to keep him around. Some way she was going to have to feed this old boy. She'd rake up something.

They'd get along even if she didn't get any extra work with the folks around the area. They always had. Maybe Uncle George could shoot them a jack rabbit. That'd be good. A person could make a lot of meals with a big jack.

"More tea?" She didn't look directly at him. Everytime he looked at her his brown gold eyes seemed to see right inside her. She poured for everyone then returned to her chair. She loosened her worn leather belt and leaned back with a grunt.

"Evenings sure is nice. Your work's all through for the day. Everyone at the table is full of food and feeling happy." She smiled at Uncle George and the old man nodded and smiled. He was ready to pull out of it now, she thought.

"You gonna feel like putting your shoulder to it tomorrow, Uncle George?"

He nodded again and looked down. He would be too shaky to work outside she thought. Plenty to do inside, helping Ary, anyway.

"You and Ary can get some of the work done around the house here, I reckon." She looked about her. Pride filled her chest. "We sure got us a good little place here. Gonna make us a summer kitchen, Uncle." She smiled at her sister. "How does that sound to you?" He nodded a third time.

"Got this old boy, John Matlock working with us now, Uncle George." She didn't look at John's eyes but at his hands. His fingers curved around the handle of the tin cup. Long, powerful looking fingers. She felt herself staring. Those fingers could put a shock through a person iffen they touched her. She pulled her gaze from his hand. Could a man's hand be beautiful? Shoot. Bunch of silliness. Better get herself on down to business.

"It's awful hot right now, John. After breakfast in the morning, soon as the stove cools some, let's move that thing outside and make us a summer kitchen."

"Arbor for shade?"

Her turn to nod. Still she didn't look at him.

"Ary can't go on working in this heat. She's gonna have us a baby, you know."

"Yes. I had noticed..." He let the word end with a sort of questioning sound. Trying to learn something. Annie knew that. He was curious all right. But he didn't need to know nothing. It wasn't any of his business, anyway.

She'd already told all the neighbors around them that Ary had run off and married a soldier boy and he got hisself killed just before they come on the run. No one questioned that. No one but old Henry Trent's boy. Junior Trent was the onliest one who kept on asking questions about things. Him being just a big old gawky pup of a boy, them questions was easy to handle. She'd told Ary just to say, "I don't know," whenever Junior asked her something.

Ary stood and began picking up the plates and cups.

"Let them things lay, little sister. I can redd up this here kitchen in five minutes. You lean back and relax yourself." She gave her uncle a searching look. "You feel like your fiddle, Uncle George?"

The old man smiled and nodded. Annie stood and smiled back.

"You three wait right here whilst I go get them things for the old man. We got us a treat coming." She ducked into the low door that led into the dugout and returned almost immediately with a violin and a bow.

"Here you are, sir. Let's us hear something lively."

Scoundrels' Bargain

George fooled with the instrument for a few seconds then lifted it to his chin and whirled out a fast chorus of *Three Jolly Young Tramps,* smiling all the while.

After their applause died down he fiddled through *Turkey in the Straw.*

"Do us some hymns now, Uncle," Annie cut her eyes toward the stranger. "Maybe we could get John here to sing some." Let him pay for his supper that way, she reasoned. He really hadn't done no work to speak of with just that one post. Wasn't right to eat like a hungry hog and not pay for it some way. No indeed. No man, not even a real good looking one like this one, was going to get away with getting something for nothing around here. No sir. Not on the Circle Twig. She'd see to that.

"With a name like yours you probably know all them church songs. How about letting us hear you sing one of them old time tunes? What's your choice?"

The stranger looked at her with such honest amazement written on his face that it was all she could do to keep from laughing out loud. He hadn't expected that there kind of a request, sure enough. But she'd see he did it, right enough. Iffen it turned out that when he sang he brayed like a donkey maybe he could quote some verse or something, instead of singing. He'd just have to learn to do his part, that's all. Sing for his supper... or dance, or say a piece. Everyone has to contribute.

"Come on Ary. Let's you and me sing mama's favorite." She nodded at Uncle George and he played a few bars. The two young women leaned toward each other across the littered table and sang in perfect harmony.

"I come to the Garden alone, while the dew is still on the roses. And the voice I hear, falling on mine ear, the Son of God discloses."

At the chorus the two of them lowered their voices to just above a whisper.

"And he walks with me and he talks with me and he tells me I am his own. And the joy we share, as we tarry there, none other, has ever, known."

The room was silent for a long moment.

"Annie, Miss Aramantha, you are magnificent singers. You sang that in perfect two part harmony. And you're a true musician, George. The churches around here don't go begging, I would imagine, with three such talents available."

"No churches."

Again he looked surprised.

"Wasn't nothing here before we came 'cept the Indians and a few buffalo." She turned her cup in a slow circle against the scrubbed wood table top. "Maybe we could start us a church or something." She nodded to her own thoughts. "Yeah, a church might really be good.

By the time four more years pass we got to have this place looking like civilized folks live here." She braved looking into the enticing amber brown gaze once again.

"That's why we was so glad to have you here a working for us. Help us prove up our place so's we can all live here forever." She forced herself to break the eye contact. She looked at the dishes as she began to gather them from the tabletop. Ary hummed a tune that the old man played softly.

Annie spoke above the pleasant sounds. "Now you see why I need another strong back on the place?"

"*Another* strong back?"

"Besides my own, I mean."

He did see. It had been a long time since he'd sung in public and he couldn't believe he was doing such a fool thing now, but he guessed he could probably make it through "Shall We Gather At The River?" And he did. And they all three clapped for him.

He'd watched Annie roll out a bedroll for her Uncle George on the dirt floor of the kitchen. The old man slipped into the pallet with a sigh and was asleep before John could thank Annie for the good food and the entertainment. She was a caring woman. There was no question of that. Maybe she just cared for people who were her family?

Later, in the barn with the bundle of quilts Annie had shoved into his arms as he left, he shook his head in amazement. Had he really taken part in a "hymn singing?" If his friends back home ever heard about this evening's "performance" he'd be a ruined man. He smiled and spread his bed on the waiting hay. It took him a long to time to get to sleep. Thoughts of blue, blue eyes, masses of pale golden hair and a radiant laughing face kept him wide awake for a long, long time.

After Annie used Uncle George's straight razor to cut off chunks from the front of her golden hair, she laid the pale strands across the shelf she'd put up in their bedroom for Aramantha's "pretties." She weighted the blonde hair down with her Mama's Bible. Aramantha's "rat" could wait.

They'd all been too tired for the new hairdo tonight, what with Uncle George heading back into the land of the living and all. Plenty of time. Thinking about getting her hair fixed would give Ary something to look forward to. Maybe get her mind off her fears.

Annie crawled onto the straw tick laid across the bed she and George had built into the side of the room with some cottonwood posts and the rope they'd brought from Arkansas just a few months before. She was mighty proud of that bed. She patted the post nearest her head. It was sure some comfortable place to crawl into after a hard day's work. Best bed she and Aramantha had *ever* had. That was for sure.

She stretched arms and legs and took a deep breath of the spicy air from the drying plants strung overhead. She closed her eyes then turned over, then over again. She tried to keep from tossing back and forth in the space she shared with Aramantha. Her poor little sister needed her sleep. She took a deep breath. It was as if there was nothing to breathe.

Like the room smelled kinda dead. Musty. And it usually smelled so good in here. It was like they wasn't no air in the room. For some reason it was gonna be mighty hard to get to sleep tonight. She turned once again and arranged the pillow more comfortably under her cheek and neck.

She couldn't think what in the world was wrong with her. The tick mattress seemed so noisy under her fidgeting turns. Usually she just had to lay her head back on her pillow and she was dead-and-gone sound asleep. Unless there happened to be a mouse or maybe a centipede in the bed. And there wasn't nothing like that in with them tonight. It was her own head keeping her awake and she knew it well enough.

Tonight, the searching amber brown eyes, the powerful touch of his hands and the square jaw of a stranger kept her company in the darkness of the dugout bedroom. Her ears could still hear the pleasureably low sound of his bass voice singing... "Shall we gather at the river? The beautiful, the beautiful river..."

"Ah, Annie," she remonstrated with herself, "He ain't nothing but another drifter just like them four others you hired on before him." She flopped over onto her stomach. "You ain't never laid around awake at night and thought of them there others. 'Cept'n how mad you was at that old Calvin for dying. Close them eyes and go to sleep, girl. Plenty to do tomorrow."

But it was a long time before she slid off into her dreams. Dreams that disturbed her. Dreams that made her smile in her sleep.

In the pole barn, the slow even breathing of the horse and the two mules were finally joined by the gentle sawing sounds of a tired man's snores.

Everyone on the Circle Twig had found sleep and so they missed the light sound of the beginning rains. Water dropping from the skies was a surprising sound in the summer in Oklahoma Territory.

Chapter 4

Rain during the night had cleared most of the red dust from the air. The sky glowed a clean bright blue behind the morning sun. Annie looked out at the beautiful morning and smiled before she spoke about the cold biscuits, sliced tomatoes and cold herb tea which she'd decided was enough to get them started for the day.

"I didn't want to fire up the stove this morning. Iffen we was to try to dismantle hot iron we'd likely get mighty little done for several hours so we're gonna be eating camp food." Annie flushed as she made her explanation and then looked over her shoulder at John Matlock, who had already taken his place at the table.

His hair was wet. A little long but not overly so. Mayhaps she'd cut it for him sometime. For a common drover he looked awful clean. He smelled a sight better too, than when he'd first rode up. He smelled sweet and spicy. Like some kind of fancy, good smelling soap. Must have bathed in the horse trough before coming down to eat, she decided. He had on puredee clean clothes. She quickly turned her glance back to the food on the table. He was staring at her in an awful funny way.

"I promise this is the last pick up meal you'll have to eat on the Circle Twig... lessen we're really out on the trail somewheres. I do know a man needs hot vittles." She handed a cold biscuit-tomato sandwich to her uncle. "Right, Uncle George?"

"Right you are, Annie Lee." Her uncle's words were muffled by the bite of sandwich he'd taken. "Could I have a little of that there pepper sauce?"

"Your middle name is 'Lee'?" John made his own sandwich from the plate of biscuits and the platter of ripe slices of tomatoes, both of which sat in the middle of the table. "Annie Lee. Lee's a pretty name. Famous too." He continued to stare at her.

"Call me Annie." The words sounded shorter than she'd meant them to be. This cowboy got her goat, somehow. Everything he said. Everything he did. Looking a whole lot cleaner and prettier than a man ought. Staring at her and all.

"Uh huh, here we are, Uncle George." She put one hand on each side of the crockery jar of fiery peppers put up in vinegar, then lifted it from its usual place on the shelf. She held the lidded jar above the table. "This here was Mama's." With her eyes she traced the blue line that decorated the lip of the jar before she placed it in front of the old man. When she looked up John was staring again. "Why you looking at me so hard this morning?"

"My God, Annie..." He had the grace to color just a bit. "I'm sorry, but you look... what happened? To your hair, I mean?" He looked at the top of her head then at her face. "Your beautiful hair... Yesterday it was the most gorgeous silken..."

Oh. Her hair. Annie laughed.

"I'm sorry. I done forgot to say anything about it. I cut off the front and sides last night. We're gonna use it to make a rat for Aramantha's new hairdo." She ran her hand over the inch long hair. "Feels kinda strange but, for sure, it'll be a whole lot easier out in the wind."

"God, I'm so glad you didn't cut it all. You really have no idea how lovely your long silvery hair was, have you?" He shook his head, still staring at her. "You don't even realize that you're a truly beautiful woman, do you Miss Annie Twig?"

Annie took a deep breath. And almost forgot to let it out. There was a stunned silence between them for a long moment. They stared at each other. Uncle George continued to munch at his biscuit and tomato and pepper sauce in oblivious silence.

Annie lowered her gaze first and laughed self consciously.

"Hunger must be affecting your brain, John Wesley." Her hand smoothed across her patched and worn shirt. "I reckon this here shirt that used to belong to Uncle George is about the closest I can come to beauty."

He shook his head once again.

"You think of yourself as some kind of beast of burden, some kind of working animal." He crunched down on the biscuit he held in his hand as he kept her imprisoned in his brown gold gaze. He chewed and ruminated. "You're a true beauty, Annie Lee Twig. A true beauty would still look beautiful if she were wearing a gunny sack for a dress. Beauty has nothing to do with clothing."

"Beauty? Huh. I reckon little Aramantha is the beauty in our household." Annie stood. "I told her to rest up this morning." She felt her face flame. He must be making fun of her. Fury rose in her. Better get this old boy to moving. Get what she could out of him before he learned the truth about his job. She took a deep breath. She didn't need to hear no more of his smart alec remarks about her looks.

"Well, John, you and me is the ones going to be making a mess around here anyway. Ary can do without breathing in all that soot today, I reckon."

John watched the old man sprinkle the hot pepper sauce onto his next tomato sandwich. He decided to try the combination. *When in Rome do as the Romans do,* he told himself. His first bite was tart, strange, peppery... but good. Maybe they had something. He fixed another pepper sauce-tomato-biscuit-round. Pretty good.

Wait until he told the folks back home that the people in the Territory ate hot pepper sauce for breakfast. No one would believe him. He stopped his fifth biscuit on its way to his mouth, realizing that the woman's blue eyes were staring at him again.

"What is it?" He put the tomato-pepper-sauce biscuit down and leaned toward her. She seemed angry. The short silver blonde hair feathered around her pink flushed face. A bit strange looking, he thought, but it still looked quite pretty in an unusual way.

"You dang sure got you one good appetite this morning." He thought he could detect a quick glint of something in her eyes, then it was gone. Despair? Fear? Anger? He couldn't tell. "Whenever you think you can quit stuffing your face we'll get on to taking this stove down."

He nodded and ate the last biscuit in two bites, swigged down the cup of room temperature tea and stood to show he was finished.

"I'm ready when you are."

He followed her when she stepped outside to look over the area she'd chosen for the summer kitchen.

"Hadn't we better build some sort of shelter before we move the stove out?" John asked. "I noticed it rained a little last night." He looked at the sky to the west. "Some clouds out there. It may rain again today."

"Henry Trent told me it don't rain much around here at this time of year but I guess it can't hurt to start with that." She ran her hand across the front of her newly short hair. "Old Trent is a liar, of course. You got to consider that." She let her own gaze roam the sky. "But you're right. Shelter sounds like a good idea. What'd you have in mind?"

"Well, I thought, if we could bring down a couple of saplings we could set them at the two corners, string some boards between them." He strode to each outside point to show where the tree trunks would stand, then he sketched all the items with his hands as he talked. "After that we could frame a shed roof and cover it with shakes or arbor or something."

Her blue eyes followed his every move. He felt himself stumbling on a word because of the intensity of her gaze. The short silvery blonde strands around her face trembled in the wind so the cropped hair made her look as if she were wearing a halo. He stepped one pace toward her. Should he say something? Could the Fleury's be wrong about these people? Better wait. Time would tell.

"That would put some protection over the stove and the person cooking..." His voice trailed off. He'd have to get hold of himself. "It will keep the cook dry and the stove..." There. He'd lost it again. He needed to concentrate. This was a job, nothing more, nothing less. He couldn't let himself be drawn into starting some kind of entanglement here. He was investigating this family. That's all.

As if it had a mind of its own his foot moved another half step closer to her. He watched her eyes widen just a fraction.

At the periphery of his vision he became aware of a cloud of dust on the trail. A youngster's voice sounded across the prairie and then they could see a child riding a brown pony racing toward them.

"Annie. Annie Twig. Come quick."

The brown pony stumbled, caught itself and came straight on. Annie ran toward the moving messenger.

"Mama's having the baby. She says she needs you and Grandma's ailing and wants some of that painkiller. She been having trouble in her back again."

Annie reached for the reins when the boy skidded the animal to a stop and slipped to the ground.

"Grandma can't help Mama. You gotta come Miz Annie."

Annie nodded and before she turned to go in the house she looked at John once again. "I'll just get my yarb sack and I'll be right with you, Billy Ray." John stepped even closer. She backed away an inch or two. "You go on ahead with the summer kitchen, John. Whatever you want to do." Her voice sounded flustered to her own ears. Like she didn't know what she was saying. "Maybe Uncle George can help you some." She backed another inch toward the door. He followed.

"You treat sick people?"

She nodded.

"You do that a lot?"

"Mama taught me some about curing. I learned some from my Great Aunt Thesalonia and a little bit from Uncle Cornish and some on my own." She swallowed, still staring into his eyes. "Some folks hereabouts calls me a "granny woman." I mostly know about using yarbs and such."

"Yarbs?"

"You know, plants that grow wild or that you grow in your garden? I fix up Billy Ray's Grandma with poke root that's been cured in a jar of George's alcohol. Helps her reumatiz real good. We ain't had much luck with a garden so far, so mostly I do my medicine with growing stuff I find out on the prairie. Mama taught me which ones was for what sickness as much as she could... like bringing in a certain kind of milkweed for easing childbirth." She gestured at Billy Ray. "I use that one a lot. Aunt Thesalonia Fleury taught me about how to make curing salves with the dried leaves and such."

"Oh. *Herbs.*" He smiled. "I wondered what a 'yarb' was when we drank our tea last night."

* * *

She flushed again and lowered her gaze from his. Had her mama told her the wrong name for all that there stuff she gathered to treat people? *Herbs*, was it? She filed the correct word in her head.

"I guess 'yarbs' is just a downhome Arkansas word for 'herbs.'" She forced a laugh, then kicked herself mentally. What do I care what this here worthless drifter is thinking?

"Annie. Hurry!" Billy Ray Broughton inserted himself into their exchange.

She looked down. "Keep your shirttail in, Billy Ray. Your mama's gonna be all right and so's your grandmother."

Annie yanked herself away from her hired hand's gold sparked, brown eyed surveillance and stormed into the house to pick up her sack of yarbs... uh, herbs. She grabbed a clean apron and a wooden box that had its own special place on the kitchen shelf.

She was pretty sure she knew what Billy Ray's mama would need... and what Grandma Broughton would accept. They were pretty good patients... always paid something, too. One of these days she would have enough saved up to put wooden floors into the place. Think of that! No more dirt floors.

At the pole barn she whispered into Lucifer's ear as she saddled him. The stranger stood watching. Apparently while she had been in the house he had tried to help her by getting Lucifer harnessed but the wily mule had kept well out of the cowboy's way.

"Old Lucifer is a pretty fast runner. He can beat lots of horses I seen." Annie tried to keep her face straight. She knew John hadn't been able to lay one hand on the big old four-legged devil. But a smile would be wrong. It wouldn't do to hurt the man's feelings anyway. She had to keep him happy... keep him working here just as long as she could before he went on his way like all the others had. 'Cept'n for poor old dead Calvin, of course.

She looked down at him before she rode away.

"You just go on with getting that shed up, John Wesley. I don't know when I'll be back. Aramantha can rustle up something for you two old boys to eat."

"Annie!" Billy Ray Broughton's voice carried up to where they lingered just outside the barn. "Annie. Mama said to come on."

"See you later." She touched the mule's spotted haunches with her bootheels. "Let's go, Lucifer." She carried away with herself the feel of that last look from the bright brown gold gaze of the man. He was the kind of person who was always looking straight through a body with them bronze colored eyes, she thought. When them eyes locked onto you it was like he was telling you something important without saying nothing out loud.

On the trail toward the Broughton dugout she asked herself the question that had been rummaging around and through her mind. She let Lucifer go full out like he liked to do and she just came along for the ride. When he got too obstreperous she had to rein him in a little. She needed some time to think.

The Broughton place wasn't far so she wasn't going to have too much time to muse on the problem. She'd like to wait until later, when she had a moment of privacy and some time. But she couldn't seem to help herself.

With nothing but the jangling of Lucifer's harness to keep her company her mind just wandered onto the hired man. Even though she didn't want to think about the new hand's words right now it was as if she couldn't make her mind quit, as if she just had to let herself go over and over everything that had happened. The whole thing kind of made her belly feel funny.

John Wesley Matlock. Good name. He'd scared her just a little out there in the yard. And even there in the house. for all that it was just a short time he'd been with them it was as though he was always watching her. And he'd moved right up to her. A couple more inches and he would have been right up in her face.

Had he been agoing to try to kiss her? He'd sure looked as though that was what he'd had in mind. When he wasn't looking into her eyes he'd been looking at her mouth. What kissing she'd ever done or had done to her wasn't all that wonderful. But maybe his kiss wouldn't be so bad even if it wasn't wonderful?

She made a face of distaste and curled her hand into Lucifer's mane to remind him she was aboard and still running the show. Surely not wonderful at all, but this old boy kinda drew her, made her want to pay real close attention to him somehow. Different from any of them other dudes she had hired.

She ought to be putting her mind on Mary Broughton's apprenticeship. The girl was doing real well for a seventeen year old. Maybe the girl had sent for her just because she felt helpless when it came to working with her own Mother and Grandmother.

Even though Mary was getting awful good at the healing trade, maybe that was the problem. Mary was afraid. Trying to cure family, or see to the birthing of family babies was scary sometimes. Annie knew that. She got a little twinge of fear whenever she thought of bringing Aramantha's baby into the world. She couldn't let Ary know that, of course. Ary was too scared herself.

And there was Uncle George. She wished she could do something about curing his drinking but she supposed she should be happy for the fact that he wasn't drunk except in monthly bouts. Lots of days and weeks he was real sober and then he was good help around the place. And they sorely needed the dollars and foodstuffs and other things he traded for his moonshine. Just last month he'd traded for a beautiful quilt that she and Ary put on their good bed. Looked real nice, too. Yeah, Uncle George more than carried his share of the weight of looking after their family.

Not that the old man could compete with John Matlock in the strength and skill department, even when sober. Too little, too many years behind him and too long on the jug. But old George was real good at cooking and such stuff. She didn't know what she and Aramantha would do without their sweet little old Uncle. He was sure hell on the fiddling and singing. They needed some fun as well as work at the Circle Twig and George could sure supply that. George just couldn't measure up to John Wesley Matlock insofar as real labor was concerned.

The thought of John threw her instantly back into the moment when she'd thought he was trying to kiss her. And that sweet talk. Kinda nice to hear. He was a man she'd have to be real careful of. He wasn't like all them other men she'd hired to help her prove up the place. Should she thank God for that or curse her fate? She didn't know. She'd try to be cautious in her dealings with him.

Shoot. She coughed slightly because of breathing Billy Ray's dust. She slowed Lucifer so she could breathe better. All that talk about her being beautiful.

Annie couldn't decide what she would have done had the drifter really tried to put his lips on hers. His lips were perfect. Like lips that were made by an artist. Kind of like the lips on the statue of that there confederate soldier from the War Between the States. Pap had said it was made out of bronze. She'd first saw the statue over in Ft. Smith when she was just a little girl and Ary was still almost a baby. She remembered she'd thought then she'd like to feel them smooth, carved, real looking lips.

Pap had been drunk that day and she'd had more than a plenty of time to stand around and look up at that soldier boy's face. She'd had the time to climb up on the pedestal and run her hands over the metal monument as high as she could reach. It had felt cold to her fingers. But the sculptured lips hadn't looked cold. Not at all. She would have climbed clear up to his beautiful brownish green metal face and looked that bronze soldier boy in the eye, but Ary was below her there, just a standing on the ground a crying for her to come down, so she did.

She thought again of John's face. His eyes. His sculptured lips as he had stepped closer to her. She bet his lips weren't cold. Maybe she wouldn't have let him do it... then again, maybe she would have... maybe she would even have kissed him back.

Maybe.

Chapter 5

On the third morning after she'd left home, Annie said goodbye to the Broughtons; the now well-as-could-be-expected Grandmother, the happy mother, the new born infant, the proud father and all the rest of the family. She'd had a hell of a time convincing the new mama that she couldn't name the little girl Flowery. Ugh. Huh uh. No. Too much like you-know-what. She could not have stood to have a neighbor girl named something that made her sick every time she heard it. Too much like Fleury. They'd finally settled on Blossom.

When she got on the trail toward home she carried a part of her fee for birthing little Miss Blossom Broughton in her arms. Another part of her pay lay against each side of Lucifer's neck in the two cloth totes she had tied to her saddle horn. And she had three coins in her pocket. She didn't have to urge Lucifer to head on home, he clanked and galloped all the way. Annie understood how he felt. She felt even more eager to get home than she usually did. She brushed aside the thought of golden eyes looking at her. *Hell, just anxious to see the new summer kitchen,* she told herself.

She just hoped that Aramantha or Uncle George had been able to find something or other to stir up three times a day, something for the man to eat. She thought about the new hand for a moment. For just that second she felt as if she could see John Matlock's amber colored eyes looking at her. She looked down the road toward home and blinked Lucifer's trail dust from her .own eyes. She hoped the hired man was still there.

For a second she felt a twinge of guilt. The fellow had looked to be a hard worker and she needed him even if she would have to cheat him on the money come payday time. The only way she was going to be able to keep that old boy working to get the summer kitchen put together and to help finish the fencing was through feeding him extra good vittles.

If he was somehow able to sit down to three square meals a day she was pretty sure he'd keep working. Every day. Maybe George had killed them a rabbit while she'd been gone.

She laughed and hoisted her payment. Maybe tonight before they ate supper she'd go put on one of her two dresses. The brown flowered one was the one Ary had worn some before she got too big in the middle. They'd just pinned up the hem for the littler girl. Or she could wear the blue striped one that had belonged to Mama. Surprise everyone. Have a little singing.

If she could keen John Matlock around and iffen she could keep on bringinq such good stuff home things was for sure gonna get better for the Circle Twig. She nestled the Broughton's payment a bit closer to her body and called it by name. Annie had to laugh again when it answered her.

29

* * *

Aramantha stood at the edge of the swept yard, her hand shielding her eyes. She wore one of the two old petticoats she and Annie had altered so the white cotton garments would be large enough around. New waiststrings did the job real easy. She also wore one of Pap's striped shirts.

Annie had said, "That there shirt is plenty big enough for you and the baby and a couple of other people." The shirt reached below Aramantha's knees and the petticoat hung to her shoetops. Atop the shirt and petticoat she wore a tattered apron. Ary wished she could have a prettier something or other to wear when Junior came riding over but what could you do? If there weren't nothing there weren't nothing.

Anyway, Junior didn't seem to mind the petticoat and shirt get up. But he'd sure liked the idea of a New York hairdo. He'd said it would make her the prettiest girl in both territories.

Annie had promised her a dress just as soon as she could get one for her after the baby come. Once they got that there cloth she knew Annie Lee could whip up a dress that looked like one of them pictures in a catalog.

"I think that's Annie a coming." She stepped toward the trail, "Yep. It's her and," She stared hard, both hands screening her eyes now. "Uncle George, I do believe she's a carrying a dog or something."

"Pray God she ain't accepted no damned dog as her payment for her curing the Broughton's womenfolks." He shuffled to stand beside his niece. "We be the ones needing something more to eat around here. Sure God we don't need something that requires us to feed it." Uncle George raised his own hand to keep the sun from his eyes. "You're right child. She sure is a carrying something, something about the color of your hair, Ary, something kinda redgold."

They looked at each other in silence for a second.

"Better go get Junior Trent and the new hand, Uncle. I'm pretty sure Annie'll be wanting to talk to them when she gets in."

The old man turned without another word and trudged up the steep trail toward the pole barn and then on into the stand of trees.

Ary absently smoothed the mound of her stomach as she watched the telltale moving dust feather upward into the sunwarmed air. A strong kick from the life inside her caused her to frown and look down.

"I reckon they ain't no use in you kicking out at me. It sure ain't my fault you're stuck inside there." She flipped her apron against herself as if to quiet the babe. "The sooner you come on out the better for both of us." She flipped the apron again. "Anyways, you don't need to get yourself all in a twitter. Annie says you'll be here soon enough." She smiled in the direction of her stomach. "Annie says we're all going to like you real well."

***

Junior Trent, Uncle George and John Matlock came down the path from the barn, moving quickly and carrying a long, peeled sapling. All three men stopped when they were within the dooryard. They lowered the pole. George and John turned their attention toward the returning Annie and her burden. After a second of watching Annie's dust from the trail, John hoisted the long sapling by himself. Balancing it easily on one shoulder, he carried it on the few feet to the partly roofed summer kitchen.

Junior Trent stepped closer to Aramantha and touched her arm with his hand. He smiled down at her and Ary smiled back before he turned to look at Annie and Lucifer racing toward them. Junior's mouth dropped open in surprise.

"Looky there, Ary. What is that your sister's a carrying. Ain't that a pig?"

Annie skidded Lucifer to a stop just at the edge of the newly swept yard.

"Everything looks real nice." She took a moment to survey the house and the new addition. She wondered where they'd gotten all the cedar shakes before she lifted the pig to introduce her.

"This here is Gulliver, folks. The Broughtons say she's a girl so I reckon we should call her Miss Gulliver... uh, Mrs. Gulliver. They say she's maybe gonna have some babies for us before too long."

"Why ain't she squealing, Annie?" Uncle George didn't move from where he stood. "What'll we do with a pig? We ain't got no pen."

"Well, she's a pet, George. The Broughton kids kept her with them inside the house or wherever they went." She waved one of the pig's hooves toward the watching group. "See? She's saying hello. We won't need us no pen. Billy Ray and them other kids always took her with them... walking or riding on the horse with them when they went to bring in the cows." She signaled Lucifer to dance her and the pig in a circle. "See? She loves to ride. And she'll follow you everywhere you walk."

Annie tightened her grip on the hog. "Someone of youall come on over here and get hold of old Miss Gulliver. She's getting mighty heavy." She looked over the watching group. "You want me to just drop the poor thing splat on the ground?"

John moved carefully around Lucifer's bared teeth and took the pig. He placed her on the ground and she looked up at him and squealed.

"See? She's mighty spoiled. Wants you to pick her up and carry her, John Matlock." Annie laughed.

John made a wry face.

"She'll have to get her ride some other way." His amber gaze moved from Annie's boots on up to the old campaign hat on her head. "I'm a lot of things but I'm no carrier of pigs." He looked at her face as if memorizing her every feature. "Welcome home."

Annie felt her face color with pleasure.

"Thanks. It's mighty good to be home." She looked across at the framed-in kitchen. "I see you been working right smart whilst I was gone. Where'd all them cedar shakes come from?"

"Junior Trent said his papa would let us have them in trade." Ary reached up for the cloth totes. "Did they give you good stuff, Annie?"

"They sure did. I did a good job for them, too." She reached for her medical supplies that she'd tied behind the saddle. "I wonder what Henry Trent was a thinking of trading. He say?"

Ary shook her head.

"No matter. We'll take them shakes and thank you very much. Now, allst I have to do is find another wagonload or two so's we can finish up." She reached for her own bags. "Here. Take these inside, too. And be real careful of them eggs in one of them sacks."

When Ary had moved a few steps away Annie whispered a question.

"What's Junior Trent doing here?"

John watched the stocky, red haired younger Trent take the bags from Aramantha and follow her toward the house.

"I'm not positive but I think he's courting Aramantha." He smiled up at her. "He's been working here for three hours this morning." He lifted his hand as if to help her from the saddle. "He has had to go inside the house a lot... for drinks and such, but even so he has been a big help."

"Courting her?"

"That's what it looks like to me." He laid his hand on the saddle horn, at the ready to help her down.

"Nah." She waved away his offer. "I'll just ride this here sweet old devil on up to the barn and give him a handful of grain." She turned the mule's head toward the path to the barn. "Courting, huh?"

John nodded.

"Hmmm." Annie slowed Lucifer to look back at Ary and Junior who had stopped at the doorstep where both stood peering into one of the opened cloth bags. Ary lifted a ham from the bag and Uncle George gave a glad cry and trotted toward them to open the other tote.

Annie let her gaze move to the golden eyed cowboy who stood looking back at her. She wondered if his eyes really were gold colored or if that was just the morning sun reflecting in his vision. She was afraid to allow herself to look at him for too long. He might think she was taking a personal interest in him.

And of course she wasn't. All she wanted out of him was plenty of work so no use letting him get the wrong idea, now was there? She flicked her heel against Lucifer's haunch. She'd get right on away from him, just hurry out of his sight. That was the best thing to do.

It was really hard to tear her own stare away from the man's intent look. Must be the sun or something. Yeah. That was it. The sun was in her eyes.

All the way up the hill she could feel his gaze touching her. Like a heated brand on her back.

Mrs. Gulliver trotted to stand closer to John Matlock and then squealed up her need to be carried. He never looked down at her, not even when she butted her head against his leg. He never even heard the pig's cries. He stood stockstill, considering some new ideas, something deep inside himself. He wondered why seeing Miss Annie Twig's return home made him feel as if an empty place in his life had just been filled.

He continued the distance to the shed where Annie stood passing a corncob over Lucifer with short hard strokes. She lifted the make-do curry comb, her blue eyes round with surprise.

"Well, you're a good provider, Annie Lee." He looked at the corncob as she turned it in her hand. "Clever of you to think of using that for a curry comb. Most everything you do is useful one way or another. I think you must be what is known as a *good woman* such as they mention in the Psalms."

They stared at each other for a moment. Matlock stepped toward her.

"You're some kinda sneaky bastard, John Wesley Matlock. You think you can use them words to come in under my guard."

He stepped closer and she moved back.

"Hold on there. You think that fancy talk is all that's needed." She ran her fingers across her lips. "And you think iffen you say sweet words a girl'll just let you do about anything."

Mrs.Gulliver squealed and grunted, then settled to steady snorting as she discovered the bonananza of fallen grain that lay on the ground between their feet.

"Aren't you afraid to see this pig snorting around your mule's hooves?"

"Oh no. Lucifer likes her. See? He's twitching his ears. That's how he shows he's happy about something. And Gulliver loves old Lucifer. Wants to take a ride on him."

Matlock had to laugh.

"The Circle Twig is certainly an interesting place. Mainly due to you, ma'am. I think you set the tone for all of us here, Miss Annie." He reached to take the corncob from her hand. "I wasn't sure I wanted to come here. It might have been a mistake."

"You trying to tell me something?"

"Well yes. I did want to talk to you. Ask you a few questions."

Annie's blue eyes darkened.

Good woman, am I? But not good enough for the likes of you, John Wesley Matlock. Is that what you're saying?

"Don't know as I can answer any of your questions, John Wesley." Wariness caused her to tighten her lips. She shoved Gulliver aside with her foot. "I ain't as educated as some folks." She wasn't answering any questions this pretty boy might ask. This was no beautiful bronze statue in the town square. This was a curious man. A stranger. Her place and her family were her business and no one elses.

"No need to get on your high horse before you even know what I'm going to ask."

"I ain't." She grabbed the corncob from him and continued Lucifer's grooming. "On no high horse, I mean." Where her fingers had touched his hand they felt as if they'd come too close to the fire. Slanting her vision up through her eyelashes she saw that he was leaning on the manger rail, just taking his ease. "Folks in the Territory don't cotton much to being asked questions." He was watching her. Her gaze went past him to the sky above the surrounding trees.

"Actually, I'd rather be watching you than questioning you."

She felt her cheeks redden under his gaze. "You don't have to do neither."

"Somehow I think I do."

"Starting to rain again." She used her foot to shove the pig away once more. "You better try to get that summer kitchen covered over as best you can. Pretty unusual for this time of year they say, but it looks like wet weather done set in."

She tried to keep from looking at him.

"Could even be a mite wet here in the shed iffen it comes up a toad strangler. Maybe you oughta plan on sleeping inside iffen it don't let up."

He could sleep in the old kitchen... the newly intended parlor, alongside Uncle George. He'd be dry there. There was room enough for another pallet if he'd lay out his bedroll partly under the table. The pig could sleep in that room too. At least for tonight. They was sure as hell no room for the animal in the bedroom where she and Aramantha slept.

For a second Annie thought wistfully of John's words and how they'd sounded when he said them. He talked awful pretty.

It'd be real nice to know **how** to talk fancy and educated and bookish like that, now wouldn't it? Annie shrugged the thought away and moved to Lucifer's other side.

She wasn't likely to be getting educated any more than she already was. Not at her age. Her schooling days was over. Most folks she'd met didn't talk much different than she did. All of them in both Arkansas and the Territory had always understood what she said. Henry Trent had even told her she was a hell of a talker. She could read iffen she had to. Write a little. She sure knew a lot about curing up folks. And cooking. And working. Most anything that had to be done with her hands she could do. Wasn't that enough?

She didn't have no time for learning that elegant kind of talk nor any other kind of frivolity. There was too much work to do. Better keep her mind on the proving up. They could even lose the place before the next four years was gone by. She shivered.

"You cold, Annie?"

"No." She ducked her head.

It had happened already to some of the folks around her. Look at all the places old Henry Trent was buying for little or nothing when people had to give up.

"Something bothering you, Annie?"

"Nothing that a lot of work around this place wouldn't cure." Maybe that'd shut him up. She bent to smooth under Lucifer's belly.

"You're a good worker and I'm willing to do whatever you ask me to do." He bent to peer under Lucifer so he could look at her again.

Well, that was good news. She hoped he meant it. She could use all the help she could get. They needed to get busy and prove this place up. She wasn't leaving here and neither was any of her family. She'd never give up the Circle Twig.

Huh uh. Not her. She wasn't giving up. She'd have this place for her own or die a trying. Oh, hell yes. This place belonged to her and to her family and to all the creatures that depended on the Twigs. She set her lips in a determined line. Circle Twig it was and Circle Twig it would remain.

Gulliver grunted loudly and moved around the mule with her. Annie was aware that Matlock also moved down toward her to once again lean against the manger rail so he could continue to stare at her. He didn't even look at the pig when it squealed a loud pig sound of gratitude for the grain that was falling from Lucifer's mouth.

"Watching me with them there gold colored eyes of his." She muttered the words into Lucifer's ear.

She knew Lucifer's yellow-toothed smile at her whispered remark looked very much like an offer-to-bite to the cowpoke. Annie smiled inwardly and rewarded Lucifer with a pat on his nose. She was pleased to see the tall man move a few inches down the wooden rail, away from her and her animal. She was sort of glad John Matlock had stayed in the barn with her. It was nice to have company. But she was even happier that he wasn't standing where they could real easy touch one another. He bothered her when he looked at her as if he knew everything about her.

"You don't want to get too close, John. Lucifer can be set off real easy." She'd noticed that when the man was too close to her it was kind of hard to think.

Chapter 6

Mrs. Gulliver tried to go with any of the Twigs or with their hired hand wherever any one of them walked for the next few days, but she seemed to have developed a special fondness for John Wesley Matlock. She squealed to ride... either in his arms when he walked or up on the horse with him when he rode. Mostly he ignored the spoiled pig's entreaties. Sometimes he shouted at her and shoved her out of his way. Ignoring his displeasure she continued to trot alongside him, grunting and snorting her own piggy version of a happy companion's song.

"We can't have us a pig in the house, Annie," Ary had said early on, "Pigs is dirty."

"Look at this fine looking shoat, Ary." Annie had lifted the nearly full grown animal and scratched at the space behind her ears. "She ain't a bit dirty. Them Broughton kids scrubbed her down about twice a week." Annie gazed into Gulliver's friendly little pig eyes.

"Why, she was a sight cleaner than them kids was. Still is." Annie lifted one of Gulliver's ears and flapped it gently. "We'll keep her clean, too." She smoothed the bristles on Gulliver's neck. "See Ary, she's the same color you are. Strawberry blonde."

Ary's grunted answer had sounded almost like something Mrs. Gulliver would say.

Gulliver liked to sleep out in the pole barn with John and Lucifer, her favorite human and her favorite animal. But now, several days after coming to her new home it seemed it was getting a mite damp for a pig's comfort in the open shed. She let them know that she'd decided to sleep in the house by plopping herself down in a cozy corner and staying there when John left the house.

"John, it's raining pretty steady now." Annie talked to him after supper as she worked on the long promised new and fancy hairdo for Aramantha. "I reckon you better bring your quilts inside here and bed down in the house." She ignored the stricken look on the man's face when she pulled and twisted the long strands of her own cut-off pale blonde hair into a ratted form which she fitted on top of her sister's head. "Lay your quilts out in the kitchen with George, I reckon."

"Junior says this is awful strange weather for the Territories." As Aramantha spoke she sat as still as she could for the framing of the pompadour. "Supposed to be dry now, dry and getting cooler now, Junior says. But the rain will be good for the crops, Junior says."

"Junior says all that, huh?" Annie looked across the newly washed red gold edifice of hair in front of her and smiled and nodded as if to say to the hired hand, *Reckon you was right. We're hearing a lot about Junior Trent these days.* Aloud she said, "This Junior, he ain't by any chance a drinker, is he, little sister?"

She had to smile at Ary's angry head tossing, "No" Quickly she pulled a strand of the girl's strawberry blonde hair loose. She twisted the loosened hair into a curl using a long strip of brown paper to tie and hold the ringlet just in front of Ary's right ear. "Well, iffen he ain't a drinker I reckon he ain't coming here to visit Uncle George. Could that old Junior boy be sweet on you, little Ary?"

Ary ducked her head and her cheeks reddened.

"Honey, you gonna have to sit up straight whilst I get this do all set up." Annie twisted another curl paper in front of the other ear. "You feeling something for little Junior Trent, baby sister?"

"Oh, Annie." Ary giggled and twisted on the bench.

"What do you think of this Junior Trent, Mr. Matlock? Is he worth shooting, you think?" She and John exchanged smiles. "Is he good enough for my Ary?"

"Maybe not." John's eyes gleamed with their shared mischief. "I doubt we could find a young man you'd think fine enough for your little sister." He rose from the cleared table and stretched, his raised hand pressed flat to touch the ceiling shakes. "Anyway, I think Aramantha will have to answer that question." He bent to look into the young girl's eyes. "What do you say, Ary? Is he good enough for you?"

"Now you two quit joshing me." Ary couldn't control either her giggles or her deepening blush. "Junior's just helping out a little around here. His papa sends him is what."

"Uh huh." Annie nodded and smiled down at the red gold pompadour. "Just what we was saying. Whatever the reason, Junior Trent is hanging around here a lot." She stirred the sugar water mixture. "Don't know if old man Trent sent him or iffen the boy just can't help hisself from coming. What do you think, John?"

Ary twisted on the bench and dared a bold look up at her big sister.

"Well, what about you and old man Trent, Annie? Is he good enough for *you*?" Ary's glance turned sly. "Junior says his papa's a going to call on you right soon." She put one hand up to feel the pompadour after Annie had slicked it into place with a little sugar water. "How soon can I take the curl papers out, sister?"

"When they're dry, of course. But I reckon you could sleep on them twisted up ringlets with no problem."

"Maybe I'll take them out later on this evening." She looked anxiously at Annie. "Just so's we can see how it all really looks, you know." She smiled at Annie's murmured acquiescence.

John Matlock sat across the table and watched the sure movements of Annie's hands. Annie felt pleased that he watched. If there was one thing she was good at, that was fixing hair. She could make a person's hair sit up and take notice, she could. Make it look like a picture in a book. From the looks of them both he and Uncle George would need a haircut real soon. She'd clip the old boys into shape... maybe tomorrow night after supper. She'd show this educated man that talking fancy or even having a strong back wasn't everything. Making people look good and making them feel good was really important too.

"Annie, you surely know Junior's papa don't want to come over here to see me or Uncle George." Ary patted the top of the arranged mound of hair as she looked at each side of her hairdo in their mother's tortoise shell hand mirror. "Junior swears that Old man Trent says you're the best looking woman in the Territory. Now what do you say to that, big sister?"

Annie felt a prick of surprise. Henry Trent?

"Why Henry Trent must be fifty years old or more, little sister. What's he doing thinking about any woman... especially me?" She raised her gaze to meet John Matlock's coppery stare. "He's the richest man in the area, some say." Why did she feel that John Matlock was waiting for an explanation? "I expect he could just about pick any wife he wanted. Why in hell would he want to make up to me?"

"I suspect you've just heard one of the reasons, Miss Annie." His eyes were flat, metallic, almost like the eyes on the statue back in Fort Smith. As if a shield had been raised across the front of his face. "I'd imagine that you are just what he says... the best looking woman in the territory. I'd have to agree with him." He smiled down at Aramantha and the bronze mask faded from his face as his look gentled. "Except for little Miss Aramantha, here, who is a real beauty in her own right."

Annie felt shame at the sudden spark of jealousy that rose in her at his words. Ary *was* especially good looking. Any man with eyes would say the same. And she wasn't a little girl any more. Nigh fourteen years old. Next week when she turned fourteen she'd be a woman, sure. And a pretty one, at that.

What did she care that John Wesley Matlock thought Ary was prettier than she was? It was the truth. She swept the last few strands of hair up from the nape of Aramantha's neck and wove them into the fancy do. A quick brush upward with the sugar water dampened comb and the hairdo was finished.

Annie sighed. Ary looked so grown up. So beautiful. If the child had something pretty to wear she'd sure enough be the most beautiful girl in Oklahoma Territory.

"Thanks, Annie. I don't even look like myself, do I, John?" Ary twisted from right to left trying to get the whole effect with the small hand held mirror. "What do you think, Uncle George?"

"Lovely as a flower. Like your mama at your age, Ary, child." The toothless smile was wistful. "Onliest woman I ever seed that I'd trade my jug for." He frowned. "Your pappy beat me out there, right enough, darling." He smoothed his gray hair back. "Milford got all the looks in our family, I reckon."

"Milford is your father?" John's question came a beat too soon for Annie's taste.

Annie gave him the look that said he was poking around where he didn't belong.

"Oh, yes. Milford was their father and Lela Mae was their mother." George continued his reminiscence, never noticing the stiffening of Annie's backbone. "Him so big and blonde and her so small and red headed. Both with blue eyes that looked like the cleanest, clearest water." He licked his lips. "That's where you girls got them blue eyes."

"I don't know, Uncle George." Talking about eyes couldn't hurt anything. "Our eyes is real different I think. Mine is a lot darker nor Ary's."

"Yes sir, you, Annie, your eyes, well, your eyes are dark blue like the sky when a summer storm's coming on and you, Ary, your eyes are light, light, blue like the morning sky on a sunny day." His own faded blue eyes smiled with memories. "But you both got them blue eyes off your two blue-eyed parents, right enough."

Ary let the hand holding the mirror slowly lower to rest on the table as she listened to her uncle.

"Prettiest couple in Arkansas, people said. And they could dance..." George looked into the air above his head as if he could still see Annie and Aramantha's parents. "Aye God, they could dance." He swiped at the corner of one eye. "I surely do miss old Milford. Seems like yesterday he died even though it's been months."

Annie sat up even straighter. Surely Uncle George wouldn't let any cats out of any bags. She wanted to hear about Mama and her Pap but she didn't want the old man giving any of their secrets away. She kept silent and let the old man talk.

"It almost killed me to bury him and I still miss that little Miss Lela Mae after all these years. Your mama was a lady." The two sisters were as still as statues as they listened to the words about their parents. George

Scoundrels' Bargain 41

looked first at Ary, then at Annie. "They observed the old ways, you know."

"What do you mean, 'the old ways,' Uncle George?" Annie whispered the question, afraid of what he might say but hoping to keep him talking about her Mother and Father.

"Oh, your mam was never alone with your pap until they was married, you know. Aye God, Miss Lela Mae come from a right good family."

Both Aramantha and Annie nodded as if they had heard those words many times.

"Their Father, Milford, was your brother, Uncle George?" John's words were almost a whisper. Annie woke from her reverie, once more on her guard. The hired man's voice had intruded upon their family's dream of the beautiful past.

George nodded and he swiped at another tear with the cuff of his sleeve. "I thought God meant it for me, Annie Lee." He sobbed the words. "But it wasn't. It hit Milford. I watched him keel over, just keel over and die."

"Your father died recently?"

Annie frowned at Matlock's question and made a gesture to Ary with one hand. Ary stood and began her search of the room.

"George Cameron Twig, are you drinking again?" Annie grabbed at her uncle's shoulder and made him turn to face her. "I thought we agreed. You was going to make it to sell to help us out some, but not to drink yourself." She glanced across at John. "Wouldn't you know it? Just when I thought everything was going so well." She raised her eyes to look at her sister scurrying about the room.

Behind him Ary was shaking her head at Annie to show that she couldn't find the jug. Annie moved a couple of steps to the sidewall where the old man kept his bedroll. She raised her heavy, high-topped work shoe and kicked at the clump of coverlets with all her might. A hard thud answered her question. Mrs. Gulliver, who lay in the corner nearest the bedding, grunted, but didn't open her eyes. Annie bent to remove the jug from the roll of old quilts.

"I'm taking your hooch, Uncle George. You're getting back into this drinking business just a mite too soon to suit me."

The old man moaned and tears streaked his cheeks.

"Don't take my little jug away, Annie Lee. I was just a wishing Milford was here, is all."

"Well, he ain't. He's dead. And you will be too, you old coot, if you keep drinking this stuff." She touched his shoulder again but the touch was gentler this time. "I'll just keep it until we get the new kitchen finished and we can invite some of the neighbors to a Sunday School." She flipped the quilts and lifted the crockery jug toward John. "Here, John. You hide this little old jug of firewater somewheres where this old bastard can't reach it. He's gonna make hisself sick."

"We going to have us a Sunday School?" The old man breathed the tremulous words with an air of wonder. "And the neighbors are aye God, coming? Right here to our house? Can I play my fiddle for it?"

"You sure as hell can. We'll have us a high old time, Uncle. And we'll all sing, too. Won't we, Ary?"

"We'll sing all your favorites, Uncle George. Mama's too. And Annie says the new hand will teach the Sunday School. Says he's a real religious Methodist." Ary smiled at John. "Oh Uncle, don't you just love to hear the new man singing them old hymns? I've just got plumb used to hearing him sing." She smiled shyly at the open mouthed hired man. "Last night Annie done told me she loves to hear you sing, John, and so do I. We both do. I most surely do feel charmed by that deep voice of your'n."

"Teach the Sunday School? What... How... Why..."

"Why not?" Annie looked at the sputtering cowboy. "You always did sound like a preacher to me. From your very first day here. That bass voice. All them pretty words. That smooth way of talking." She held out one hand to her little sister. "We could maybe take up an offering. All preachers does it, you know. Why, we might even have us a dance." Ary stood and took Annie's hand.

"Shall we dance?" Annie bowed to the shorter girl before she placed her hand at the spot which had once been Ary's waist. "I 'member mama said the Methodists didn't have no problem with dancing. We might make this a *Methodist* Sunday School and dancing class."

She and the elegantly pompadoured Ary solemnly danced through the small space around the table as if they could hear an orchestra tracing out the steps for them. Annie spoke to Matlock above Ary's head.

"Might be you could put us in a wood floor in the new room. Make it a fine place for dancing and a good place for your preaching."

"Annie Twig, you've gone too far." John Matlock heard his own words but he already knew there was no way out. He lifted the old man's jug as if to hit her with it, then smiled and let the thing drop to his side once more. If Miss Annie Lee Twig wanted herself a Methodist Sunday School Dancing Academy he was very much afraid she would have herself one and there wasn't much he could do about it. He suspected he'd better prepare a sermon. He was caught here like a tropical fly in a piece of amber and he couldn't even think about leaving. Not yet. All he had was a few names and a little family history. He still hadn't learned much of anything. Nothing really.

The slow, silently graceful dance of the two young women continued and Annie smiled into the baffled yellow gold eyes of the hired man.

Scoundrels' Bargain

It was a good idea to always keep a man off balance if you could, she thought. If you didn't they'd try to rule over you. She'd learned that over the years even if she hadn't learned anything else. *Pap had been a pretty good teacher when it come to what men were like and all.*

It was like she had said to Ary when they were first trying to get some man passing through to help them build themselves some kind of shelter. "Ary, if they is one thing I learned in this life it's that you can divide men up into three groups... some sweet, some drunk, and some mean... and the most of them mean."

"Why do you say that, Annie?" Ary had let the reins slacken so she could turn from her driving to listen to her sister.

"Just look at Uncle George... sweet and drunk. That's the trouble with the sweet ones. They probably either end up taken over by the whiskey or run out of town by the mean bastards."

Ary had laughed at what Annie was telling her but they only had to look over at old Uncle George drunk and snoring and tied into the wagon seat to see Annie was telling some truth.

"Just look at what they did to Mr. Calendula, back in Van Buren," Annie had continued, "He was nigh onto the sweetest teacher I ever did have and the smartest, too. And then them big old boys in the school made it up amongst themselves they was gonna run him off 'cause, they said, he was a Eyetalian dago and a Yankee from Chicago. A damned Yankee, they said, and they purely did just put the skids to that real good, smart man."

Annie had looked at Ary to see if she was understanding. She was trying to explain some of the things that had happened back in Arkansas while Ary was still a little child.

"They ran him right off, little sister. That was the last time I went to school. And you know Ary, some of them old school boys was most as big as men even iffen they was just in the fifth grade. And even iffen they wasn't full growed, some of them was already drunkards. Mean and drunk. Just what I been telling you. Mean and drunk goes together, mostly."

She hadn't said any more just then but she'd silently considered their own Pappy. Now Pap was sweet when she was real little and Ary was a baby. She could remember that. Then he was sweet and drunk. She could remember that, too. Then he turned drunk and mean. She sure as hell could remember that. Look at what had happened to him. Addison Fleury had been sweet and drunk and hidden mean. She shoved that thought from her mind. Drunk and mean or sweet and drunk. Men was mostly useless or dangerous or both, she'd learned.

She'd just have to keep her eyes on old John Wesley Matlock. See which group he fell into. She couldn't yet rightly decide, though she was pretty sure he wasn't a drunk. Sometimes he was kind of sweet. Other times he nettled her something awful. Sometimes his bronze stare just rankled her good, but she wasn't sure yet. Not about him. Time would tell.

Meanwhile, she'd keep him on his toes. Keep putting him through his paces. Singing, working, spouting a few Bible verses. Make him preach a sermon or two. She might even have him dancing ere long. She laughed to herself at the thought.

She felt so pleased with her plans for John Matlock that she whirled the smaller girl several times and she only stopped when Ary cried out and clutched at her belly with both hands.

Annie froze in place. "Oh, Ary, is it the baby a coming?"

Ary straightened and took a deep breath.

"No. I don't think so, Annie. Not now, anyways." She smoothed the front of her apron. "I think the little thing was just a dancing a reel or two in there. I think our baby could might turn out to be a Methodist instead of a Baptist."

Annie laughed and caught John's eye as he too laughed. He returned her gaze, his lips slightly parted. When their eyes met his laughter died at the same time hers did. Something crackled between them. Something like lightning. For a second the two of them were caught up in the exchange. Annie drew in a long, frightened breath. She felt stunned. Had something strange happened between them just now?

She was brought back to the moment when Uncle George's tears turned to laughter, as well. She had only a second to ask herself about the strange exchange between them. What *had* happened? Was that what was making her skin tingle?

From the earthen floor in the corner, Mrs. Gulliver raised her snout and launched a loud and happy squeal. There was so much mirth in the tiny room that in her hidden preoccupation with the "something" she'd exchanged with John Matlock she almost missed Ary's next words.

"Anyways, this here baby can't come and join us tonight, big sister." She laid her hand at the back of her head and smoothed upward in the age old feminine gesture of a woman demonstrating awareness of her womanhood. "I just puredee wouldn't let our baby come out right now." She giggled at her sister's look of amazement.

"Why wouldn't you let the baby come? What do you mean, girl? I thought you was wanting this business of having a baby to be all over and done with." Annie frowned a perplexed look down at her sister.

"Well, this morning Junior done told me he was going to ride over tonight just especially to see my famous New York hairdo. So he'll be here." Ary giggled and looked at Annie from the corner of her eye. "Could be here any minute. He said his papa was a coming with him. Said old Mr. Henry Trent was a coming to bring you a real nice present, Annie Lee."

Chapter 7

No sooner had Ary said the words, "He's bringing you a present," than they all realized that they could hear wagons driving up in the yard. John watched Aramantha spring for the door as quickly as her swollen belly would allow.

"It's him. It's Junior Trent and his papa.

Junior's driving one of the wagons and Mr. Trent is a riding that big old gray horse of his'n." She smiled back over her shoulder, her voice full of excitement, "Glory be, Annie, that's some present. He's brought you two wagons piled full of cedar shakes."

"Well, invite the folks in, Aramantha. Don't just stand there gawking out the door like you ain't had no learning." Annie ran her fingers through her hair and headed toward her sister. Uncle George crowded through the door to stand in the entryway right behind the two young women.

John Matlock rose from the table, a black look on his face, his brown eyes shooting amber fire. It was about time he met this Henry Trent. Next time he sent a report back East he'd have them see if they knew anything about this "rich farmer." Fleury was the man he was trying to find, of course, but it wouldn't hurt the people in the office in Little Rock to do a bit of investigating for him. Sure, he'd admit it was personal. He'd tell them so if they asked.

He cleared his throat to catch Annie's attention.

"Why does Trent feel he must bring wagonloads of shakes to you, Annie? Did you tell him we wanted to shingle the new room?" Matlock's low voice was almost a growl.

Annie turned and looked at him in surprise.

"I didn't tell him nothing. I ain't seen him since the last time I went into town. You're the one who told me Junior Trent was a coming over here all the time. That he was the one brought them shingles you already nailed down." Her blue eyes widened. "I bet that's it. Junior must have told his pappy we was still trying to figure out a way to finish putting the roof on the summer kitchen."

"Well, why would this Mr. Trent suddenly feel responsible for your new room?"

"I don't know and I don't care." She shook her head as if she wanted to dismiss all the questions. "I can tell you this, though. I ain't looking no gift horse in the mouth and I sure ain't turning them shakes down, John."

"What if there are strings attached, Annie? Have you considered that?" He stood with his hands in his trouser pockets, looking down at the fair-haired young woman. He shrugged. "Never mind. I'll go on out and meet this Henry Trent."

45

"Now John." She put out a hand as if to stop him. "Don't you dare say nothing that'll rile old Henry." She straightened her shoulders and hitched up Uncle George's cast offs before she put a smile on her face and stepped out onto the back steps. To John she looked like a rare spring blossom wearing a weed's disguise. She looked back at her new hired hand. "I want them there cedar shakes, John Wesley Matlock." She whispered fiercely. "You understand?"

"At whatever cost?"

"What the hell you talking about? Trent sure knows he ain't going to get no pay out of anyone at the Circle Twig."

"Maybe he isn't looking for money. Had you thought about that?" He met her gaze and was disturbed by the mixture of fear and cunning he saw there. She'd do about anything for those damned shingles, it seemed. He let the quiet moment stretch between them. She lifted her head and broke the eye contact.

John's hand briefly brushed hers on the door facing. Annie snatched her hand away as if his touch had burned. He could tell she felt the same thing he felt whenever they touched, even accidentally. She spoke as if their conversational threads had not been broken by the distraction of the touch.

"Well, I sure ain't got nothing else old Trent is gonna want or that I want to give him. Cep'n for maybe a cup of tea." She absently rubbed the back of her hand. "Maybe you ain't noticed, friend. I don't trust no man no farther than I can throw him. Just look at old Calvin. He went and died on me. You just never know what a man is fixing to do." She nodded emphatically. "You don't have to worry none about some old man getting the better of me, lessen he ups and dies. Truth to tell, them shingles is probably cut from our own cedar breaks up on the ridge. Old Henry ain't likely to give anything of his own away. But I appreciate them, anyway!"

John nodded and stepped out onto the portal stone behind Annie to survey the visiting gift bearers. Mrs. Gulliver stuck her snout out into the rain for a moment, snorted her displeasure, then snatched herself back into the corner of the warm room where she settled back into her comfortable dreams. In the confusion of the arrival everyone else just ignored the gentle misting rain and the churned up mud of the dooryard.

Junior Trent unhitched the wagon he was driving and after a wistful look at Aramantha he lead his team, harness leather creaking, metal fittings clanking, up the path toward the pole barn. The other driver trailed behind him with the second team.

A large silver haired man wearing a black rubber poncho thrown across his shoulders and an expensive three piece suit the same color as his hair, still sat upon his horse. His dark narrow brimmed Stetson shadowed

Scoundrels' Bargain 47

his face but when he looked toward the house Matlock could see the man's facial features quite clearly.

At least he's not wearing a tie. John smiled grimly at his own observation. Trent wore a white shirt buttoned up to the neck but he'd left his starched collar at home. John watched the man ignore the movement of the draft horses as he looked calmly down at Aramantha and Annie. They both walked toward him with smiles on their faces. The horse he sat on was a sleek, fast looking animal, a shade darker gray than the man's suit and his hair. The man's leather gun belt was hardly noticeable under his well tailored suit jacket but John noted that the gun and the holster looked well cared for and well used.

When Aramantha looked after Junior Trent and seemed about to start up the path toward the barn her sister stopped her with a whispered sentence or two before she greeted the visitor.

"Get on down off that there horse, Mr. Trent." Annie called in her best Arkansas learned neighborly welcome. "You step down and come on in and have yourself a cup of yarb...uh...herb tea with us. Get on inside out of this rain." She looked at the parked wagons and smiled. "Where you taking them shakes, sir?"

"Did you bring them for us?" Ary was fairly hugging herself with happiness. She was trying to be a good hostess as perhaps her sister had suggested but she couldn't keep her gaze from straying toward the path to the barn.

The gray haired man nodded and stared down at Annie. The ice in his gaze melted slightly as his silvery eyes seemed to search every part of Annie's body and face. A diamond sent a flash of fire from the ring on his little finger. Only a real stone would be able to wink any light in this early evening dusk, John thought. The visitor still didn't speak.

"Well, come on in, now, Mr. Trent." Ary nervously patted her new hairdo as she belatedly added her own welcome to that of her sister. She glanced once more at the path to the barn. "That there Junior Trent can just find his own way on into the house."

The man nodded again and looked after his son who, with the other driver and the four horses, had disappeared into the trees.

"Glad to have you, Mr. Trent." Uncle George thrust his hand up toward the man in the saddle. "I'm George Twig." Trent either didn't see the gesture or he simply ignored the old man.

The rancher raised his chin and pointed with it toward the tall cowboy who stood in the open doorway watching everything from the back step. He spoke his first words.

"Who's he?"

George looked over his shoulder.

"Oh, him. Just the new hand Annie done hired."

"He have a name?"

"Name of John Wesley Matlock." Aramantha piped up with the name and further information she thought important. "Annie says he might be real religious with a name like that. She says he might help us start us a Sunday School." She smiled shyly and hung her head for a second before she straightened, then forced herself to go on. "Junior says he's gonna come to it. Maybe you'd like to come to our Sunday School, too?"

Trent nodded, then looked away from Aramantha, his eyes like flint, a slight expression of distaste on his floridly handsome face. John was pleased to note an incipient double chin under the man's pugnacious looking jaw.

"That man's no hired hand. A gun man or a bounty hunter, a lawman or someone hiding from the law, but I can tell you this for sure, Miss Twig. He ain't no down-on-his-luck, work-for-nothing drover." Trent continued to stare at John Matlock and John Matlock stared back.

Matlock decided that Trent had allowed the good life to pack a few too many pounds onto his frame but he could see the man's body still looked solidly muscled under the softer outer layers of flesh and the custom tailored suit. He watched Trent again turn his face to look down at Annie. He smiled down at her the way a wolf smiles at an unaccompanied lamb.

John Matlock tried to see Annie Twig as she must look to someone like Trent. Young? Beautiful? Uneducated? Yes. All those things and more. She must look like a young woman who could be educated and molded to become what Trent might need for his position in the community. Was he aware that if he took Annie he would also be forced to take a younger sister, an illegitimate baby niece or nephew and a drunken old uncle... plus a mule that could clear a building of any number of occupants in seconds, not to mention a pet pig?

Somehow he didn't think Trent would care for all that extra baggage. Matlock let a thin smile cross his lips. Only a crazy man would want to hook up with a woman who had all those black marks against her.

At the sound of the door closing Trent again turned his attention in that direction and looked even more intently at the dark browed Matlock who slouched his muscular body against the edge of the doorframe, his arms crossed on his chest. John Matlock stared back at the visitor with a flat searching gaze. Neither man spoke.

Ary, George and Annie stood in a row near the gray horse and looked first up at the tightlipped visitor, then back at the tall, hired man who was becoming a part of their Circle Twig.

To Matlock they looked like a line of innocent blue-eyed forest prey caught in the torchlight of an armed hunter. His protective instincts rose and caused him to take an even more probing look at the well-groomed Mr. Henry Trent.

After a second, Matlock shrugged, straightened and reopened the door to step back into the room where the building of the red gold pompadour hairdo had been taking place only a few minutes before. There had been color and laughter and singing. Now everything had gone colorless. Gray rain, gray visitor, gray future. He silently cursed Trent's intrusion into the Twig family evening.

In a matter of a few minutes his pleasure in those moments of watching Annie's dexterous handiwork on her sister's hair had been destroyed by the rich man's encroachment into their space.

He was consumed by an unreasoning fury but he knew he didn't even want to try to explore the cause of his anger. He just knew that somehow, Henry Trent was bad news... for him as well as for the Twigs... but especially for his Annie. He shocked himself with the thought... *his* Annie? She wasn't "his" and she never could be.

Without question her life was here with her family on the Circle Twig and of course, his life was elsewhere. Wasn't it?

When they were all inside and seated around the kitchen table, Annie knew her face must be flushed with excitement. When she hung the wet rubber poncho on the peg beside the door she lifted one hand to her cheek. It felt hot. She tried the other one. Hot too. It wasn't every family who received a visit from the most prominent and influential man in the neighborhood. She almost wished now that she'd taken a second or two to pull on one or the other of them two dresses that was still folded up in mama's trunk in the dugout bedroom.

And all them shakes! A gift. She just couldn't get over it. They could probably finish the roof of the other room with about ten days work. They could put the shingles on the roof and the planks on the floor and have a Sunday School meeting and an all day gathering right out there. Best do that before the room was closed in. More people could take a part in the goings on, especially if it wasn't still raining.

Her gaze swung between Henry Trent and John Matlock. She felt her flush deepen. They were both acting like two strange dogs sniffing around the same female. Both shooting looks that could kill back and forth and back and forth across the little room. And it seemed mighty like she was the female in question. She couldn't help but smile. It was kind of nice to have two grown men acting like they were going to fight over who got Miss Annie Twig's attention. It surely was different.

"You say you're from Arkansas, Matlock?"

"I didn't say."

"Annie Lee and Aramantha and me. We're all from Arkansas." Uncle George was still trying to do the right thing.

Annie saw that neither of the two other men even gave the old man the courtesy of a glance. *Bastards. Both of them*, she added inside her mind.

"Junior says you folks have family in Arkansas, Mr. Trent." Aramantha now tried to do her part. One of her curls had lost its spring from being out in the rain. The lock of red gold hair hung damply lank against her neck. Annie wondered where Ary had put the curl papers. She'd have to redo the ear curls.

John at least smiled at little sister but Trent just looked at her as if she weren't anything but trash. It was kind of like he smelled something bad.

Annie kept the smile on her face but she felt it losing a lot of candlepower. Anyone who didn't like her family could just move it on down the road so far as she was concerned.

Even a man with two wagonloads of cedar shakes? She asked herself. What if he took the shingles back? Mmmm. She considered the idea for a second. Better be nice for a little spell longer, she told herself. *I want them there shakes.*

"John, I wonder iffen I could trouble you to get the jug? Maybe Mr. Trent would care for a drink a little stronger than y... herb tea."

"Maybe I better go see whatever happened to that there Junior Trent." Ary rose and moved toward the door and had slipped out before Annie could say a word.

"Yeah. A drink now, Annie. That'd go real good." Uncle George looked around the room as if he were searching out the proffered jug.

"No. No drink for me, tonight, Annie. I would like to talk to you in private if you ain't got no objections." The steely gray eyes swept the people still at the table. "If your family and friends would excuse us just a few minutes."

John Matlock stood so abruptly he almost turned over the bench. He put his hand under George's arm and practically lifted the skinny old man from his seat.

"Come on George. You and me'll go find that jug. Leave 'Mister' Trent alone with 'Miss' Twig."

"What? We all ere, aye God, going to get the jug?" George almost skipped toward the door. "John Wesley Matlock, you ere a right good man as I was a..." His voice was cut off by the door as it was slammed behind him by the tall hired hand.

Annie felt almost dizzy at the swiftness of the change in the feel of the room. Mrs. Gulliver was the only member of her family left in the house. And that little redgold sow was dead asleep. Snoring just a bit. Gulliver broke wind and Annie had to smile at her. That was nothing but good healthy pig smell, anyway. Such a pretty fat pig. Them baby pigs would

Scoundrels' Bargain

sure be good eating. They'd probably have long bellies like their mama's so's they'd be plenty of bacon on each one. 'Course she'd never say any of that right in front of Mrs. Gulliver. Pigs was smart.

"You keep your pig in the house?" The gray eyes looked as if they were measuring Mrs. Gulliver for a shroud. Annie didn't much care for the look or his tone but he was a guest... a gift bearing guest, she reminded herself.

"She's a pet pig. Name of Mrs. Gulliver." Annie kept her tone mild. "Was they something I could do for you, Mr. Trent? Was you a needing some curing or something?" Maybe he was sick. Sure. That was it! He had some kind of sickness and he didn't want folks to know about it. Probably wanted to buy some ginseng root. Some men were like that. Secretive. Of course. That was surely the reason for the wagons full of cedar shingles.

"No, no." His voice was impatient. "I'm never sick." His eyes took a quick survey of the room, including the snoring, farting pig. "I had heard that you had a man living here with you and I..."

"You mean my Uncle George?" Annie felt like putting the candle up real close to the man's face to see if a little fire would warm him up somehow. "Why would you be at all interested in me and my family?"

"No, no. I knew about your uncle. I mean the stranger. John Wesley Matlock, I believe you said?"

"I can tell you this, Mr. Trent. Mr. Matlock ain't 'living' with me. He's our hired man. But even iffen he was 'living' with me it wouldn't be none of your business, now would it?" Annie tried to keep her voice down. Keep things civil. If he wasn't careful this old boy was flirting with real trouble.

Shakes. Shingles. New room. Don't lose your temper, Annie Lee. She heard her own words admonishing herself and yet she proceeded to ignore all the calming words as they buzzed right through her head and straight out again.

"And iffen that was what you was a wanting to talk about, I guess our talk is over." She stood up and made an angry move toward the door, her hand lifted to take the visitor's old hat and his damned ugly wet black rubber thing from the peg so she could throw it at him.

"Now, now, Miss Annie. People talk, you know. A young woman alone has to be real careful." He touched the gold chain that hung from his watch pocket above the leather gun belt. "I was just going to offer you my protection. I thought maybe I could call on you sometimes so folks could see that I think you're a credit to our neighborhood."

"I think the neighbors like me just fine without your help, Mr. Trent." She turned and seated herself again. "I appreciate you bringing me them shakes. I really do, but I been taking care of myself and my family for over ten years now, part of one of those years was spent right here next door to the Trent ranch. People in the neighborhood seem to like me. I reckon I can carry on... without any testimonials from you."

"Yes. Um. Well. Your family." He looked down at his right fist which he rested on the wooden table top as if he was about ready to break the well scrubbed boards in half with the big ham-like thing, Annie thought. "When is your sister's baby due?"

"Our baby is our own affair, Mr. Trent. Was there something else you wanted?"

"Well, I suppose the girl and the baby and your uncle could continue to live here quite happily without you, couldn't they?" He placed the other doubled fist on the table about a foot from the first. "Then this Matlock person could stay or go as he pleased."

Annie felt a chill crawl up her spine.

"Live here without me? What the hell are you a talking about?"

"Protection, Miss Annie. It doesn't do your own name or your reputation any good at all to live here with an obviously pregnant younger sister and that sot drunk uncle of yours and now a man that no one in this world knows. I want to protect you from all that." He lowered his head and peered up at her through thick black and silver eyebrows.

"And how was you aiming to do that, Mr. Trent?" Annie's lips felt so stiff with anger she could barely get the words out. "How was you gonna 'protect' me from all then awful things?"

"Why, I'll just take you to live in my own house, Miss Annie. What else?"

Chapter 8

Before she could control herself, laughter simply burbled out of Annie's mouth. She tried to stop the burst of loud snickering, but she couldn't.

Go and live with Old Man Trent? Wait 'till the others heard what this barmy old man had suggested. She let her giggling die down and she stole a look at her visitor. Ah oh, his face was so red it was almost purple.

"I'm sorry, Henry. I wasn't laughing at you." She looked at the corner where Mrs. Gulliver still snored and only occasionally passed gas. The rude sounds weren't so loud now and the smell wasn't so bad. Anyway Junior's old dad didn't need to pretend like he never in his life heard a pig let wind. "I seen your house... not inside, of course, but I'd reckon that you have wooden floors and lots of fancy furniture. Maybe even carpets on them floors." She smiled into his red face. "I was just thinking of Mrs. Gulliver taking her ease in your... you know, the room where you eat?"

"The dining room. And who is this Mrs. Gulliver?"

"Yeah. The dining room. That's it. The dining room." She pointed at the relaxed red gold sow in the corner. "That there is Mrs. Gulliver. I done told you. I was just thinking of that little shoat a sleeping in the corner of your fancy 'dining room.'" Annie chuckled again. "Somehow I just don't think we all would fit in." She leaned slightly toward him. "I was thinking about us. That's why I was laughing."

"Believe me, your pig will never sleep in my dining room, Miss Twig." Henry Trent rose and frowned down at her. "My invitation was for you and for you alone, not for your pig, your drunken uncle, your slutty sister, your hired man lover nor any of the other strange creatures of your household." He lifted the black rubber poncho from the peg by the door. "The invitation was for you alone."

Now Annie felt the angry color rising in her own face.

"Well, then, I reckon you and me don't have nothing else to say to each other, do we, Henry?"

She'd let this old boy get on out of her kitchen in the most polite way she could manage. Never let it be said that the Twigs weren't mannerly to guests in their house. Just being regular polite was about the best she could do, she told herself. She had always told Ary that anyone who came to their house was to be treated right... like a guest... just the way their mama had taught them so many years ago. But as his words sank in she just couldn't control her mouth.

"Slutty? Drunken? Hired man lover?" She rose slowly from the chair at the end of the table. "You can say all that to me right here in my own kitchen?" Her hand swept a gesture around the room. "You can insult me and my family, whilst at the same time you was a asking me to come and perch myself in that there big old ugly house of yourn?"

He stood looking down at her. He nodded.

"I feel you show promise, Annie. With a little work... well, I think you could be worthy of me, of my place in the community, with just a tiny bit of polishing."

"Worthy of you?" Annie felt as if she were bursting at the seams. "I reckon any one of us Twigs is worthy of any two of you Trents. My mama was a Fleury... of the Arkansas Fleurys." She tore the dark gray Stetson from the wooden peg and thrust it out toward the visitor. "My Great Aunt was Mrs. Thesalonia Fleury, a sought after hostess in the City of Little Rock. My Uncle Cornish Fleury was a judge in Little Rock." She shook the gray hat in the air. "And my Pap weren't no slouch neither when he was hisself."

"You think about my offer, Annie. I'll be back."

"Ain't no use in that, Henry. This here is my home and I ain't leaving it for the finest mansion in Oklahoma Territory... which I guess your house ain't, anyway, is it?"

Trent stood staring at her.

"I never take 'no' for an answer, Madam."

"You better take it this time, Henry Trent. They ain't never going to be no other answer from Annie Twig. And don't call me Madam. Call me Annie."

"We'll see."

"We done already seen, Henry. You just better get on along home to your polished wood floors, now."

Trent dropped the poncho over his shoulders, then clapped the Stetson on his head.

"I'm going to have you, Annie." The words were a savage murmur. Annie shivered. She'd heard that kind of talk before. After she'd left Arkansas she'd never thought to hear it ever again.

"You *ain't* either going to have me, Henry." Annie's words were shouted at the man's back as he stepped off the small porch.

John immediately stepped into the light from the opened door.

"Trouble, Annie?" He looked up at her, his golden eyes full of hope. She could see his hands were doubled into fists. He was just a looking for an excuse for a good fight.

"Get out of my way!" The older man brushed against the cowboy without looking at him.

"Just a minute, Mister." John reached to clutch at the back of the neckline of the black poncho to drag Henry Trent to a stop. "He bothering you, Annie?"

"No, no, John. Let him go. He ain't bothering me. He's just a going home." She stepped out onto the back step. "Turn him loose now, John. Everthing's all right, I tell you."

John released his handful of rubber but he gave the man a slight shove forward as he did so.

Henry Trent stumbled toward his horse for a step or two before he turned and stared up at Annie then back at John Matlock. His hand rested on the holster at his waist.

"I won't forget this, drifter," He muttered the words without looking at John. "And I meant what I said," He spoke those words with his steel gray eyes trained on Annie. "I'll be back."

"You come on back, anytime." Annie said the customary hospitable words she'd learned so long ago back in Arkansas. She spoke through clenched teeth. "My neighbors is always welcome here. I'll be right where you left me. Right here in my own little house on the Circle Twig." She glanced up at the young couple who were ambling down the trail from the barn. "Junior, you better bring your pappy's teams down. He's a going home."

She couldn't hear what Aramantha and Junior were saying to each other but it was clear that they were disappointed and weren't ready to part from each other. Junior touched Aramantha with one hand and smiled down at her.

"I'm sure sorry I'm going to have to leave, girl." Junior couldn't keep his hand from reaching toward the little strawberry blonde. He touched her lightly on the shoulder. God almighty, she was about as pretty as a new budded rose. And she was promised to him. Just like he was promised to her. Joy coursed through him.

He took off his wide-brimmed hat and looked solemn for a moment. She liked him to kid around with her.

"Now, if my Daddy was to marry your sister, that would make you..." He looked off into the rainy twilight sky. "I guess that would make Annie my Mama and you'd be my Aunt. Ain't that a gallimaufry of a thought? My own little Aunt Aramantha."

Aramantha giggled and slapped at his shoulder with the corner of her apron.

"Silly."

"Can you marry your Aunt, do you think?"

Ary looked up at him, her eyes full of love. That what he liked most about her. She was just like a pretty little redbone puppy who wanted to sit in his lap and go wherever he went and who felt bad when he left her. She liked to tease him, too.

"Maybe we'll get married before they do and that'd make me your wife and Annie your sister-in-law, Junior."

"Guess we better do it like that." He looked at the people in the dooryard below. "I guess I better go. Daddy is going to stomp my guts if I don't get myself on down there."

He inclined his head toward the New York hairdo.

"I sure liked your new hair style, Ary. I'm sorry you was having all them aches and spasms up in the barn. I sure don't want to hurt you none."

"Oh, it was just our baby wiggling around, Junior. He does that all the time. Maybe the little thing will be some quieter next time you come."

"I'll see you tomorrow, for sure, Ary honey. 'Bye." He moved ahead of her down the path, ready to do his Father's bidding.

"Come on in now, Ary," Annie called, "Let Junior get his father's rig ready to go."

"No." The man settled his gray hat more securely on his head. "The cedar shakes are yours, Miss Annie. Someone will come for the wagons in a few days." Trent gave her a frosty smile. "When I give something, I never take it back." He turned the smile toward John as if to say, "I don't take back *anything*, not even my threats."

"I'll come over tomorrow and get the wagons, Annie. I'll see you then, Ary." Junior threw the words over his shoulder as he turned once more toward the barn. Ary waddled into the light from the open door.

"Why they leaving so soon, Annie?" Her voice was plaintive.

"Another promise, Miss Annie." Henry smiled again. "My son won't be setting foot on this place again. Please tell your sister she can look elsewhere for her pleasures." He tipped his hat and walk mounted his gray horse to disappear into the darkness.

Junior and the Trent hired hand, riding on the wagon horses, clanked down the hill and then off into the darkness behind Henry Trent. Junior's "'Bye Ary," was almost lost in the noise of the moving animals.

Annie looked into the puzzled face of her younger sister.

"My pleasures?" Ary repeated.

"I think he means he ain't going to let Junior Trent come a courting over here on the Circle Twig, anymore, little sister."

"But Junior's my best friend." Ary sniffled and dragged herself up the step as if her body weighed a ton. She grunted with the effort of lifting herself. "Junior'll come back to see me. I know he will. I don't care what old Henry Trent says."

"Maybe so, honey. I just hope if he does come he don't bring that pappy of his with him."

Scoundrels' Bargain

John Matlock stood silently staring into the darkness where the Trents had just disappeared.

"That Trent is a dangerous man, Annie."

"I know, John. but he ain't likely to come around here anymore." She smiled up at him. "I done sent him packing."

John smiled.

"You turned him down?"

"Sure did."

"Turned him down for what?" Ary's curiosity overcame her discomfort. She twisted at the lank strands of hair that fell in front of her ear. "What'd he want from us?"

"Nothing from us, Ary girl. That was the problem. He just wanted something from me." Annie pulled Ary's hand away from the straight red gold hair. "Where'd you put them there curl papers? I'm a going to have to do you back up."

Aramantha pulled the limp brown paper strips from her shirt pocket and handed them to her sister.

"Sister! You mean he came over here to ask you to marry him?"

"I don't know iffen it was marriage he had in mind. Wanted me to go live with him in his big old house... without nobody. Without you nor George nor Lucifer nor nobody." Annie grinned at John. "He 'specially didn't want you, John."

John returned the smile.

"I consider that a compliment." He touched Annie's shoulder as she worked. "We'd better keep an eye out for him, just the same. I think he's a dangerous man who is used to getting his way." Annie could feel the print of the hired man's hand all the way through her body.

Uncle George let the door slam behind him.

"Where's our visitors, aye God?" He swayed a step or two before he dropped to sprawl on the bench. He slammed the jug down on the table. "Got old Henry Trent some of the best stuff he never tasted."

"Mr. Trent's gone, Uncle."

George's eyes filled with tears.

"I'm sick, Annie Lee. You gonna have to cure me up some. I'm feeling mighty bad." He swiped his eyes with the sleeve of his shirt. "Get out that sack of yarbs and get to doctoring on me, girl. Little things is a crawling in under my skin."

"Oh, my Lord, John Matlock. You done gone and let Uncle George get at that jug too strong." Annie forced the jug from her uncle's hand and lifted it to the other man. "You go out and hide it again."

"Ow-ww-w-w." The scream from Aramantha stopped everyone in place. Even Gulliver kept silent. The pregnant child stood open mouthed, her curl papers now tightly wound against her head at each ear, one hand pressed against her lower back. "Oh, Annie, I'm scared. What's a happening to me?" She looked down. "I told Junior I was a having these here funny twitches whilst we was a talking out in the barn but I didn't pay it no mind. I didn't think it was much of nothing."

Her petticoat, her shoes and the dirt floor all around Aramantha's feet were drenched with liquid.

Annie spoke as quietly as she could.

"Looks like you was already in labor, little sister. Your water done broke, honey. That means the baby is ready to come." She stopped John before he stepped out the door. "Never mind about that there jug right now, John Wesley. Just set it up there on the highest shelf by the pepper sauce." She glanced at her Uncle George who now sat on the bench, his mouth making silent words, his unfocused blue eyes roaming the air above Aramantha's head.

"For sure he can't help me none with this." She indicated the seated Uncle George with her chin. "And I am gonna need some help mighty bad. No time now to send for Mary Broughton. I think, Matlock, that *you're* the one who's gonna have to help me birth this here baby."

Chapter 9

"Annie. My God. I don't know anything about helping a baby to be born." Matlock's voice held pure horror at Annie's demand that he become her assistant. "Couldn't I just go get the Broughton girl? Or her grandma? I could be back in less than an hour."

Annie smiled up into his wide brown gold eyes. She saw that the man's pupils were abnormally wide and darkened by fear. If she didn't calm him down right away he'd be running hysterical. She tapped him on the chest with her forefinger.

"No time for Mary now. And even iffen you don't know nothing about birthing, John Wesley, it's all right." She let her hand again touch, then pat his chest lightly, trying to calm him the same way she calmed old Lucifer when he spooked. "You don't have to be scared. You say you don't know nothing about babies getting borned." She patted him lightly once more. "That's perfectly all right. I know *everything* about getting that baby borned." She turned and reached up for her medicine sack. "I got me some chamomile and nettle and shepherd's purse. Them's all for easing childbirth."

Uncle George groaned against his folded arms but he didn't raise his head from the table. He began to snore almost as loudly as Mrs. Gulliver in her corner of the room.

"Why don't you help me get this old geezer tucked into his bedroll?" She took one of George's arms and waited for the hired man to take the other. They hoisted the old man up from the bench to help him wobble the few steps to his pallet which waited to be laid out against the wall, next to Mrs. Gulliver.

Annie let the hired man take all of her uncle's weight while she spread George's bedclothes. John then lowered the spare old man to the nest of quilts. George smiled a toothless smile, closed his eyes and fell instantly asleep. John was surprised at the sudden twinge of affection he felt for the older Twig. He patted the man's shoulder after lifting the top quilt to cover that bony protuberance. When he looked up he saw that Annie was watching him. Her blue eyes said something which held him silent for a second.

"Now ma'am, what else shall I do?" He gave a slight self-mocking bow.

"Well now, Mr. Matlock, sir, how about you just take hold of our little Mother here and walk her around and around the room whilst I get things ready?"

A sharp yip from Aramantha caused Matlock to blanch. "She's hurting, Annie. Shouldn't I give her a little taste of George's potion? That would cut the pain a bit, wouldn't it?"

"No, no. That's just an old wive's tale. I learned a long time ago that moonshine slows the birthing down. Ain't good for the baby, neither. You can give Ary a drink after she does her job, iffen you're still a mind to and she wants it."

"Her job?"

"Yes. Her job. Having us our baby. That's her work right now. You've surely heard of 'labor pains' haven't you?"

"Oh. Well. Yes." John Matlock looped his arm through Ary's. "Do you really think walking is best? Shouldn't I just take her in and tuck her in bed?"

"Bed's the worst place for a birthing mother to be. Walk her, sir. Walk her."

Aramantha walked in the same area where she'd danced with her sister a few hours earlier, now with John Matlock at her elbow. Annie dipped hot water from the pan on the stove and poured it into a basin. Working up a lather with a bar of lye soap made by Grandma Broughton, she scrubbed down the wooden table top.

Both Ary and John stopped their pacing and stared at her frantic cleaning.

"Sister... you gotta move." Annie gestured with her chin. "Get her walking, John."

Ary groaned, bent and held her belly with both hands.

"Oh-h-h-h, Annie. I'm hurting."

"I know, honey. You keep walking." Annie had moved to the shelf beside the stove. She didn't look up from the grinding motion she had begun with a battered mortar and pestle. "It won't be long now. I'm a fixing something that'll be good for you."

By the time John Matlock found himself almost dragging the weeping mother-to-be about the room, Annie had her hand-picked herbal medicine ready. She lost herself in thought for a moment.

"I'm going to need me some rags, clean rags. For afterward." She gave the hired man a pained smile. "I know you never did see me in such a thing but I got a dress in the bedroom." She nodded. "Yeah. I guess I could probably use that. I might as well tear that dress up. I don't never wear it anyways."

"Would a clean shirt do?"

"Yeah. It'd be about right. You offering one of them fancy shirts?"

"I wouldn't mind. I guess I'd rather you didn't tear up your dress." He smiled a golden smile at her. "I think I'd very much like to see you in that frock." He guided Ary to the bench. "Sit right here. I'll just be a moment."

"Your pains a coming faster, are they now, sister?" Annie asked the youngster as John searched through his saddle bag and lifted out an expensive looking white cotton jacquarded shirt to wave it in the air like a flag of triumph.

Annie thanked him with her eyes. She used a knife to start the first tear in the garment. In moments she had a pile of clean white cloth beside her other materials.

"Everything all right, honey?" She placed one hand on Aramantha's mounded belly.

Aramantha nodded. "I think the baby's ready to be borned, Annie."

"Ain't you glad?" Annie grinned widely at her sister. "We gonna have us our baby in just a little while and you gonna get rid of that great big belly you been complaining about."

Ary nodded, smiled and again groaned loudly.

"Honey, you don't have to be polite. You can scream iffen. you want to." She smiled at Matlock. "You just go ahead and think of John Wesley here as family. Right, John Wesley?"

The cowboy nodded. His lips were caught between his teeth. His face paled at another groan from Ary.

"Call me John." His voice had deepened to a growl.

"Oh, all right, iffen that'll make you happy." Annie's voice held laughter. "Take that old apron offen her. That shirt, too. I'll go get her clean shift and petticoat. You stay right with her." Annie ducked into the low door to their bedroom and returned with the worn white garments.

"He's undressing me, Annie." Aramantha's whine made Annie laugh.

"No he ain't, honey. He's a helping you get ready for the baby."

"Oh. Well. Okay. Thank you for helping me, John." Ary smiled her trust upward into the dark eyes of the man. "'Cause you're helping me it'll be partly your baby too, won't it?"

"Yes, Ary. I think you're right." He looked to Annie for direction. She motioned with her fingers that he should turn around.

"Let's put on these here clean clothes for to welcome the baby, Ary." When she'd covered the younger woman she touched the back of the man's shoulder to assure him that modesty had been served and that everything was all right. "You can turn around now, and hoist her on up there onto that there table, *John* ... And get her shoes off."

"The table!" John and Aramantha spoke in unison and both stared at Annie.

"Ary, you been with me ten times at least, when I was a birthing babies." Annie let out an exasperated breath. "You know I always use a scrubbed down wooden table iffen I can. Ain't no better medicine than good lye soap." She gestured at the man to lift the small girl up to the tabletop. "You can't get a bed really clean. Them beds is like death traps for little new mothers until after the baby comes. I done told you all that."

John nodded.

"It makes sense, Ary."

"Yes. Thank you John Matlock." Aramantha's eyes again sent messages of trust to the tall man before she cried aloud at a fierce contraction.

"Annie. Can't you do something for her?"

"I am doing something for her." She gestured across the table. "Now *you* can do something for her. Get her up there on the table, then you get behind her and help her sort of half sit, half lean up against you, there." She watched the man help Aramantha up. He stood behind her and held her against his chest. "See that she's kinda close to the end of the table."

When he'd moved her down, Annie raised the tail of her sister's worn petticoat to have a look. "Nature does most of the work and nature takes its time, mister." She gently arranged Ary's legs so her feet were wide apart and flat against the table, her knees bent. Annie reached behind her and lifted one of the heated herbal potions to pour into a tin cup.

She handed the cup to the man.

"Hold this for her to drink.",

Before Ary had downed the half cup of greenish liquid, another huge contraction almost lifted her body from the table top. Ary grunted, then panted.

"Here it comes, little sister. Looks like it might be another little strawberry blonde." Annie passed the back of her hand across her own sweating forehead. "You been doing a real good job, but now you gonna have to push, Ary. Push." She looked up at the wide eyed girl and winked. "It's kinda like going to the outhouse, little sister. You gotta keep pushing when you feel something. Understand?"

Ary nodded and lay back against John.

"Did you see the baby, Annie?" Her voice held fatigue.

"Yeah. I saw just a little of the crown of its head and then I guess it decided to go back for another look at its mama before it comes out for good." She felt Ary's leg begin to stiffen against her hand. "It's a coming, now. Push, girl, push."

The birth lasted only minutes but to the three participants hours passed, worlds changed, the universe buckled and a new baby was born.

Annie lifted the tiny crying mite still attached to its mother and said, "Here's our little girl, Ary, our baby girl. Not very many mothers get their babies as easy as you did, sister." When Ary held the baby against her the child quieted. John helped the young mother lie back on the table. Annie poured more warm water into the basin. She dipped one of the white pieces of cloth into the hot water and handed it to John.

He raised his eyebrows in a question.

"Well, Ary says it's partly your baby too. I thought you might like to give it it's first little bath with some of this here fancy cloth you donated."

He smiled and took the cloth. Annie could see the tenderness in his eyes as he swabbed the newborn who lay at her mother's breast. Ary was checking the baby's toes and fingers to see if she had everything.

"She's perfect, Annie, just perfect. So tiny!"

"Yep. You made us a real pretty little girl, Ary. And in record time too. What you gonna call her?"

"Am I the one who gets to give her her name?" Ary's eyes widened with surprise before she smiled up at the man still supporting her, then at her sister.

"Sure do. You're her mama, ain't you?"

"I like the name Wesley."

John groaned and rolled his eyes.

"Yes. I got it, sister. I'll name her Wesley Ann. That's pretty, don't youall think so?" She appealed to the other two. "And Wesley is a famous name, Annie says. I'll just name her after you two."

"Sounds right nice to me. Thank you little sister."

"Are you sure you want to saddle her with the name *Wesley*?" John rolled his eyes but continued his gentle wiping of the baby. When he'd finished he slipped his arm under Ary's shoulders

"I'm sure." Aramantha lay back in the big man's arms and sighed. Her eyes fluttered closed.

"I'll cut the cord when Ary's ready, John. I'll clean up the afterbirth then you can carry her on into that there bed. I bet she and the baby will be plenty able to sleep now."

Later, after mother and baby were safely tucked into bed, Annie flopped onto the bench next to the kitchen table and yawned hugely. John slid in beside her.

"I guess I could take a mouthful of that stuff you was wanting to offer the little mother," she said and yawned again.

John stood and retrieved the jug.

"I'm surprised that you drink."

"I don't 'drink,' as you put it. I'm just plumb beat down and I'd like a taste for medicinal reasons." Annie reached for the jug, took a small drink and held it out to her hired man. "You better have one, too."

He took a longer swallow and set the jug on the table.

"I've never had a baby named after me."

"Kind of a nice feeling, ain't it? Having a baby named after me is always nice. They's several Annies and more than one Twig, around here and back in Arkansas, who has me to thank for their names."

"It's just as I said. You're a good woman, Annie."

He trained the focus of his gaze onto her face. He slipped one arm behind her shoulders and bent his head so he could touch her lips with his own. She had a natural fragrance, spicy and feminine, the smell of a woman who had been doing the work of a woman.

What started as a gentle, almost brotherly, kiss, suddenly heated. He pulled her closer and drank deeply from her lips, her delicious mouth. The moonshine she'd tasted made a tangy overlay for what he had known would be a wild sweetness. He felt as if he could never hold her closely enough, never have enough of that sweetness.

To Annie, the beautifully sculpted lips of the statue came alive against her own. Her defenses were down. She wanted this man. She opened her mouth to his questing tongue. Her hand lifted involuntarily to tangle in the shaggy black curls at the nape of his neck. She pulled him closer and yet closer. She felt him groan deep in his throat. She answered with a murmur of her own. Her blood sang in her veins. She was awash with desire for this man. She squeezed her thighs together and rubbed gently at the thrill between her legs. With her eyes closed she felt herself floating on a sea of pleasure that she hoped would go on forever.

When he was the one to pull away first she felt shocked, disappointed, almost betrayed. She had wanted the thrill of their kiss to go on and on.

"I'm sorry, Annie." He drew a deep, shaky breath as he spoke.

"Nothing to be sorry for, John." Was he apologizing about the kiss or was he sorry about quitting so soon? She didn't know. She only knew that she had liked his mouth on hers, his body near hers. "I kinda liked what you was doing." She glanced at the sleeping Uncle George and the gently snoring, Mrs. Gulliver. "I guess you're right though. It's about time we both hit the hay too." She stood and walked toward the corner where his saddle bags and his bedroll lay. As she walked she could feel the imprint of his mouth upon hers almost as if he were still kissing her. Maybe she'd always feel his lips against hers.

Uncle George snorted loudly and flopped over in his sleep. From under the corner of his quilt something metallic glinted in the candlelight. She bent to pick up the item.

"When you was pulling out that pretty shirt something fell out'n your bag, I expect.". She turned the object in her hand. "What's this here?" She held up the silvery metal shield. Her fingers felt cold where they touched the thin official looking symbol. "I reckon this here thing is yours." She stretched out her arm and tossed the shining item toward him as she forced her next words from a jaw gone rigid with fear.

"Was old Henry Trent right? You some kind of damned lawman, Mr. John Wesley Matlock?"

Chapter 10

For a long moment the word "lawman" rang harshly in the air of the small room before John silently placed the silver shield into his shirt pocket. Annie narrowed her eyes and waited for his answer.

She raised her hand to touch her lips. The kiss that she'd thought would brand her lips forever had already disappeared. Her lips felt stiff, cold. So did her heart. The lips and heart of a statue, now. How could she have been so wrong about this man? She wouldn't say another word to him until he explained himself. Damned sneaky marshal or sheriff or deputy or whatever the hell he was. Come here to harm her family, she just knew.

How could she have let him help her bring their new baby into the world? And now the baby was branded with the man's ugly name. This here Matlock was nothing but a low down, lying, carpetbagger marshal or maybe something even worse.

John Matlock cleared his throat. His ginger colored gaze flickered across her face then his lids lowered. He searched the dirt floor as if looking there for words to say to her. He enviously watched Mrs. Gulliver shift and fart loudly, then sigh with contentment. His night would probably not be so restful. He might even be ordered out of the tiny house. He'd have to watch his tongue and he must find a way to sooth this pride wounded beauty, Annie Twig, if he could.

In the long silence that lay between them, a huge clap of thunder caused each of them to take an involuntary step toward the other. He forced himself to raise his gaze and look directly at her. He couldn't bear the pain and anger he saw there in those blue eyes, the bluest eyes he'd ever known.

"Annie..." He held his hands out toward her.

She shook her head and let her glare say it all. She was telling him there would be no going back. No touching of her hands. No kissing of her lips. Nothing of that kind would ever be able to make up for what she saw as a kind of betrayal. He had to tell her something... maybe not everything, but he had to make *some* sort of explanation and he had to do it now. Until he did he knew she would not let one word pass her lips.

"Annie, I'm not a marshal, nor a deputy. Not even a real lawman. I don't work for any branch of the government." He smiled as he pleaded. He opened his hands toward her, palms up as if asking for mercy. "Hell, I don't even work for the railroad. Can you believe me when I tell you these things?"

She took a deep breath and released it to let some of the suffocating fear escape from her chest.

"I don't know iffen I can or not. If you ain't none of them things then what's that there tin badge thing all about?"

"I'm what is called a 'Pinkerton' detective." He took the silvery badge from his pocket and traced the word Pinkerton with his finger as he read. "See? It says so right here. *Pinkerton.*"

"What's that word mean? What does Pinkerton mean?" She looked at the boldly engraved metal words he held out to her on the metal shield. She read aloud. "*Pinkerton Detective Agency.*" Her voice quavered on the last word. "I think I heard of them. Ain't a detective some kind of police?"

"A Pinkerton detective is a little bit like a lawman, but not exactly." Matlock inwardly cursed his own carelessness in ripping the sacrificial shirt from his saddlebag only to reveal himself much too early in the game. He'd have to tell her something. He wouldn't be able to stay if he didn't calm her down. "Mr. Allan Pinkerton started the agency years ago back East. I work for the agency so I am called a Pinkerton detective, not a lawman."

"What does that mean, 'not exactly' a lawman?"

"Well, I'm a detective, which means I was hired from the agency to search out what the client..."

"What's a client?" Her blue eyes were wide and searching as if they held lights somewhere deep in their depths. No. She wasn't buying his explanation. Her eyes were still sending angry signals. The blue glitter resembled Oklahoma lightning flashing from behind a cloud.

"The people or company or group that hires the detective would be called the clients. Like when you went over to help your neighbors, the Broughtons, the Broughtons were then your clients. Understand?"

"Yeah. I see." She ran her fingers through the short blond hair at her temple. "I was just curing folks, my *clients*, I guess you'd call them, but I'm not rightly sure I truly understand what *your* job is for your clients, John."

He gestured to the bench and she sat down beside him. That was some headway, he supposed. She was at least willing to talk.

"I'm supposed to find out what the client needs to know. My agency is paid by, and I owe my allegiance to, the private party who hired me." The blue eyes were still stormy. He could see she needed more reassurance. Somehow he had to regain her trust. "Annie, what I'm doing is legal but I'm not working for the U.S government nor a state government nor even any city." He took a deep breath. A small lie couldn't matter. "I can't actually put anyone in jail."

Uncle George snored loudly, then quieted. She rose to look at the old man, then she put the kettle on to boil. Good. She was acting as if she were ready to capitulate.

"I'm sorry if my little shield scared you, Annie." He slipped a question in as she spooned dried leaves into the teapot. "Are you afraid of the law for some reason?"

She turned to him, fury again mounting in her face.

"There you go again. Asking them questions. I ain't telling you nothing, *Pinkerton Detective Matlock*, until you come clean and tell me just what it is you was a nosing around for, here on the Circle Twig."

"Do the Broughtons trust you to keep quiet about what their medical problems are?"

"The Broughtons? Are you investigating that there bunch of Iowa farmers?" She smiled and lifted the hot water and poured it into the teapot. Spicy herbal steam rose in the air. "They ain't never done nothing wrong in this world. I can tell you that." She giggled. "Grandma Broughton gossips an almighty lot but other than that they ain't no harm in that bunch of folks. Might as well look into Mrs. Gulliver's activities."

"Annie. Annie." The call from the bedroom froze both of them in place. "Annie. Come here. Hurry!"

"Oh, my God. Something's wrong with Ary or the baby, Annie." He whispered the words. His panic stricken amber eyes searched hers for reassurance.

"We don't know that." She whispered back and waited a beat more before she moved toward the dugout doorway. It seemed as if he really cared what happened to little sister.

"Ary, honey. What's wrong? Are you paining bad?"

"No, sister. It hurts a little between my legs but not real awful bad. I'm tired but I'm feeling some better." The young mother lifted the precious bundle wrapped in the back section of John Matlock's expensive white shirt. "I called you in because I think our baby smiled at me, Annie. I just wanted youall to see it, too."

"Oh, little sister, that's wonderful, but you and Wesley Ann better go on back to sleep." Annie smoothed the reddish pompadour. "Your hairdo is staying right nice, Aramantha. Maybe that's why the baby was smiling at you."

"Can a baby smile at you at this age?" John's whisper was incredulous. He stood stooped in the low doorway and peered over Annie's shoulder. Ary had obediently closed her eyes and was immediately asleep once again. The baby had never wakened.

Annie pushed the tall man back into the other room. He blinked in confusion.

"That baby was asleep, Annie.... how could it have been smiling at her? Is she maybe delirious?"

"It wasn't and she isn't. But I learned a long time ago not to argue with new mothers. Iffen they see their baby smiling at them, who am I to say they didn't see it?" She poured the tea into two cups and moved around the table to sit across from him. "A little story like that don't hurt no one." She put a teaspoon of sugar into her own herbal tea then held the teaspoon in the air and looked questioningly at him.

"No. No sugar. I like it just the way you brew it, Annie. The same way I like everything you do." He had to grin at the scathing look she tossed him. "Let's talk about little stories... some people call them 'lies.' But I guess you don't?"

"I'd say about anything that seems necessary to keep a new little mother quiet and happy right after she's just give birth."

"Well... my job is a little like yours in that I am expected to keep my client's secrets while I'm ferreting out the answers to his or her questions. You keep the Broughton's family secrets and I keep my client's secrets." He drank a swallow of the herb tea. "In other words I'm keeping them quiet and happy the same way you do a new mother." He lifted the tin cup as if to toast Annie. "Good stuff, Miss Twig."

"Call me Annie," she said absently. "So you're telling me that keeping secrets is just a part of your job, too?"

"Yes. It's called *confidentially* in the detective business." He took another swallow. "I'm really sorry I kept things from you, Annie. I felt I had to."

"Lied to me, you mean?"

"Well, you weren't lying when you didn't tell Ary that her baby can't smile yet, were you? My lies aren't much bigger than that." He drank again and held his cup out for a refill. "I just can't tell you any more about what I'm doing here. I wish you could accept that."

"You ain't no cowpoke, huh?"

"Well, I'm doing a pretty good job for you here on the Circle Twig, I thought. You have any complaints?" He watched for her headshake. "In that case what does it matter that, while I work for you, I'm also working for the Pinkertons?"

He was astounded to see Annie's face redden, her gaze drop to her cup of tea. She moved restlessly on the bench. She actually looked rather embarrassed. She opened her mouth, then closed it. Her blue eyes looked up at him again. She wanted to say something and she was... what? Afraid? Ashamed to speak about whatever it was?

"Well, what do you say? My work here on the Circle Twig is all right?"

"Uh, yeah. You're for sure doing a good job for me. Better'n nary a one of any of them others I hired. Uh, John Wesley," she shifted again and the next words came tumbling from her lips, "Seeing as how the Pinkertons is a paying you to snoop around out here... uh, do you think we

Scoundrels' Bargain 69

could kind of overlook your first month's pay?" She turned the tin cup in circles on the scrubbed wood of the table.

He had to laugh.

"I've been here nearly six weeks. Exactly when were you planning to tell me you weren't going to pay me for my first month's work, Annie?"

She felt a ripple of surprise at his laughter then she let her own laughter join with his.

"Never, so long as you was willing to keep on working without mentioning it." She took his empty cup and carried it with her own to the basin in the corner. "All of them others asked after awhile. Cept'n for old Calvin. That old boy only worked for two or three days 'fore he up and died."

She slid once more onto the bench and looked boldly up at the smiling golden glance across from her.

"I ain't never... I *didn't* never tell them drifters nothing lessen they asked." Maybe she could quit saying "ain't." She'd heard old Henry Trent say "ain't" and iffen that old boy said it she could do without it. She remembered Mr. Calendula telling her that the use of "ain't" was "incorrect" and Mr. Calendula was the best teacher in the world even iffen he was from Chicago. Matlock never used the word. It'd probably be easy enough to watch out for the word itself without her having to take some kind of long-term English and diction lessons from this old boy. All she really had to do was pay attention to what he said and how he said it.

"In other words, you lied to those men?" He couldn't control his delight with what she'd revealed. That would make the whole thing much easier. The glimmer of candlelight in her eyes echoed his amusement.

"I guess that's about it, John. Reckon we all got our secrets, ain't... haven't we?" Her pert smile and her quick correction of herself were too much for him.

"Sometimes more than one, Miss Annie." He leaned across the table and lightly kissed the smiling rosy vee of her lips. She kept smiling and she didn't move away from the kiss.

"Here's Uncle George's jug, Annie." He stood and reached across her for the crockery item. "I believe you and I must drink to seal our bargain." He took a quick nip and handed the jug across the table to her. "How about this as a mutual pact? A mutual pact means we both must agree to it." He raised his eyebrows in a questioning movement. She nodded her understanding. He continued. "I won't tell you my secrets if you won't tell me yours."

"A scoundrels' bargain?" She nodded again and took a drink to seal their mutual agreement. She leaned forward and kissed the perfect set of male lips that didn't taste at all like she believed the lips on that metal man in Fort Smith might have tasted. Matlock didn't move away. In fact, he caught her head in his big hand and returned as good as he got.

She leaned back from the kiss and smiled at her still unpaid hired hand. This here good looking John Wesley Matlock was hardworking and puredee fun to be with but she'd have to watch what she said. And she'd better make real sure that Ary and George minded their P's and Q's around him, too. She'd make sure the old man was sober when she explained it to them. They were just two innocents in a sinful world. They needed protecting. Anyone asked them anything they'd answer right off, just blurting out the truth.

For sure, this here John was the kind of a man who could worm the deepest secret right out of them two, they were so wet behind the ears.

She'd bet this old boy could even get secrets out of old Lucifer and without any question Mrs. Gulliver would tell him anything he wanted to know iffen she but could. That little sow just rightly loved this big sweet talking Pinkerton man.

Later, when she'd slipped into the bed beside Aramantha and the new baby she helped the baby find her mother's breast. It was soothing to hear the little cooing sounds Wesley Ann made as she nursed. Aramantha barely woke to welcome Annie into the bed with them.

After the baby had finally dropped off to sleep, Annie let herself relax and smile up into the darkness. She was determined to keep her secrets but it would be mighty good to have them Pinkerton folks a paying for the work she sure as hell had to get done on this here place.

Iffen the Circle Twig was ever going to be hers *someone* was going to have to work alongside her like a good hired hand was supposed to. That someone might as well be John Wesley Matlock. Yeah. She had to say it was right generous of them northerner folks, them Pinkertons, to fork over the money for the job.

She was still smiling when sleep overtook her.

Chapter 11

"I'm kinda worried, sister." Ary held the new baby to her bared breast and smoothed and patted the newborn's back as it suckled. "Wesley Ann's been with us for nigh onto two whole days now and she ain't done number two yet." Ary smiled down at the nursing child. "She acts like she feels all right. She eats a bunch." The young mother turned a gaze of appeal up to her sister. "I guess that's what bothers me, sister. Lots has gone in but nothing has come out."

Uncle George frowned and moved to add his patting motion to Aramantha's on Wesley Ann's tiny bare back.

"Poor baby." He rolled his eyes to see what Matlock and Annie thought of Ary's bad news. "Now me, aye God, I can't go more'n a day without squatting out there in the woods." He patted the babe again. "Iffen I do skip more'n a day I get the bellyache real bad." He looked at Annie for confirmation of his complaint.

John Matlock leaned forward to look at the baby but he didn't say anything. He examined the busy baby's back very carefully before he also turned his tawny eyed, questioning gaze toward Annie.

She felt pleased to see the tiny line of worry that appeared between his brows. *He cares about that, there baby, don't he? Looks at me now like maybe he thinks I know a little something he don't know don't he?*

Annie dug her needle securely into the white cloth before she put the garment on the table to hold up both hands as if quelling an angry crowd.

"Don't worry, any of you." She gently raked the rumpled front of Ary's New York Pompadour with the fingers of one hand. "New babies usually don't have their first movement for three, maybe even four days." She took up the small garment she was finishing off, lifted it to her lips and clipped the thread with her teeth. She thought she could still smell just a trace of John Matlock on the white cloth. Smelled like a city man. Smelled rich. She held the tiny white cotton shift toward the candlelight so the others could admire the finished garment.

"You didn't know you was making a contribution to Wesley Ann's wardrobe, did you, Mr. Detective?"

"Is that from my shirt?"

She nodded and smoothed the miniscule garment over the head of the now sleeping infant. Ary helped pull the child's hands up through the sleeveless arm openings.

"Annie, why're you calling him Mr. Detective? Why you doing that? What's that mean?" Ary turned her puzzled face to look at Matlock then at her sister.

"Well, I was a wanting to tell you Ary, you and Uncle George need to know that John Matlock here is a detective. That's a sort of a lawman."

Ary's eyes opened wide and her lips made an O. George frowned again.

"Lawman?"

"Yep." Annie threaded her needle from the precious spool of white linen thread that Mrs. Broughton had shared with her. "'Course he says he can't *arrest* no one." She held the threaded needle up with one hand and slipped a knot into the long end of the thread with the other. "Just the same, all us criminals here on the Circle Twig gotta be careful." She laughed lightly but she gave Ary and her uncle a meaningful glance. "He works for them there Pinkertons, back up there in New York."

"I thought he worked for us." Ary kept her eyes fixed on the baby. "Lookie here. See? Like I said. She's a pretty good eater, sister." She smoothed the baby's reddish hair. "What's a Pinkerton?"

"Well, it's the name of them people up North who is paying him to work for us. Ain't that nice of them?" Annie grinned across the table at the golden flash of the hired man's aroused glance. She suppressed the laughter that wanted to answer his accusing stare.

Both Ary and Uncle George nodded agreement and lost interest in the conversation. The new baby and what she was doing was their main concern.

"Aye God, look at little Wesley Ann. She's all dressed up right pretty now, ain't she?" Uncle George let a gnarled finger trace the rounded neck of the garment. "For sure, little girl childrens shouldn't have to go around naked as jaybirds."

"I cut out two little things for her just from the back part of John Matlock's shirt. Not to mention a world of pieces left over for starting a quilt one of these days." Annie pulled the second unfinished shift from her basket. "I may try to get me some pretty pink embroidery thread and put two or three rosebuds on the front of this here one. She could wear that for the Sunday School." She smiled at the hired man. "We all thank you for the use of your nice shirt for our little girl, John."

"You're all welcome," He leaned forward, "Especially you, little Miss Wesley Ann." He placed his finger into the baby's grip. "O-o-o-oweee, lookie here at you." He gently bounced the tiny fist in his huge hand. "You're strong like your Aunt Annie, pretty blue eyed baby girl." He grinned at Annie then turned back to the baby. "O-o-o-o-oweee. Aren't you a pretty little redhead?" He made a series of little clicking sounds with his tongue as if to catch the newborn's attention.

It pleased Annie somehow to see the big educated man playing the fool for the new baby. It was clear that the youngest female in the family had already securely wrapped both her old uncle and the other male at the table, right around her little fingers.

Aramantha pulled the front of what had been her pappy's shirt up to cover the breast she'd been giving Wesley Ann. The strong prickle of worry that Annie felt had no place to go. Her little sister was still wearing the same old petticoat, shirt and apron get up. Maybe there was something she could do.

"Next thing I'll do is get that brown dress of mama's out and we'll cut it down to fit you, Ary. Ain't no more need for you to run around in that makeshift outfit cept'n for dirty work around the place." She was rewarded by Ary's radiant smile.

"Could you fix my hair again, sister? It done got all frizzed out." She turned to let Annie see the partly ruined red gold edifice.

Annie nodded.

"Could you do it tonight... just in case Junior or Mary Broughton or someone might come by to see our baby?"

Annie let her gaze meet John Matlock's level stare. He raised his eyebrows. She shrugged. She knew he understood what she was thinking. Both of them were remembering Henry Trent's last words before he'd left the yard. He'd said Junior wasn't to be allowed back on the Twig place.

Well, she was pretty sure Junior Trent wasn't a coming back here anymore but she could at least fix the girl's hair. It'd stay up real good this time since Ary wouldn't be twisting around a having a baby and all. Probably best if they let Ary learn about Junior on her own. No use hurting her feelings any more than necessary right now whilst she was still feeling delicate and all.

"I'll do that directly, honey." She stood and moved toward the bedroom. "Let me get my hair fixing stuff."

"I don't think Junior has ever saw me in a dress." Aramantha called after her.

Annie silently brought out the dress and her comb and brush and their mama's mirror. She looked once more at the tall cowboy and shook her head almost imperceptibly. He kept surprising her with his understanding. He probably also understood that she was trying to keep Ary's mind off Junior Trent.

"You go put on this here dress and I'll get the sugar water ready for you." She gestured toward the bedroom. "Let Uncle George take the baby."

"Let me take the baby." The hired man's cultured voice brooked no interference. "I haven't had a turn to hold her yet and you did say she was partly mine, didn't you, Aramantha?"

Ary looked at Annie to see if it was all right, then smiled at Annie's nod and placed the baby in the arms of the waiting man.

"I won't be but a minute."

"Take your time, Aramantha. Wesley Ann and I want to get acquainted... don't we girl?" He smiled down at the unfocused blue eyes. "She looks a lot like Annie Lee, don't you think, George?" He held the infant out so the child's great uncle could look at her. "She has Annie's blue eyes." He made a smooching sound toward the baby. "Have you noticed George, see her little fingernails? She's so tiny but everything about her is perfect. Look at her little feet."

"Aye God, all the Fleury's has blue eyes, son. This'n couldn't a had nothing else. Why Addison..." He opened his mouth to say more when Annie interrupted.

"Why don't you go get your fiddle, George, and we all can sing whilst we're prettifying up little sister?" Annie let her voice rise and override what the old man had been saying.

Her Uncle's face lit with delight. He bobbed his head "yes" and scurried into the dug out bedroom to bring back his music maker. Ary followed a moment later, wearing the brown calico dress she'd worn some before she'd gotten too large around the middle.

"Look, Annie. That there milk for Wesley Ann is a making me bigger in the chest. The dress fits real well there now." She smoothed the flounced apron drape at the front of the garment. "And this here stuff'll hide my belly. Last time I wore this un we was in town. Remember, Annie?"

"Yeah, sister, I remember. Looks like we can just nip it in a teensy bit at the waist and take that there ruffle off the hem and it'll do just fine." she frowned. "Course, I may have to make the back the front so's you can button up or down for Wesley Ann."

Annie pointed to the bench. "Sit you down here in front of me and we can sing and make our plans for our Sunday School." She dipped her comb in the sugar water. "For our festivities you could wear this here dress and your fancy New York do and you'd look just as fine as frog hair."

"When we gonna do that, sister?"

"Soon as John here has the roof on the new room and Wesley Ann is old enough to meet all them folks, hon. I don't hold with them as would keep you in bed for a week or more but I reckon you need to take it a little easy around the house. Don't suppose you're quite ready to dance anyway just now, are you?" She patted the red gold hairdo. "But it won't be very long."

George played and he and Ary sang a lullaby to the baby as she burped milk bubbles against John Matlock's shoulder, then her head wobbled back into his big hand. Annie knew the baby felt security there. A baby could tell. Those were strong hands that were holding her. It was amazing that such a small person could have such a strong hold on a

Scoundrels' Bargain

roomful of adults. Annie felt her own heart melt as she looked at the infant. John was smiling down at the little mite as he spoke.

"You're putting her to sleep, George, you and your nieces. Those two wonderful voices with that fiddle of yours make a powerful combination. You lullabying could make me want to go to sleep while it's still light out."

"Aye God, the Twigs can sing, the Fleury's too. You girl's old Great Aunt Thesalonia Fleury, she was Addison Fleury's great aunt, too. Let's see. That made Addison your cousin. Don't know why I forgot about that. Why that last day him and me, we was a..."

"Uncle George, get that there peach basket from behind the stove and we'll just let Wesley Ann sleep here on the table with us whilst I work." Annie raised her head abruptly and pointed the dripping comb at the door. She tried to keep the sharpness out of her voice. "Fold up two of them there dish towels and lay them into the basket and it'll make her a fine bed." She smiled down at Ary. "Is that all right, sister? We can always carry her in that basket, too, was we a needing to."

I got to get George and Ary alone somehow and tell them to be mighty careful talking about the Fleurys or the Twigs or Arkansas or our family or anything. They ain... haven't understood a single word I been saying about John Wesley Matlock being a law man.

She let out a long breath and looked at the tall man rocking the baby against his chest and murmuring nonsense syllables to the sleeping child. Not that he's all that crazy about the law right this minute. Looks to me like he done been smitten by a little redhead. Which suits me fine. We do want to keep him happy to stay around here, at least for awhile.

A crash and a harsh bray stopped everyone in the room.

"That was Lucifer. Probably kicking out at a wolf or a hyena." Annie went on with the arranging of the younger woman's hair.

"Hyena? Here in the territory?" Matlock felt a moment of shock. "Are you sure?"

"Sure. Them coyotes is everwhere."

"You call coyotes *hyenas*?"

"Aren't they the same thing? When it's wet sometimes they'll try to get in under the roof of the shed." She combed a long strand of hair over her hand. "That old devil of a mule just can't stand to have them wild animals in the shed with him." She patted the last red gold curl into place. "Now, you're all new again cept'n for them two ear curls, little sister."

"If you don't mind I'll just go up and look, Annie." John stood with the baby in his arms. His eyes turned dark as the night outside. "Here George." He handed the sleeping child toward the old man. He looked down to take one more glimpse of the infant. "Now, don't you wake her up."

George laid his violin and bow on the table to reach for the baby. A louder series of crashes and brays and the sound of metal smashed against wood roused them all to action. Mrs. Gulliver squealed. George thrust the baby into Ary's arms, John stepped out the door and Annie put down the comb and followed just after him.

"What is it, John?"

"I'm going to find out."

"I'll come with you."

"You better stay right here, little lady."

"This here is the Circle Twig. My place, and don't you forget it. And I ain't no 'little lady.'" She jostled ahead of him down the two stone steps. "I'll go with you. It's probably nothing but Lucifer getting his licks in on some lowdown intruder."

"Exactly what I'm afraid of but I don't think it's an animal ... a lowdown *human* intruder is what I think we might find." He'd already swept around her, his long stride easily outdistancing her up the path toward the barn. She hurried along behind him. The misting rain had stopped for the moment. The air was clear even though the ground was still muddy.

She didn't know where such a thing had come from but it looked mighty like the moonlight was a glinting off of something dark and metallic, something held in the hired man's big hand. Uh huh... she could see it real clear now. That's just what she'd thought it was... a gun!

He'd been expecting something like this ever since the night of Henry Trent's visit. Probably some of that rancher's goons sent to make trouble. He smiled into the darkness. Bet no one had told them about that mulish nightmare Annie kept in the barn, the nightmare called Lucifer.

The animal wasn't in the barn but John could distinguish three sets of prints just outside the shed. Looked as if there had been two men on foot... and the mule. Lucifer was still on their trail, likely as not.

"Was it a painter?"

"A painter?" What was she talking about?

"Yeah. You know, looks kinda like you."

"A painter?"

"Yeah. Your eyes is gold. Like cat eyes. And you prowl around in the dark, kinda like a painter, too."

A cat? Oh. A *panther*.

"No, not this time. No pug marks I can see." She acted as if she were ready to bound up the hill after her lost animal.

John held Annie back with one hand.

"They're gone, I expect. Let's not walk around out there just now. First thing in the morning I'll come up here and track them. If we flounder around out there in the dark we may erase all the signs."

"Can you tell what it was?"

He gestured toward the sets of prints he'd seen just outside the shed.

"Looks like two men walking. Both wearing heeled boots."

"Maybe them two bastards stole my good mule."

"If they'd wanted a mule they'd have taken your biddable one." He pointed to the gray mule that calmly munched hay from the filled bin of the manger. "Believe me, no one but you would want old Lucifer." He touched her arm. "We can tell a lot more about who and what and why in the morning. This muddy ground has made a record of everything that happened here tonight... I'll just follow it in the morning."

"You read sign? You an Indian?"

"No. A detective... remember?" He stepped a bit closer to her. "Detectives are supposed to detect." He smiled down at her. "But the truth is I learned a lot about tracking from the Indian Scout in my regiment."

For a moment there was silence in the dark barn.

God I want to kiss her. And I think she wants me to kiss her. He moved even closer.

She took a step back.

"Are you afraid of me, Annie Lee?" Her blonde hair was his only light in the darkness. He couldn't see her features well. Her face glowed darker than her hair but lighter than her brown shirt. He could see that her blue eyes were wide and watchful of his movements.

He watched her luminous hair shake to signal the negative. She wasn't afraid.

He moved a fraction closer. She didn't move away from him this time.

You're not supposed to get mixed up with a suspect, he reminded himself. You just now heard her Uncle start to say something about "Addison" before she interrupted him. You need to be delving into what may be something really messy. Be careful of involvement, John.

I'm already involved, he argued inwardly. Somehow I've allowed myself to become thoroughly mixed up in the life of this strange family. Hell, I'm even worried about her stupid mule.

"I hope nothing has happened to Lucifer, Annie." Her smile gleamed whiter than the halo of her hair.

"You don't have to worry none about Lucifer, John. I reckon he can take care of himself."

There. He cocked his head and reviewed what she'd said. In almost perfect English. Both sentences. Was she changing her language patterns or was he just becoming used to her speech? He felt like cheering. But he had to be honest with himself. He had to admit that it wouldn't matter if this woman spoke only gibberish, he'd still want to touch her, to kiss her... to love her.

"Could we sit down here for a few minutes?" He gestured toward the pile of hay in the corner where he'd first made his bed. "Talk for a minute before we go back to the others?" She smelled like a fresh peach. Now how did she do that?

"You think they're a coming back or something?"

"Maybe." He entrusted the gun to the grain shelf above the manger.

She bent in a graceful movement and rested in the pile of hay. He followed. Another strained moment of silence stretched between them.

"Annie..."

"John..."

They spoke simultaneously and then laughed. Another long moment of silence followed. He leaned toward her. She swayed toward him. Their lips met, then they drew back from each other. She put her hand on his back and felt a tremor run through the hardened muscles there. She heard a sigh and knew it was her own. At last. She'd wanted these lips on hers for so long. The remembrance of the banished, drawn out kiss they'd shared in the kitchen came flooding back into every nerve and fiber of her body memory. She arched her back and let herself sink more deeply into the surge of desire she felt for this man.

I can have him for this moment, she told herself. Who's to say no?

I need this man... and he wants me. It ain... isn't as if I were thinking about marriage or anything like that. This man ain't wanting no uneducated farm woman for a wife but he wants me right now, right enough. For sure with all the stuff I got piled on my back, I'm never going to have what regular folks have, a husband, kids, love. Might as well take whatever comes down the pike iffen it's something I want. First man since Addison... and I don't remember never feeling like this with Addy... not even at the beginning.

All I have to do is let all that there turmoil in my mind just slip away. Forget about all that there past stuff. That was then and this is now. A whole other life. So this man hadn't been honest with her? Still wasn't. Sure. She knew that. But he wanted her. She also knew that. Just quit thinking, Annie, she advised herself. Just let whatever happens, happen. Take what you can get if it's what you really want and be glad of it.

She lay back against the hay. She took a breath filled with the dust from the hay and with one hand on his shoulder, the other on the back of his neck, she pulled his face down toward her own. She opened her mouth to his entreating tongue. His mouth offered salving honey to her hungry heart. She lost herself in the heated, swirling, demanding kiss. A kiss that went on and on. A kiss that somehow seemed to open her soul. She let herself sink deeper and deeper back into the hay.

She'd moved beyond conscious thought. The sound of hoof beats hardly penetrated the brown velvet cocoon of longing that together they'd wrapped around the two of them until abruptly, John jerked away from her with a loud wordless cry then a curse. He jumped to his feet.

"What the fu...? Jesus. Your goddamned mule just bit the hell out of me, Annie." She sat up to see John Wesley Matlock rubbing his injured backside. "I'm lucky I had on my trousers." Behind him Lucifer danced, eyes rolling, gleaming teeth clacking, ears laid back in a rage of warning. "I think I'm going to have to kill that devil's spawn you call a mule and I'm going to do it right now!"

He reached for the gun.

Chapter 12

The lawman let his hand drop away from the gun at Annie's scream of horror.

Annie raised her hand to touch his as she questioned him.

"Did he draw blood, John?"

"No, but I'm sure he meant to. Bastard animal." He. continued to rub his backside.

"Well, John, iffen Lucifer didn't draw blood he wasn't mad at you."

"Mad at me? Annie, what in hell are you talking about. I'm the one who's angry with your hell-ridden animal and I don't give a damn about how he feels."

"What I'm saying John, is that you don't want to shoot an animal who just gave you a playful little nip. He may be learning to like you." She could still see a lambent fire in the man's eyes just as she had before he kissed her but now the light was different. Now, she knew it was the glow of puredee anger.

John stared at her in disbelief.

"You're telling me that he nearly bit my rump off because he *likes* me?"

"Well, yes. I'm saying he may be beginning to like you iffen he didn't draw no blood. When he wants to hurt someone old Lucifer hurts them real bad."

John rained down muttered imprecations on the head of the evil mule all the way from the barn to the house. Annie erased her secret smile when they stepped up onto the back step. *It wouldn't do no good to let an angry man see a woman a laughing about his troubles. especially iffen the troubles was funny.*

After listening to John's story about the strange sets of footprints, Ary and George continued their musical entertainment.

"Annie, why don't you and George sing that song about me a sleeping beside the crick. I always loved that song. I can even remember mama singing it, Sister. Can't you?"

Aramantha looked down into the face of her newborn. "I want Wesley Ann to learn it."

"This here music was set to a poem writ by Old Bobby Burns hisself, long years ago, away across the waters." George announced before he lifted his fiddle to his chin. "I learned this song when I were just a boy in the hills of Arkansas."

* * *

Scoundrels' Bargain 81

John listened in amazement to the song of "Ary sleeping by the creek." No question about it the Twigs were magnificent singers. Amazing. Now how had the old man known about Burns, a poet who had lived in Scotland back in the 1700's?

"*Flow gently Sweet Afton among thy green braes.*
Flow gently, I'll sing thee a song in thy praise,"

Oh. *Sweet Afton*. Why did Ary think *Sweet Afton* was a song about her? He listened to the plaintive notes of the old Scots folk tune and smiled in recognition when they harmonized on the next lay.

"*My Ary's asleep by thy murmuring stream,*
Flow gently sweet Afton disturb not her dream."

John loved their substitution of "Ary" for "Mary." What an unbelievably strange mixture of knowledge, ignorance, erudition, benightedness, pride, poverty, beauty, superstition, secrecy, talent and love this family held.

In some ways Annie was right. They had no doubt descended from good blood, from a good family background, perhaps generations back, even though this particular branch of the Twigs and the Fleurys or one of them at least, apparently had plenty to hide. He'd better get on into Guthrie right away. The people in Little Rock would be waiting for his report.

He just might get some pink embroidery thread and a few other little things if such items could be had in the axle deep mud of the tent city that the Territorial capitol offered.

He looked at the enticing rosy vee of Annie's upper lip as she sang with an easy grace. She was a flaxen haired picture of the epitome of innocence. He felt himself harden as he relived the instant when she'd pulled him down to lie against her as she lay in the hay. He swallowed. For those few minutes he'd completely forgotten his mission here. All he'd wanted was to have her mouth under his, her body pressed against his. He groaned aloud and covered his indiscretion by clearing his throat.

He glanced at each of the Twigs' faces. The singers hadn't noticed his discomfort. They were too busy concentrating on their close harmony patterns. A quick picture of how Annie's lush breasts must look when not covered with that confounded old brown shirt rose behind his eyes. Better not dwell on that right now.

Yes, Annie was the one... the one he'd really have to work hard to get around. Too clever, by far. And she drew him toward her as no other woman had ever done. Even when they were working on the fence or on the shingled roof for the outside kitchen it was almost as if his hands had a mind of their own, it was very nearly impossible to keep his hands from circling her slim waist whenever he came close to her.

With that pale blonde hair haloing about her head she looked like an angel but the truth was, he suspected she was very far from being one.

Sometimes it was hard to even think of her as a suspect. When she smiled it was as if the sun had come out from behind the cloud.

Of course, getting information from little Ary and old George would be almost too easy, like shooting fish in a barrel. They would need very little prompting to fill him in on whatever they knew. They probably didn't know much. Probably background stuff about the family mostly.

He rubbed his hand against his backside. Rotten mule. That animal had ruined everything. He wondered if Annie had taught the devilish creature that trick?

Only a few minutes after Mary Broughton had brought congratulations and some peach butter and some tiny gray moccasins made by Pa Broughton, every eye turned to the door at the soft sound of scratching against the frame. Junior Trent stood silhouetted in the doorway.

"See, sister. I told you Junior would want to come and see me and the baby."

Annie nodded at Ary. "Well, go let the boy in, sister."

"Miss Annie I can't rightly come in, I reckon. I had to walk across the fields and my boots is some muddy. Mess up your house."

"Hey, get your little old muddy self right on in here, Junior. We ain't got no polished wood floors like your papa's." She pointed to the floor. "See. Dirt. Just like that stuff you been a walking in but a little drier."

Junior nodded at Mary Broughton as she left with a wave at Annie.

Ary stood to move to the open door.

"You come on in here, Junior. I done got me my baby." She held out the little girl for his inspection. "Name of Wesley Ann." She looked down at the mud that Junior was trying to scrape off on the doorstep. "How come you had to walk over?"

Annie shot a glance at John. She could tell he was having the same thought she was. Junior just might have been one of them onery no-goods who'd been trying to steal her mule. She moved to the door, also, dripping comb in hand. Why would old Junior Trent want her mule? His daddy owned a plenty of riding animals and pulling stock, too. They didn't need Lucifer.

"Yeah, Junior. How come you been walking through all that there mud?" She put the second curl paper into Aramantha's red gold hair. "You fall off your horse?"

Ary reached out and pulled on Junior's sleeve.

"Quit that stamping around now and come on in. Annie don't care. It ain't as if we have to mop it. Anyway, I want you to look at our new baby."

"Yeah, Junior. Come on in." Annie smiled and used the polite phrase she remembered from her mother's time. "And how's everybody up your way?"

"Fine ma'am." After he'd given the time worn answer the red-haired youngster looked all around him and stepped into the room. He wore heavy high top work shoes. He reached toward the wooden door.

"Miss Annie, you mind if I close this here door?"

"Why go ahead iffen you want. It's a little warm with it closed. You cold?"

"No ma'am." He looked down at his muddy shoes and scraped one toe against the dirt floor. His voice lowered to a murmur. "Don't want no one to be able to look in here and spy me sitting here, Miss Annie."

The candle on the table flared briefly then shuddered and drew in upon itself as if in fear, turning the flame into something small and wizened as compared to the brilliance of seconds earlier. Annie stared at the strange phenomenon and shivered even though the room was warm.

John Matlock stepped to the door, opened it and looked out into the well swept mud of the moonlit yard.

"No one out here, son. Who're you expecting?"

"Well, papa... uh... papa..." He dug his toe into the floor once more then looked apologetically at Aramantha. "He says I can't come see Ary, anymore. I just walked on over so no one would know I was gone." He lifted his chin and smiled at Annie. "I heard him tell one of the hands to keep an eye on me. I didn't want no cowhand nanny a staring in at me from your dooryard."

Annie immediately leaned over and blew out the candle on the table. The acrid odor of smoke and hot wax lingered heavily in the air of the darkened room.

"We don't need us no light anyway. We can see by the moon. It'll be good to save on candles. Ary and me hate making them things anyway. Open that there door, Ary and let's us have some air and light in here." Moonbeams rode in on the cooling Oklahoma breeze when Ary swung the wooden door wide open once more. "Reckon we can sing in the dark good as we can in the light, can't we Uncle George?"

"You betcha, Annie Lee. Moonlight is free." The old man used his fingers to strike a chord on the strings of his fiddle. "Aye God, boy, you sound like you might be a singer. Are you a tenor like me? Maybe you could follow along with me? Can you sing?"

"I don't know, sir. I like to sing when I'm out with the longhorns. The cows act like they like it." He chuckled and looked at Aramantha to see what she thought of his joke.

"But Junior... why... I don't see why your... why Mr. Trent don't want you to come no more to the Circle Twig." Ary stood in the open doorway,

Wesley Ann in her arms. Anxiety rode in her voice. "Does that mean he ain't never going to want you to come and visit?"

Annie put her arms about her sister's shoulders.

"Come on and sit down, honey. Don't you worry about Mr. Henry Trent. I'll bet Junior thinks you look real pretty tonight." She guided the younger girl to the bench to sit next to their visitor.

"You do look right pretty to me, Ary." Junior grinned at the young mother. "You wearing a nice dress and your New York hairdo and all. And I like your baby... much as I can see of her." He leaned around to look directly into Ary's face. "I'm sure glad you're up. I always thought you had to be abed when you was birthing babies."

"I was in the bed but Annie tells me I need to get up some now. That's better for me, she says." She jiggled the baby. "She don't hold with them old fashioned ways, sometimes."

Junior smiled and moved just a fraction closer to the young mother. She smiled and moved a tiny snippet closer to the red headed male visitor.

As if to break the tension George twanged a string on his instrument.

"Let's us sing some of them good old songs. John, you pick up the bass and you, Junior, you follow along with my tones. I'll teach you a little about making pretty music." He pointed to Annie and Ary. "You girls just do your usual." He turned to Junior. "We'll weave in and out amongst their pretty patterns. What do you say, boy?"

Junior nodded.

George lifted his fiddle and began to play.

At first light John traced the intruders' boot prints over the ridge to the cedar break. All the signs showed that the two had mounted horses and headed toward the trail that ran near the Trent spread. He had to laugh when he saw the confused mishmash of prints that covered a wide circle around where the men had tied their mounts. He'd just bet old Lucifer had done quite a bit of damage to both horses and riders before they were able to get away from him.

He followed their clear trail for a few yards just as that wicked mule had done. The signs were very clear. No doubt those old boys had ridden out of here convinced that the devil himself was after them. At the place where Lucifer had turned and pranced back to return to his pole barn John reined in his horse to do the same. Four hours trailing "sign." He'd better get back. Annie would be eager to hear what he'd learned.

He passed the shed and shouted a few rude words to the invisible Lucifer before he walked his own horse down the path to the little house. He again felt a touch of surprise that the intruders hadn't shot old Lucifer. Either they hadn't been able to get to their guns or they had been afraid of

Scoundrels' Bargain

the trouble the noise of a gunshot would have brought their way. Or maybe they'd been *told* just to scout out the place?

Should he tell Annie he suspected Trent had sent bullies to scare her or should he just keep quiet? He'd have to decide. She was sure to want to know what he'd found. Maybe he should just ride on into town and see if the office had been able to find out anything about Trent. No use raising a fuss if it wasn't necessary. He thought of how Annie's blue eyes would sparkle when he brought back some little geegaws from town. He'd go by and tell her and the others where he was going. He felt a longing to see the feisty little woman before he headed out. He smiled and lightly kicked the horse to speed him up a bit.

At the house he found only Ary, Uncle George and the baby.

"Aye God. One of them there Smith brothers was injured in a accident... runaway, the boy said. Annie had to go see about him." Before George started peeling a second large potato he reached across to turn the three sizzling slices of ham that lay frying in the black skillet. "She said she didn't know how many days she'd be. Smith's bones is all broke up I understand. Blood coming out of one of his ear holes. Pretty serious hurt." He pointed his knife at John. "How many taters you think you could eat, boy?"

John felt his heart sink with disappointment. He had really needed to see her, to talk to her. He always looked forward to talking to her, hearing what she had to say. Damn. He twirled his hat with impatience. He didn't know if he could stand to wait around who-knows-how-many-days to see Annie once again. Might as well do something to pass the time. He needed to contact Little Rock anyway... maybe he'd just go on in to town so she'd be here when he returned. Make the time go faster.

"Thanks George, I think I'll skip eating." He shoved the adoring Mrs. Gulliver away. Damned pig was always *leaning* against him. "Will you and Ary be all right here if I leave too? I need to ride into town for a day or two."

"Aye God. We'll do just fine. All them Broughtons are just a couple of miles away and you know that little Mary ain't a going to stay away from this here baby for very long." He looked at the wall behind the stove as if he were seeing something written there. "Time for that girl to start getting herself her own babies, I reckon." He cackled with laughter then gestured to the rifle hanging on the wall. "Got my long gun right up there. My old pap give me that. Aye God, no, I won't let nothing bad happen to these here children."

"Yeah. You go on John." Ary smoothed her hair up from the nape. "But we sure gonna miss you. Junior said he was going to slip back over tonight or tomorrow night. We're going to practice up for our Sunday

School." She smiled with pleasure. "I think he's a getting the hang of that there singing in harmony."

"Great. I'm glad he isn't paying any attention to that old dad of his." He twisted his hat in his hands. "Ary, is the baby asleep? I'd sure like to see her before I go."

Ary grinned and ducked into the bedroom to bring back the drowsy child.

John bent and pressed his lips on the soft round of the little girl's cheek. A sweet, milky fragrance drifted up from the infant.

"'Bye sweetheart." He tickled the little toes that waved in the air. "I'll bring you and Annie... uh," He slanted his gaze up to the face of the baby's mother. "I'll bring you and *everybody* a present from the city."

Ary's eyes widened. "Me too, John?"

"Presents for everyone. Especially for you. Even for Mrs. Gulliver and her friend, that mule from hell. Don't you know that that's the rule when you go to town? You have to bring back gifts."

Ary smiled happily at her uncle and he winked at her.

"See girl. Wasn't I telling you? See what happens when you have a pretty little baby girl? Ain't that what I done told you?" George sliced potatoes into the grease. "Everyone's happy for you, hon. They be bringing you presents and stuff." He winked at John, who smiled and nodded.

"Now George, don't you be trying to get those shakes nailed up. I'll finish that roof in a couple of days when I get back." John slapped the old man on the back. "You hear me, now?"

"I hear you, boy. Aye God, you wait one second and I'll pack you up some biscuits and a tomater or two for the road." He wiped his hands on his shirt front and hefted a flour sack of leftover biscuits from the shelf. "I'm real sorry I ain't got no way to send pepper sauce with you. I know how you like that stuff." He swept two tomatoes into the bag as well and handed the lunch to John. "You'll be getting mighty hungry ere you get into Guthrie, boy."

As he rode up the trail John left Ary on the front doorstep waving goodbye with Wesley Ann's chubby hand.

He'd felt badly about leaving George and Ary alone but he'd felt an even deeper twinge about leaving that baby. She already acted like she knew him. Sometimes he'd swear she had sort of looked like she was smiling at him, no matter what Annie said.

He'd never known a baby really well before... and Wesley Ann, well she was so pretty, and so smart and she *was* partly his. They'd said that, hadn't they? That's why he'd hated to leave her. She might even forget about him. How long could a baby remember anyone, anyway? He'd have to ask Annie. He just hoped George and Ary would know how to take care of that little darling while Annie and him were gone from the place.

He turned the horse's head toward the Trent spread. He had to pass that way to get to town anyway. Might as well ride on in and look the place over on the way. Maybe look over old man Trent too while he was there. You could always tell a lot more about a man in the daylight than you could at night.

Not that he needed to know much more. He already knew that Trent was a double-dealing backwoods crook of some kind. It shouldn't take much to learn what sort of Machiavellian schemes that underhanded old rancher was involved in. Not that he cared. He was just curious.

What Trent was doing was really not important, it wasn't even his business... not so long as the old bastard stayed completely away from Miss Annie Lee Twig.

Chapter 13

"Can I help you with something, stranger?" A tall, thin, scraggy faced cowpoke stood by his mount, his questions directed toward Matlock. "What's your name? You looking for anyone in particular?"

"My name's John Matlock and I was hoping to see Henry Trent."

"Well, well. I done heard of you, Matlock, and no, you can't talk to him." The man's eyes swept him from head to foot then back. "*Mister* Trent ain't here."

"You work for Trent?"

"Yeah, I work for the man and now I'm a going to do one of the things he hired me for and escort you right on back to the road." He swung up onto his hungry looking cow pony. "Me and Sharky, there, we're gonna help you find your way back to where you come from, Matlock." He gestured to another gaunt faced man who sauntered his horse toward them from some distance away.

The two men rode behind him until he reached the stone posts of the entry gate. When Matlock turned right to continue on his ride toward town, both men moved their horses forward to ride in tandem with him. They said nothing. Nevertheless, Matlock could feel purposeful menace in their silence. He slowed and stopped his horse. They also stopped.

"Oh, don't mind me." He waved them on with one hand as though brushing insects aside. "You boys go on. This little chore always takes me a minute or so." He reached into his shirt pocket and with great deliberation pulled out his silver badge and fastened it to his shirt pocket. "Can't do this while I'm riding. Got to get this on right." He pulled one side of the front of his shirt out of his trousers and made a ceremony of polishing the badge with the tail of it. "This is an official errand I'm on and I'd forgotten to pin on my shield." He tucked his white shirt back into his trousers.

"Hey, you some kind of lawman?"

"Yep." He clicked to return his horse to a slow walk. Hesitation was evident in the eyes of the one called Sharky. The two seemed to come to an unspoken understanding as they reined in.

"I ain't fooling with no marshal." He heard the first man mutter to his friend Sharky. Matlock smiled. Apparently Sharky felt the same trepidation and without another word, both of Trent's cowpokes wheeled to return the way they'd come. Matlock wondered if either or both of the men had mule shoe shaped bruises or bites somewhere on their bodies. He chuckled. He'd like to think that both carried Lucifer inflicted wounds... wounds where blood had been drawn!

Scoundrels' Bargain

In town he let himself be directed to the new telegraph office. Aware that in a small community like Guthrie there would be little security for any messages he would send, he deliberated carefully before he wrote out the words and pushed the form and a few silver coins across the counter to the bearded man who waited on him.

"Is this enough?" He indicated the money he'd put on the paper carrying the message.

"Looks like a little too much, Mister," the telegrapher grunted and pushed back two of the coins. "Your message ain't very long."

Matlock pocketed the money and straightened from the counter.

The man read the message aloud.

Fleury not here stop Found his relatives.

Signed John Matlock

"That sound the way you want it to, Mister?"

Matlock nodded and stepped out of the telegraph office to start on his promised shopping.

"Now, Uncle George, just 'cause our Annie's gone, that ain't no reason for you to be reaching for that jug again so soon." Aramantha walked to take the crockery jug from the old man. She could feel the brown dress swish across the tops of her shoes as she worked to clean up after their supper. She loved that feeling. It felt so grownup, what with her hair up and all. Annie had talked to her like one woman to another just before she left.

"Ary," she'd said, "With mama's dress made over to fit you and with your New York Pompadour, you're just puredee a woman now. A pretty one." She'd whispered right over the top of Wesley Ann's head, "You're gonna have to take care of everyone whilst I'm gone. Take real good care of our baby. Try to keep George busy and out of the hooch. And I hope you can depend on old John to know what he's supposed to do."

Ary had nodded understanding of her sister's instructions.

"And if Mary comes over for some herb gathering, just tell we'll do it when I get back. Maybe John should ride back home with her if he could."

But Mary Broughton never came and John Matlock was gone now, too, so it was just her and Wesley Ann and Uncle George. And Junior. She felt a thrill run through her. He'd said he might come a little after sundown. She sure wanted to see him. She pushed her longing for Junior Trent to one side. She had to keep things together here. Maybe she could keep old George from getting drunk if she said she needed him to help with the baby.

"Uncle George, you know Wesley Ann just loves it when you carry her around against your shoulder." She pinched the placid infant lightly on the back of her leg to make her cry. "See, she's so fretful... could you do something with her, do you think?"

"Why sure, that's my darling girl." George held his arms open, his face beaming down at the sniffling infant. "Uncle George loves you, honey." He jounced the child up and down and the change caused her to forget her tiny hurt. He walked about the room singing and talking a mile a minute. The baby gurgled with pleasure.

Ary couldn't help smiling. Maybe there was one little bitty someone that the old man loved better than he loved his homemade liquor. She'd have to remember to tell Annie about what she'd found out, about how she'd kept George sober by putting the baby in his arms. Or maybe not. Annie might not like it that she'd had to tweak Wesley Ann's leg. Annie didn't want nothing harming their baby.

A crash against the doorstep turned both Ary and George into statues for a second. Through the open door both could see the huge clod of red dirt that had shattered and broken into dusty chunks there. Without a word, the old man handed the child to Aramantha and reached for what she'd always heard him call "pap's long gun." The rifle hung above the spot where Mrs. Gulliver liked to rest.

He padded toward the door opening. Ary clutched the baby as closely as she could while she crept to stand behind the old man.

"What is it, Uncle George?" She could hear the tremor in her own voice.

"I don't know, girl. I ain't even looked outside the door yet." He gestured to the space beside him just at the door. "You stand right there." He frowned down at the egg sized clumps of dirt. "And don't you dare stick that baby's head out of this here house unlessen I tell you to."

Ary nodded agreement and pressed her back against the log wall. Wesley yawned and leaned against Ary's chest.

The old man put his finger against his lips and stepped out onto the stone step where the clod had landed. His gaze moved to the right of the house. Ary couldn't stand it. She had to peek out over his shoulder. Against the setting sun she could see three riders silhouettted. Braids? Feathers?

"Them're Indians, Uncle George?"

He nodded.

"What do you fellars need?" He held the gun loosely in one hand and squinted into the red and gold of the sunset.

One of the men held up his right hand as if greeting them.

"We wish speak gold hair white eye woman witch."

"You want to talk to me?" Ary peered over the old man's shoulder but she didn't move from her place behind her uncle.

The man on the horse snorted amusement.

Scoundrels' Bargain

"Not you. We want gold hair woman. Witch doctor. You just little girl."

"What do you boys want with our Annie?" George shaded his eyes with his free hand.

"We talk with her. We give her our message. You send her out."

"We ain't sending nobody out until you injuns speak up about what it was you was a wanting."

Ary and George watched the faceless black figures of the three men lean together to talk. Before they turned their horses the spokesman shouted a last message.

"You tell gold hair woman we come back to speak to her, tomorrow. We come back every night to see her. We ain't quitting until we speak to woman."

"She ain't coming out to talk tonight so you old boys better head on down the road." George lifted his hand to the barrel of the gun and laid his head against the stock as if aiming at the men who were already riding away.

"You ain't a going to shoot them Indians in the back, are you, Uncle George?" Terror sent Ary's voice up a notch. Wesley Ann made a grunt of protest at being squeezed so hard.

"Naw," The old man's voice was calm. "Aye God, them wasn't injuns no ways, girl. Just some bastards a trying to torment us'ns or maybe our Annie, I reckon."

"How could you tell they wasn't Indians?"

"I got me a heap of Injun friends, child. Lots of them redskins like that there rich tasting firewater I make. Ain't a one of them Indians that talks like that there man was a talking. Them was white men masquerading, missy."

Within minutes after the men had gone, Ary put Wesley Ann into her peach basket on the table so she could have her hands free to sweep off the doorstep. Before she'd finished Junior Trent came riding up. Ary grabbed the baby from the table and the two of them stood waiting for him on the path from the barn. Ary felt so glad to see him that she just had to let him wrap his arms around her and Wesley Ann for a little while.

When she told him what the men had said she saw something flicker way in the back of Junior's eyes. Something like shame? Or embarrassment? Or maybe it was something else. Maybe it was just the sunset in his eyes.

Just having him there smiling at her made Ary feel light and happy. When they went into the house she didn't even light the candle lest someone look in on them from the dooryard. She sat close to Junior on the bench and the three of them whiled away the evening singing all the old songs they could think of. Uncle George said Junior had a good ear and that Annie was going to be real happy that Junior could sing harmony right along with the best of them. He said the boy's good voice made Junior Trent seem like family.

"I am real sorry about your brother, Mr. Smith." Annie shook the claw-like hand of the wisened old man. "I done the best I could. His body was just too broke up, I guess. It wasn't just his legs and arms. Something inside him got broke." She hoisted her medicine sack and the wooden chest. "Are you sure you don't want me to lay your brother out? Mary Broughton and me could stay and do that sad chore for you."

The old man shook his head.

"I don't blame you none for his death, Miss Annie. I was just hoping against hope that you two ladies could do something for him." He reached into his overall pocket and brought out a worn leather clasp purse. "What do I owe you and Miss Mary, ma'am, for all your work?"

Annie took a step back from the man.

"No sir, Mr. Smith. You don't owe me nothing. I'm always glad to do what I can for the folks around these parts."

"Me too, sir." Mary was learning real, Annie thought. She'd given the right answer.

"I'm in your debt, Miss Annie. You too Miss Mary. I know you two ain't had but mighty little rest since you got here that day before yesterday." The older Smith brother lowered his gaze to stare at the floor. "Gonna miss old Jim." He raised his head once more and tried to smile. "You tell that uncle of yorn that I'll be by to see him ere long. Mayhaps He and I can do us a little business. You tell him now, Miss Annie."

"I'll do that Mr. Smith." She stepped outside and turned toward the impatient mule. Mr. Smith followed. "Iffen I go on now I can be home just after midday. I'll stop by with Mary and tell Grandma Broughton about your loss." She swung up into the saddle and Lucifer toe danced past the elder Smith and onto the trail. Annie waved once then turned her face and her thoughts toward home.

They may not be so glad to see me this, time since I'm not taking good stuff home. Nothing to take back from this here batch of doctoring. Nothing but bad news and sorrow.

After she left the Broughton's house she felt her heart lighten as she rode along under the hot autumn sun. Can't stay sad with God's sun a smiling down on you, she thought. Won't be long 'til I see Ary and the baby and Uncle George and Mrs. Gulliver and... She wouldn't allow herself to name the person she wanted to see most. But she smiled. *He'd* be there, too.

And he was. He stood in the dooryard watching her ride in, as did Aramantha and Uncle George. Mrs. Gulliver trotted forward to greet Lucifer. Oh, it was good to be home after all that useless doctoring.

"Did you bring something, Annie?"

"No, sister. I lost Mr. Smith's brother. I couldn't bring myself to take nothing from him."

John Matlock stepped closer.

"Let me help you down." He raised his arms toward her. Lucifer didn't seem to resent the man's presence. Annie swung her trousered leg over the mule and felt a twinge of pleasure. Sometimes it was real nice to let yourself be cared for by someone, even if you knew you could take care of yourself.

She smiled down at the detective. "I'll not be too heavy for you, John?"

He put a hand on each side of her waist and lifted her with ease. When her feet touched the ground he stood looking down at her, his hands still at her waist. Annie's eyes were the sky and she smelled of the sun.

"I'm glad to see you, John Wesley Matlock." she said and smiled.

I don't think I can live happily without this woman. He heard his own unspoken declaration as if it were a vivid pain lancing through his chest. *I may even be in love with her.* He stared down at her trying to fix her face and this moment in time, in his mind and his memory.

As they stood gazing at each other the sun slipped behind a cloud and light sprinkles of rain once again began to fall. He silently reminded himself that he would probably have to be taking Annie Twig into town to the authorities one of these days and he understood in that instant why the sun had needed to go into hiding, and why the rain drops pattered a mournful melody on the brim of his hat, a tune that drummed a song of despair into his ears.

Chapter 14

Matlock stood paralyzed with shock for just a moment. Shocked by his own inner declaration. He loved this woman? Couldn't live without her? He must be mad to be thinking such strange things.

Annie Twig was special. Beautiful. Very special. He'd always carry her memory, of course, as well as the memory of her most interesting family and strange farm animals but to think he couldn't live without her? That was sheer nonsense. There was no woman *anywhere* who could command his attention all day, every day, not even Miss Annie Twig, as beautiful as she was. That was one of his unbreakable personal rules... wasn't it, to take women as he found them and to leave them the same way? Anyway, to become infatuated with a suspect was unthinkable.

"I brought you a present from Guthrie, Miss Annie."

"You been into town?"

"Yep. And back again." He held up his hand as if defending himself. "I got the roof finished. Don't worry. Already started on the floor." He let his hand drop to her shoulder. "We saved the ritual of the gift-from-town-opening until your return." He searched her face. "We heard your patient had died. I'm sorry."

Annie felt a flash of surprise. They'd already heard of Jim Smith's death? Bad news traveled mighty quick, didn't it?

"Yeah. Mr. Smith died." She shrugged. She'd liked the old man. She wished she could have saved him. Nevertheless, she'd done her best and that was all she could expect of herself. His brother knew she'd tried everything she knew to do.

Matlock was continuing.

"Yes. Even before I rode out from Guthrie I heard that you weren't going to be successful with your patient."

"Yeah, sister. The Broughton's middle boy come over and told us about it. And there was them Indians. And..." Ary couldn't keep from smiling. Her dimples always showed up when she spoke Junior Trent's name. "'Course we'd done heard about it from Junior Trent." She giggled just a little. "He's been over here every night since you been gone, sister."

"What does Junior have to say?" Annie asked the question of her sister but her questioning gaze rose to John Matlock's face. He shrugged as if he didn't want to be the one who answered.

"Oh, not much. But them Indians. It was all so silly, sister. Them men saying you was a witch and all."

Scoundrels' Bargain

"Aye God, I shoulda shot them there play Injuns." Ary nodded agreement with her Uncle's words.

"What in hell has been going on here? Indians saying I'm a witch? You heard this kind of stuff, too, John?"

He nodded silently.

Annie tried to shake away the foreboding that swept through her. Everyone in the neighborhood talking about her? Something about being a witch? Now, her homecoming didn't seem quite as radiant as it had seemed earlier. She raised her gaze. The sun had gone away, also. She held out her hand and felt the misting rain.

"It's starting to pour." Annie grabbed her bag and her box from Lucifer's back and turned toward the house. "Could you put Jupiter up, John?"

"If you give me a long rein." John gingerly took the leather strips in his hand and stepped ahead of the animal. He walked with care, frequently glancing back at the devil spawned animal but Lucifer had apparently decided that he wasn't worth biting or kicking. The mule went up the trail behind him with an unheard of docility, Mrs. Gulliver snorting welcome right at his heels.

Maybe this demon-in-mule's clothing is learning to tolerate me, John told himself, but he didn't allow the mule to get too close to him.

Back in the house he piled his saddle bags onto the table while the old and young Twigs waited in their usual places at the kitchen table.

He pulled out a small paper packet.

"Embroidery thread, my lady." He bowed and handed the package to Annie. Her eyes opened wide as she pulled out silken skeins of pink, green and blue thread. "I thought you might like to make some leaves to go with the rosebuds you planned for Wesley Ann's dress." He pulled out a second tiny package. "And the needles for the embroidery." He bowed.

Her eyes gleamed with pleasure. He felt a strong spurt of joy. Wait until she'd seen the hidden gift.

"A toy for you, Wesley Ann." He held out a bright pink rattle toward the child. Ary took the plaything and looked it over curiously.

"What is it, John?"

"It's a little noisemaker for her. They call it a 'rattle.'" He shook Ary's arm. "See, it rattles."

"What's it made out of? This here thing is as light as a feather. It ain't glass and it ain't wood and it sure ain't iron."

"It's a new material called *celluloid*. Back East they've started making lots of things out of it. They even make men's collars out of the stuff so the men can save on shirt washing." He held the rattle high. "Just run a wet cloth over the celluloid and it's all clean again."

"That'll be handy for a baby's toy." Annie peered closely at the precious new toy. Neither she nor Ary had ever had a store-bought plaything that she could remember. They'd made their own dolls out of corncobs and leaves whenever they'd had a few moments to play.

"Aye God, now ain't that something?" Uncle George took his turn at shaking the rattle and he grinned at the baby. "You can play your rattle whilst I fiddle the tunes, Wesley girl."

Wesley Ann promptly put one end of the wondrous new toy into her mouth and closed her eyes.

"She sure likes it, John Matlock." Ary said, "Thanks for bringing her the little fancy."

John delved into his sack and brought out an oval shaped tin box which he handed to Uncle George. "No hard candy and no nuts, George, just soft bonbons straight from St. Louis." He drew out another box of the same shape.

"And a box for the house. It has all kinds of bonbons, some with nuts." He laughed and handed that box to Annie. "George, I just wanted you to be able to be selfish with yours, old man. You can eat every piece of candy in your box all by yourself without guilt."

The old man struggled to get the tin lid off his candy box then popped a sweet into his mouth with a moan of pure pleasure. Annie opened the other box and set it in the center of the table.

John used both hands to lift the next item from the saddle bag. He lifted a length of creamy silken material high in the air and let it drop like a shining waterfall onto the table in front of Aramantha.

"New dress for Ary. It looks like clotted cream to me but the dandy who sold it to me said it was called 'ecru, my good man.'" He made his voice falsetto the word as he pulled out a handful of lace. "And 'ecru' lace to trim. And buttons, and thread and slippers." He pulled another handful of things from the bag. "I hope they fit. I measured your foot with my eye before I left."

Ary sat speechless.

Annie felt as if Lucifer had kicked her in the chest. John Matlock had brought her some embroidery thread and some needles and then he had brought all this here gorgeousness for little sister? She reached to just touch a corner of the cloth. Her work-roughened finger seemed to snag in the softness and she yanked her hand away.

She wanted that dress material for herself!

She looked at Ary's stunned expression and found herself torn both ways. She wanted her little sister to have at least one beautiful thing in her life. Of course she did.

But she wanted that dress for herself!

Why was she being so silly? She never wore dresses, never even *wanted* to wear one... and now here she was a wanting this here pale silk dress length as she'd never wanted anything in her life. The impractical color seemed to hold the faint, faint, faintest, touch of peach. Oh, glorious beauty!

She silently sneered at herself.

"You could sure set a lot of fence posts in that there get-up, Annie Twig." But still, she wanted the dress, wanted to put her own hair up, wanted to wear the pale silk slippers with the tiny curved heels instead of farmer work shoes, wanted to dance and see herself reflected in the eyes of the man who held her in his arms.

Oh, she wanted Aramantha to have the dress. Aramantha actually *needed* the dress. The child might be getting married ere long once she got acquainted with all the neighbor boys. Or maybe John was thinking about courting Ary hisself? Oh no. She couldn't live with that. Sure she could, she reassured herself, she'd lived with lots of things that she had thought would kill her and they didn't. She wanted Ary to be happy.

But telling herself that didn't seem to matter. She still felt a desperate longing to feel that vibrant, creamy, palest peachy silk, slipping, sliding down her naked body like cool spring water on a hot summer day. She wanted some beauty in her own life. she wanted to be a girl... a woman, for just a little time.

She wanted to see what it would be like to feel silk against her skin, to see admiration in the eyes of a man, even if only for a moment of time.

It was difficult to smile. She smiled.

"Why Ary honey, I reckon I could make you the prettiest dress in the territory with that length of silk. My, ain't...aren't you the lucky one?"

Ary nodded but still she said nothing. The young woman's blue eyes filled with tears. She rubbed the back of her hand across her eyes.

"Is this really all for me?"

"Yes, little Ary. I bought it just for you." Matlock's voice was gentle.

"I ain't never had a new dress before, not one bought at a store and made up just for me. And this here is the beautifulest thing I done ever seen." She looked at the detective. "Oh, John. You're just about the best man in the world, I reckon. And you too, Annie, for sewing this pretty stuff up into a dress for me. I'll help you and I'll do all the housework and I'll..."

"Now that's enough promising." Annie put her hand over Aramantha's but she didn't look up at the gift giver. She didn't want him to see the pain in her eyes. She kept her smiling gaze firmly fixed upon the leaning tower of shimmering silk.

Ary stood and rushed to the bedroom and returned with a crumpled piece of paper which she spread out on the table beside the cloth.

"See sister. See, this here is how I want my new dress made." She turned her pleading blue gaze toward Annie. "It's got lace and buttons and it's so beautiful."

Annie nodded agreement. She bent above the drawing which had been taken from an old Kansas City newspaper.

"Sure, Ary. I'll try real hard to follow your picture here."

John's voice intruded into their perusal of the drawing and the silk.

"Uh, Annie. I wasn't really able to remove Lucifer's harness. Would you mind going up to the barn with me so maybe you can distract him while I finish up the chore?"

Annie nodded and left the house without saying anything to him. Annie stomped up the hill, Matlock strode close behind. She kinda wished the mule had kicked him or torn a hunk out of him, at least just a little nip.

Lucifer innocently munched on grain that had been thrown into his feedbox. He smiled a wide yellow smile at Annie and gave a gentle kick to Mrs. Gulliver's backside. The animal wore no leather trappings.

"I thought you said... He's all put away right and proper. What's going on?"

"My way of getting a little privacy, Annie. Hope you don't mind." John crouched into the hay in the corner and patted the space beside himself. "Come sit beside me."

Annie dropped wearily into the hay. Now what was he going to natter on about? She wished she were in her own good bed. An afternoon nap surely wouldn't be considered sinful after all the work she'd done at the Smith's, not to mention the long ride home. She stretched and yawned widely.

"You're sleepy?" His voice sounded like satin against her ear.

"Yes. I been working over that old boy for nigh three days without much time for rest."

"And now you're home we won't let you rest either, will we?" His words came from even deeper in his chest.

"Oh, I always want to find out what's been a happening around the Circle Twig when I been gone." She yawned again. "I don't know what to think of these here rumors about me and old man Smith. I guess I'll have to think of something." She lay back slightly against the pile of hay. "Maybe now's the time to get that there Sunday School started." She grinned up at him then dropped her gaze. His eyes were a calm and tawny amber as he listened to her suggestions. "With you as our preacher, John Wesley." She grinned up again. His eyes were no longer calm and friendly. They blazed down at her with an intensity that forced her into silence.

He reached into the straw behind him and drew out a flat black velvet box. He brushed it back and forth against the front of his shirt, then handed the box to her with a curt nod.

Annie sat up straight.

"What's this here?"

"Open it and see."

She pressed the metal button on the side and the box lid snapped open. Inside on a wine red velvet bed lay a thin, flat, metal heart strung on a delicate twisted chain. The center of the heart glowed with a large blue, heart shaped stone surrounded by smaller faceted crystals. At each side of the heart lay smaller blue and crystal heart shaped jewels set in the same kind of metal.

"Oh," she sighed the words, "A silver heart."

"Not silver, Annie Lee."

"You brought this beautiful thing for me?"

He nodded.

"I don't care even iffen it isn't real silver. It's so beautiful. It looks like silver and I love it."

Matlock cleared his throat. "It's a precious metal that is something like silver, Annie. It's called platinum."

"Is that there platinum better than silver?"

"I don't know if it's any better. It costs a bit more than either gold or silver."

"I don't know what to say, John." He watched her swallow with excitement.

He lifted a strand of her pale hair with one hand. "I was looking for something as beautiful as you but all I could find that came anywhere near your coloring was this necklace and earrings. Platinum is a little like the color of your hair and the blue sapphires are the closest thing I could find to the color of your eyes. I guess the little diamonds stand for those tears you say you never shed."

"Sapphires! Diamonds!" She took a deep breath. "Oh, John Wesley. These are real? Is all this truly mine? Can I wear it?"

"Of course. You can do anything you wish with it. The set belongs to you."

"Help me put it on." Her hands were shaking so badly that she couldn't lift the velvet bed to release the platinum chain.

John took the heart from the box and draped the chain about her throat. The shining heart hid itself inside the brown shirt she wore.

"Annie, shall I loose the top buttons so we can see it on you?" he whispered. Even before she nodded her answer he had unbuttoned the shirt. The jeweled heart lay in the crevice between the tops of the two white globes of her breasts. A pulse beat wildly at the base of her throat.

"Beautiful."

"Can you put the earrings on me, too?"

"I'm afraid not, Annie. You'll have to have your ears pierced before you can wear them. I thought you might want to do that someday when you're older."

"Some days I feel mighty old already." She closed the box on the earrings and placed it gently an arm's length away. "I'll have Ary do my ears."

"Well, you're not old. You're a lovely young woman. A woman so beautiful you make that little trinket look like something from a queen's collection."

"I wanted to buy dress material for you, too." He lifted the chain and let it rest once more against her breasts. "I decided to wait until you could help me choose. Get exactly what would suit my angel haired boss lady."

Annie reached to pull his face close to hers.

"I aim to kiss you, John Wesley Matlock, for all them sweet words you're saying." And she did.

Her kiss was soft, sweet, slow, an unhurried exploration of the man's sensuous mouth. Finally she pulled away from him and lay back smiling at him. His breath came quickly, his eyes darkened with desire.

"Thank you for thinking of all of us, John. I reckon you're about the best hired man we ever had us on the Circle Twig."

"Better than old Calvin?" John smiled and with a long straw he traced the line of the bright chain down to the hollow where the glittering heart lay between her breasts. He touched the metal heart with one finger. "You've warmed your cold platinum heart, Miss Twig. I feel your body heat inside this metal."

She pulled him to her again and placed a line of tiny, slow, kisses across his sculptured lips.

"I like your way of thanking me, Annie-of-the-sapphire eyes. If I bring more presents will I receive more kisses?"

"No more presents needed." Her voice sounded throaty to her own ears. "This here platinum doodad must have cost a ton of money. Are you rich, John?"

He bent and kissed the place on her neck where she felt her pulse beating so frantically before he gave her his smiling answer.

"Well, I thought as you've so often and so sharply reminded me, since I had all this money the Pinkertons were paying me to just lie around your place here, I might as well put my ill gotten gains to good use." He laughed and bent again to kiss her lips.

Her arms, of their own volition, twined about his neck to pull him even closer. She tasted him with her lips and with her tongue. Salty and sweet and something more. Behind her closed lids fireworks made gold and silver and platinum fountains of joy. He groaned and without taking his lips from hers he pulled her to lie on top of him. The platinum heart tumbled from her breast to rest upon his chest between them. She let her legs slide deep into the hay between his opened knees and she cupped his head with one hand while she smoothed the day old roughness of his cheek with the other.

She might as well admit it. She loved this smart mouthed man. And there wasn't a thing she could do about it. She could probably have him for only a moment but she wanted whatever she could get.

She tried to sink even deeper into the hardness of his awakened body. She could feel his manhood pressing against her leg. She wouldn't wait any longer. Today would be their day. She reached between them and tugged his shirttail from his trousers. Then his hand had done the same for her old brown shirt.

"Annie. Annie. Sister?" Ary's voice.

Annie lifted her head.

"What is it, Ary? I'll be down to the house in a minute."

"I reckon maybe you better come on in the house right now, sister. Some men is in the house there just a touching things."

Chapter 15

Annie turned her back to John Matlock.

"Quick. Take off my new pretty. I'll go see what's wrong." When the necklace was again on its wine colored bed, she snapped the box closed and dug the black velvet square back into the straw. "I'll hide my heart for awhile longer."

As she stood, he stood. They turned so they were back to back. Each saw to their own shirt and trousers before they faced one another, then John put his gun into his belt at the back of his waist.

"You think something bad...?"

"Well, there have been some rather strange happenings around here in the last few weeks, Annie."

He pressed the gun securely into the hollow at his waist. "Might as well be prepared."

She nodded agreement before she turned to jog down the path toward Ary.

"What do you mean, 'men touching things,' sister?"

"They's three men in the house and they're just a touching and a looking at everything." She turned and looked down at the house. "A laughing and talking with each other, acting like me and George ain't even in the house. They looked at the Baby's new rattle even." She looked once again at the house. "George is awful mad. That's the reason one of them took Uncle George's old long gun offen the wall." Ary looked apologetically at Matlock. "He was the same one who threw my new dress material down on the floor."

"They touched the baby?" Matlock's eyes narrowed.

"Yeah, but she's all right. Uncle George has her now. Little Wesley was crying. They didn't like that."

"I'll kill them." Matlock stepped forward and put his arm out as a barrier in front of the two young woman.

"This is my place. I'm going in there." Annie pushed past his outstretched arm.

"Better let me go in there first. I think I know who these men are. One of them is called 'Sharky' or I miss my bet."

"How'd you know that?" Ary looked admiringly at the hired man. "He's the one threw my dress material on the floor."

"Is it ruined?" Annie couldn't keep herself from asking. She had an inner vision of that pale creamy silk under the muddy boot heels of some rotten meddling cowpoke. The thought made her tremble with anger.

"It's all right. I picked it right up." Ary smiled at John. "One of them does answer to the name of Sharky and the other one is called Buell, I think."

"Does Buell look like a skeleton with jug ears?"

"Yes. Why how'd you know?" Ary's mouth opened in an 0 of wonderment.

"I believe I know both these old boys." His eyes flashed amber wrath toward the little house. "I'll just bet that they didn't expect to find me here today."

"Be careful, John." Annie felt as if everything in her world were tumbling and rushing and whirling around her. She'd just gotten home, received a handsome gift, had started making love to this man she wanted so badly and now she was hearing that intruders were inside her house. *Strangers that John Matlock knew.* And all of this in less than an hour.

"You two stay out here."

"Not likely, John Wesley. You done forgot who this here place belongs to?" Annie smoothed her damp hair back with both hands, then flicked a piece of straw from her shoulder. "Can't nobody bother my family without they answer to me."

"Do you have a gun in your belt, Miss Twig?"

"No." He was right. She needed a weapon. "We got George's long gun in the house." She shook her head. No good. They already had that, Ary said. She stood motionless for a second. "I'll go get Lucifer. You stay out here Ary. And you John, you go roust them out. Make them come outside, John, and I'll sic my mule on them." She turned back toward the barn. "Give me just a minute and I'll be ready." She nodded to Matlock with her explanation. "Don't want to take that animal on into the house, of course. He'd probably break what few little things we got in there."

John chuckled deep in his throat and returned her nod.

"Good idea. Ary and I will wait for you just outside the door." Matlock moved with quiet deliberation toward the open structure of the proposed Sunday School and summer kitchen area. He stood quietly beside the door that opened into the old kitchen to wait for Annie's reappearance with her live doomsday weapon.

He had to laugh again as she came racketing down the hill toward battle. She looked for all the world a slim Amazon, skin like sun-warmed satin, blonde hair flying, Lucifer's hooves striking sparks against the rocks in the path.

I love it, he thought. No one back in the home office will ever believe my story about Trent's old boys being chased home *again* by our resident "watch mule." Still smiling, gun in hand, John turned to the door and stepped inside.

Seconds later the intruders stumbled outside, their holsters empty. Released from the Annie's hold on his bridle, Lucifer closed in on them, feet flying, a murderous look in his rolling eyes. He emitted harsh snorts and piercing whinnies from between clacking yellow teeth. The one called Buell shouted and raised one arm to protect his face.

"Get this damn mule off me." The man tried to edge out from under the animal's attack.

Lucifer brayed triumph before he sank his teeth into the upraised arm and Buell screamed, pulled away, stared at his arm for a second then raced toward the trail. Drops of blood marked his movements.

Mrs. Gulliver squealed her displeasure with the intruders and circled as if she were a guard dog looking for an opening. Lucifer ignored the man who got away but he let his back legs fly like razor edged bullets toward the two other men. One hoof connected with Starkey's shoulder, knocking the man back against the wall of the house. Starkey grunted and crouched to try to move himself outside the range of the raging animal. The third man went down screaming under a flurry of front hoof feints.

He went down and lay silent. Starkey never even looked at his fallen companion but edged away and followed his bleeding friend Buell on the trail toward the road. Mrs. Gulliver followed the two of them a short distance, chastising them, trumpeting angry grunts and squeals before she turned back to offer more help to her friend Lucifer.

Annie calmed the furious mule with a few words, then, holding onto Lucifer's bridle for balance, she raised her foot to let the heel of her work shoe scratch behind Mrs. Gulliver's ears. The scratching served to gentle down the little sow's excited squeals.

"Good mule. Good pig." She felt awfully proud of her livestock. *Real Twigs, both of them sure enough. Any old marauders come in here them animals'd take care of the family sure.* When the two were quiet she motioned Matlock to help her lift the unconscious man.

"We'll put him inside on the table. I'll see what I can do for him." They toted the unknown intruder into the kitchen and after Ary had scooped up the gift box of St. Louis candy to place it high on the shelf, they laid him out on the table.

"He must work for Trent too, since he was with those other two ne'er-do-wells." John Matlock stood looking down at the man while Annie sponged his forehead and his neck. "Might be able to learn something from this old boy. I can't figure their game." He picked up George's long gun that they'd thrown in a corner and held it out to the old man who hung it in its regular place.

"You think him and them others was sent by Mr. Trent, John?"

"Undoubtedly."

"What's that mean?"

"That means I think your friend Trent is trying to give you a hard time because you turned him down."

"You think?"

"He hasn't really done anything... yet. Just tried to annoy you. Or scare you, perhaps." John touched the pulse at the base of her throat and slid his finger tip down to the vee of her shirt almost to where the necklace had disappeared earlier. "Perhaps he thinks that if you are frightened enough you just might run to him for protection?"

"Well, he's got another think coming." She felt the line of fire he'd traced on her neck. When he stepped across the room to examine the baby she looked around at all of them. Ary holding the baby, Uncle George and John standing in a close huddle in the corner of the kitchen as if to solace each other. She could smell the sour mash from the old man, the milky baby smell from Wesley Ann, Mrs. Broughton's lye soap from Ary and that man smell from John, a little like sweat and a little like horse and a little like that expensive soap he used. Annie figured she smelled like Lucifer and maybe like the herbs she'd used. Altogether they smelled kinda good... like a family. Mrs. Gulliver was part of her family but the little sow didn't smell bad at all so far as Annie could notice, not unless she was breaking wind and right now she was being as good as gold, just leaning gently against John's legs.

"After we bring him around and find out something from this old boy, I got to take me a teeny little nap at least and then we are going to make our plans. We have to do something to stop all this silly stuff right now."

"What you gonna do, Annie?"

"Gonna invite everybody round about to a preaching here this next Sunday or maybe Sunday after next, with dinner on the grounds and dancing in the afternoon. You seem to be coming along real well, little sister." She let her hand raise to touch the spot where the platinum heart had lain earlier, then her finger traced upward where his had traced down. "Reckon you're ready for a little fun." *Maybe find, yourself a good husband, little sister,* she added silently. "And I gotta remind folks I ain't no witch. Let 'em see we're a right steady religious bunch of folks just like the best of them." Blue twinkled toward amber. "Got us a preacher man right here in this house."

"Oh, Annie. I'm no..."

"Aye God you're right, Annie Lee. Good idea. Let folks see they ain't got nothing to fear from the Twigs."

"Next Sunday or Sunday after next?" Ary jounced Wesley Ann against her hip. "Could I have the new dress by then, reckon Annie?"

"Sunday after next." Annie nodded. "You can have your new dress and a new hairdo." She pushed her own hair back in a gesture of fatigue. "We got us a world of stuff to do twix now and then." She smiled regret at the tall man standing beside her. "We got us so much to do we won't have time for nary another thing but work this here next ten days I expect."

"I'll just run right on up to my squeezins. Folks'll be wanting a little taste when they come, I reckon. I need to get me another good big batch started." George darted through the door and on up the muddy path toward the cedar breaks before Annie could stop him.

"I'll start on the house." Ary handed the baby to Annie. "Iffen you're a going to the bed you can take Wesley Ann with you, sister."

"This man looks like he might be coming too. I reckon the old boy is all your'n, John. I'm too tired to talk to him." Annie let her sapphire glance tell John of her regret and he nodded understanding before she turned to slip through the bedroom door. One thing she was really glad about... next time she could wear her magnificence to bed. Iffen he'd a brought her a dress she wouldn't never be able to wear it much... that there pretty she could work in, eat in, and even sleep in, iffen she wanted.

She curled herself around Wesley Ann upon the luxury of her very own cornhusk mattress. Her last thought was of the amber gaze of understanding she'd received from John Matlock. In seconds both she and Wesley Ann were asleep. Annie with one hand on the baby, the other on the spot where her very own beautiful new extra special platinum metal heart had lain.

She dreamed she was looking up at a platinum statue with sculptured lips and golden eyes. The statue looked right back at her and said three magic words to her. It scared her that the statue talked but she really kind of liked it too.

When she woke at suppertime, Ary had come to get the baby.

"I done invited Junior Trent to supper with us, sister. Hope you don't mind."

"Fine. Did John get anything out of the cowpoke?"

"He said he'd tell you all about it at supper." Ary reached for the little girl. "I'll feed her in here and then I'll be right in." She unbuttoned the remade back to front waist of her brown dress. "This here dress is sure some handier, Annie. I'm glad you changed it around. I just feel like rich folks every night what with a washing my face and a putting on a real dress to eat supper in."

"Why you are rich, little sister." Annie planted a kiss on Wesley's head and another on Ary's cheek. "You're real rich. You got your good health. You're a young beautiful woman and best of all, haven't you got us this here sweet baby?" Ary smiled happily and nodded.

Annie ducked into the kitchen. John stood waiting.

"I have some bad news," he said.

"What happened to our visitor?"

"I think he's on his way to Amarillo about now. Said he didn't owe old man Trent anything, anyway." John smiled. "Of course, I encouraged him to go."

"Yeah. I'll bet. What'd he say?"

"He said Trent is going to try to use the stories that are circulating to scare you and other people." John put his hand on Annie's shoulder. "Looks like he's determined to have you, one way or another, Miss Annie Twig. It seems that Trent wants folks to quit paying you to doctor them."

"That old bastard."

"Exactly."

"Maybe Junior'll tell us something. Ary done said he was coming to supper." She felt John's hand on her shoulder sending messages that had nothing to do with their conversation. Each strong finger seemed to ripple strange waves through her body. She felt as if the palm of his hand made a mark on her. "Wonder iffen Junior Trent knows what his old daddy is a doing?"

John shrugged and let his hand fall. She wanted to lift it to its place on her shoulder again.

"Junior's growing up fast, Annie, but I wouldn't blame him with Trent's doings." He smiled down at her. "He's crazy about Aramantha and I think he's a good kid. I think he just hasn't yet decided what he wants to do about this campaign of his dad's." John bent and kissed the corner of her lips. "Why don't we give him a little time? If you want him for Ary maybe we should just let old Trent drive his boy right into our corral?"

She raised her right hand and touched the corner he'd kissed. Her lips glowed so she could hardly speak, so she nodded and whispered.

"John. Lean your head down here."

"Why?" He grinned.

"I got something for you."

He seemed to like what she gave him.

At the supper table Junior Trent stayed noticeably silent as Aramantha chattered away talking about the men "a touching" and how John had run them away with Lucifer and Mrs. Gulliver's help. Finally she asked the question they'd all been waiting for.

"Them men work for your daddy, Junior. How come he has them come over here and bother us?"

Junior looked down at the fried ham he'd speared with his pocket knife. He examined it carefully, top and bottom, before he laid it out on the flat tin pan he'd been given as a plate.

"My pa thinks he runs the world." The red haired young man knotted his arms across his chest and leaned back against the wall. "He thinks he runs me and he thinks he can run you folks."

Ary put a biscuit on Junior's plate. He relaxed and split the biscuit with his knife to lay the two rounds inner side up, next to the ham.

"I'll take some of that there red eye gravy." He poured several spoonfuls of the thin brown gravy onto the biscuits. "Yeah. I'm real sure my father isn't going to be able to buffalo you folks and I'm kinda thinking he may have a harder time with me than he expects."

"We got plenty of that there gravy, Junior. Help yourself." Ary leaned toward the freckle faced man as if confiding in him. "I made the supper tonight."

"And it's good," Junior talked around a mouthful of biscuit sopped in gravy. "You're a good cook and a good mother and a real sweet and pretty little woman. I don't know why he don't like you, Aramantha. He don't even know you."

"I don't know why neither." Ary passed the platter of sliced tomatoes to him. "Lessen it's *because* he don't know me very well. Maybe at the Sunday School I can talk to him. Get better acquainted with him?"

"It won't do no good, Ary. He's a hard-nosed old geezer. He's got his mind made up and he's stubborn as your sister's mule when he's got some idea in his head." Junior nodded down at the food in his plate. "Yep. I guess I gotta go ahead and do what I been planning."

"What you planning, Junior?" Annie handed the little jar of Mrs. Broughton's plum butter to the hungry youngster. "Can you tell us?"

"Well, not right now. I ain't got everything thought out yet."

"Your father is interfering with Annie's business, Junior." John spoke in a man-to-man tone.

"I know. He puredee loves to interfere in other folk's business. Particularly mine." He took a huge mouthful of biscuit smeared with plum butter. "I reckon I ain't going to allow that much longer, neither." He chewed pensively and stared into the middle distance.

"I'm what you might call a growed man, now. Old enough to call my own shots."

"What've you decided you gonna do, Junior?" Ary gave Junior the dishrag for wiping his grease smeared fingers.

He swallowed before he cleaned his hands then smiled thanks at Ary.

"You'll see, little girl." He tilted his head toward Aramantha and the baby. His smile died. "You and me need to get private. We got a lot to talk about." He looked at Annie. "That is, if your big sister ain't got no objections."

Chapter 16

"How do I look, sister?" Aramantha lifted one side of her creamy silken skirt and twirled to show off her first new dress.

Annie sighed. Beautiful. The child was so beautiful that she'd probably take all the congregation's attention away from John Wesley Matlock and his Bible lesson for the Sunday School.

"In that new dress you're just about the prettiest thing I ever seen, Ary." She felt a stab of pleasure at the younger girl's dimpled reaction. "Don't you agree, Uncle George?"

"She sure is growed up looking. Beautiful like your mama... and like your great aunt Thessalonia when she was young." He looked at Annie. "Aye God, Annie Lee, you're beautiful this morning, too. Got on that there dress that was your mama's and that there fancy necklace." He jounced Wesley Ann in his arms. "You two'll set the whole territory on its ear."

Annie looked down and pressed the platinum heart against the faded bosom of the blue striped gingham dress. She did feel right special. Pretty even. Maybe it was that pat of flour she'd swiped across her nose to cut the shine. Iffen you didn't notice her work boots peeking from below the hem you might think she was some society lady come to church.

She slicked her hand up the back of the new hairdo she'd made for herself. Ringlets in the front where it was short and a psyche knot on top made up from the long strands at the back. "Elegant" Ary had said. She wanted John to see her all dressed up and curled and powdered like a lady.

"John's present does make mama's dress look right up town, don't it?" She smoothed the old man's hair. "You look nice too, Uncle George." She buttoned the top button on his shirt. "Sober, too." She grinned at him and took Wesley Ann from him. "Got your fiddle?"

"Got it right here." He grinned back and lifted the instrument from Mrs. Gulliver's corner.

"Where's John, Annie?" Ary gave another half twirl.

"Said he was too nervous to hang around waiting for us. He's outside saying hello to the first comers, I reckon." Annie couldn't help her giggle. "He's scared to death to get up and talk in front of all them people."

"Ah, he'll be all right, Annie. I give him a little swig outta my jug." George twinked a string on the fiddle. "Calmed the boy right down."

"George, I'll never forgive you iffen you gone and got our fancy preacher drunk." Annie looked at the shelf where the jug usually sat. "He's been working on that lesson all week." The jug was gone.

"Aye God, he ain't drunk. He needed a mite of nerve medicine and I give it to him." George stepped toward the door and bowed. "Iffen you ladies is ready...?"

Annie waited for Aramantha and George to go first before she stepped out onto the wooden floor that John and Junior Trent had labored to finish just two days previously. The roofed area smelled so good... like new wood. It was mighty pretty, too, Annie thought. Big enough for everyone. The school bell that Mr. Smith had fastened to a corner of the roof glowed platinum in the sun. He'd said he knew that his dead brother Jim would have wanted her to have that bell from their old school in Texas. Uncle George had given him a jug of the finest to take home after that. Smith had said he might be back for the doings. Annie hoped he would come. He'd looked so old and sad and kinda dried up.

The Twig's own benches and the Broughton's chairs and benches didn't nearly fill up the space. She hoped others would bring chairs. The bales of hay that rimmed the two ends would work real well as seats for the young people who liked to be back away from the preaching, anyways. Mary Broughton was sweeping up the bits of hay that had littered the floor. Annie smiled her thanks. Mary was a real good girl.

Junior Trent stepped up onto the floor and took Ary's arm. He doffed his hat.

"You sure do look pretty, Miss Ary."

"You look kinda pretty your own self, Junior. I ain't never seen you in a suit before."

Junior smiled and reddened.

"Your daddy coming, Junior?" Even though the younger Broughton children had been told to speak their invitation at every house, Annie couldn't help wishing that they'd skipped old Trent's place.

Junior nodded.

Wasn't that the way? Well, she wasn't going to let that sorry old man ruin her fun today. She'd just ignore him.

Junior and Ary walked arm-in-arm to greet the first three people who walked into the dooryard then both waved at a man and wife and baby in a buggy. Annie kept the smile on her face but she could feel her cheeks tightening when she couldn't locate her hired hand anywhere.

"Where is John Wesley, George?" She bounced the baby frantically and muttered the words so no one but her uncle could hear her. "Is he out in the barn a drinking?"

"Might be having a little snort but he ain't going to be drunk, Annie Lee." George reached for the baby. "You calm down a mite now. Go and talk to the folks."

Annie felt more than one pair of eyes trained on her as she ambled through the gathering crowd. She didn't want to run straight up to the barn, she just planned to end up there accidentally iffen she just kept moving. She couldn't tell if the folks was a talking about her being in a dress or if they was a talking about her being a witch. Well, it didn't matter. Today's

Scoundrels' Bargain

big goings on would clear everyone's mind of that silliness. Maybe they was just admiring her. At least they was speaking civil.

Several men sauntered down the path from the barn, John Matlock among them. He looked all right. Annie heaved a sigh of relief and turned again to the newly laid floor. She and John and Junior had had a good time putting down them boards. She took the baby from George so he could tune up and in seconds he was fiddling a lively version of, "Shall We Gather At The River?"

Folks hurried to get seats. Some carried their own chairs, others sat at the edge of the floor and let their feet rest on the dirt. Mary Broughton sat with some other girls on one of the hay bales. She looked real nice. Everything looked real nice. It was going to be a wonderful day.

Annie stepped to the bell and tooled out a double series of peals that brought the few malingering churchgoers rushing on into the new open air room. Ary, Junior, Uncle George and the baby and John sat on a bench in front of their own kitchen table. Annie had decided the table would work quite well as John's pulpit.

Annie stepped to the table and smiled out at the folks. Night onto sixty people she reckoned, counting babies and all.

"Welcome to our Sunday School." She smiled and stepped around to pick up Wesley Ann. "We sure thank Mr. Thurman Smith for our nice bell. He brung the bell in memory of his brother Jim Smith who died recently from an accident, as most of you know." Annie nodded toward the wizened little man who sat astride his leather saddle right near the front. A few people applauded.

"Now, I wanted youall to see our new baby. This here is Wesley Ann Twig." Annie walked to the second row of chairs and put Wesley Ann into Grandma Broughton's arms. "Grandma Broughton is going to dandle Wesley Ann whilst we start the singing and then we're going to have us some preaching." She turned and smiled at John. His skin darkened in a flush.

"Our mama brought us up to be Baptist," she continued, "But Ary and George and me, we done talked it over and we thought we'd have our Sunday School be something else... maybe Methodist which ain't... uh, isn't so very different from being Baptist cept'n they dance." She nodded at George. "We got us some music and we want to dance here this afternoon iffen any of youall was so inclined."

She smiled broadly at the smattering of applause. "So be it."

George lifted his fiddle to his chin and twanged a note.

"We don't have us no hymn books but we thought iffen youall didn't know a song we could parse out each line and pretty soon we'll all know the same songs." She faltered just a beat when she saw Trent ride in on his big gray horse. People turned and looked but she was happy to see they turned right back to hear what she had to say. "I'm hoping we can meet like this at least once a quarter. Or maybe oftener. Let's talk about it over dinner." She turned again to motion her family and Junior to stand. "Us Twigs will start with a song or two then any of you otherns who'd like to, could come up front here and parse out some favorite songs of your own for us. How does that sound?"

"Sounds good Annie."

"Amen, girl."

"Let's sing."

The calls and shouts from the congregation were better than a handful of silver dollars to Annie. This here Sunday School was going to be a big success.

"Uncle George's been playing 'Shall We Gather At The River?' so what we'll do is Ary and John and Junior and me will parse out each line, then we'll sing the whole thing all the way through. Ready?" She stepped back to the bench and stood next to John Wesley and the music began.

"Shall we gather at the River? The beautiful, the beautiful river?" Annie could hear Thurman Smith's rumbling bass monotone below the voices of the rest of the singers. The old man beat the horn on his saddle to accompany his singing. Maybe this kind of gathering would keep him from being so lonely now. The whole congregation sang the parsed out first line of words back to the Twigs.

"Gather with the Saints at the river, that flows by the throne of God." Annie was glad Grandma Broughton still had her loud soprano voice even iffen she was awful old. The fat little old lady smiled and sang and bounced Wesley Ann on her knee. Her granddaughter Mary's clear treble swung in from the place where the young people had congregated.

By the time the Twigs had led three songs and the gathered neighbors had roared out three more hymns parsed out by Mary and Mr. and Mrs. Broughton, Annie knew for sure she'd done the right thing. Even old Henry Trent was singing all them old songs with them.

Time now to hear them fancy words from the Pinkerton man... from the preacher... from John Wesley Matlock. She felt a deep throbbing in her chest when she stood alone once more to introduce him. All these folks was gonna love him just the way she did, well maybe not the way she did, but they was all gonna love him. She was sure of that.

"I got a real treat for youall today. Our hired man is a real educated man, a religious man, name of John Wesley Matlock, from back East. He's the one gonna teach us the text from the Bible. You folks say *Amen* now for our preacher for today."

Amid a sea of "Amens" John Wesley Matlock staggered only slightly when Mrs. Gulliver leaned into his legs as he moved around the table.

Scoundrels' Bargain

Annie felt herself smiling the broadest possible smile at the end of John's lesson. Why, he had spoke so good, so educated, that sometimes she didn't even know what he was a talking about. Now *that* was rightly what she called the sign of a real preacher, sure enough. Didn't matter that he'd told the whole congregation he wasn't no preacher before he started. They sure knew better now.

She stiffened when he asked Uncle George to pray but that old man rang down the house with a prayer so loud that Lucifer brayed an answering Amen from the barn.

When it was time they'd all bring out their dinner baskets and each family would eat separately so's no one would be embarrassed about what was in or not in the family's lunch pail. Give the kids time to run and play a bit afterward and then on with the dancing. John Matlock and Junior Trent readied themselves to carry the kitchen table "pulpit" back into the kitchen. The Twig family would leave their benches on the new floor but they'd eat standing up in their regular places back in their own little log kitchen. She couldn't hardly wait for the afternoon's festivities to start.

She'd just bet that John Wesley Matlock was as good a dancer as he was a preacher. The thought of his arms around her made her smile to herself. He really wasn't drunk... he'd just had a nip or two.

After they'd eaten all the cold fried chicken they could hold, Ary and Junior excused themselves, planning to go off for a walk. Annie offered to keep the baby but Junior said he was going to carry Wesley Ann himself.

John Matlock had to show Junior how to carry a baby so it was protected. Before he'd let the baby go on the walk with the two young people John made Junior swear he'd take better care of Wesley Ann than he did of his own horse.

George wobbled to the corner and kicked his bedroll open as he muttered something about a "little nap" before he laid himself out on the pallet of quilts. Almost before his head touched its resting place he began snoring.

Annie looked across at the hired man to search for a sign that he was feeling what she had been feeling. When she looked up into John Wesley's amber eyes and saw herself mirrored there she realized that for at least a few more minutes they could be alone together even though they were in the midst of a crowd. She felt anticipation tighten within her. She looked a question. He nodded almost imperceptibly. She held out her hand. He took it into his own and she led him into the dugout bedroom. Neither said a word.

Something shiny stretched between them. Annie knew that. It seemed to be a platinum cord of love and *longing*. She knew that John Wesley felt it too. But they wouldn't talk about it. All they would really ever have was this stolen moment and others like it. She took a deep breath of the musky air in the cave-like bedroom.

Annie slipped her hand up under his vest and lay her palm against his chest. Through the heavy cloth of his shirt she felt his hard muscles under her fingers, felt his breath move in and out, felt her own blood thrum in answering rhythm to the beat of the big man's heart.

She raised her gaze. His eyes sent her a honey colored message of slow sweetness. He lowered his lips to crush hers and his hands encircled her body. Joy rose within her. It was as if they danced without movement.

The buttons. His mouth searched hers. She felt his fingers loosing the buttons at the back of her dress. She couldn't move, couldn't resist, could only move closer into the heated ring his arms made about her body. He stepped back just a fraction and helped the bodice of her dress to slip down from her shoulders, off her arms, then allowed the cotton cloth to dangle all around from the sash that cinched the calico dress in the middle. She stood nude from the waist up.

"Annie," His voice whispered from somewhere deep inside himself, "Annie girl. Let me look at you." He cleared his throat or growled or moaned. He felt the same yearning she did. Annie stood, chin lifted, wanting him to see her, wanting him to think her beautiful. She could feel the hardening of her nipples.

Part of her slipped back to the time with Addison, back in Arkansas. Nothing gentle about that go round. She pulled herself back to the territory and the shadowed room and the man she wanted so much. He took slow steps around her, caressing her with his eyes, letting his finger draw a line from the platinum heart to the space under her right breast, across her ribs and down her back to the cloth barrier of the dress then up and over her shoulder and down again to the other breast. It was as if she were clothed with his gaze.

"Ah, Annie. You are so lovely. So blonde and silvery and white and ivory." The shadows in the tiny room seemed to shift. "I want desperately to see all of you." He kissed her again. "What do you want, darling?" *Addison Fleurey would never have asked that.* The thought came unbidden and as quickly disappeared. John's hand lifted the front of the bodice to touch the cloth belt that held the dress about her. Her hand covered his and held it.

"What is it, Annie? Let me see the whole of you."

She could see his passion swelling in the throbbing of a blood vessel that stood out against the golden skin of his throat. Loving him was the center of her world but she couldn't... couldn't. Not right now. Not with all these people here. They'd have to leave their want unfulfilled.

"John, we'll have to wait. You forget there are people all around us." She memorized his sculptured mouth with greedy eyes. Maybe if she could feel their touch just once more she'd be able to go back to being the strong and capable Annie, the responsible Annie she'd left behind somewhere in the kitchen.

He bent and kissed each swelling nipple, then opened his sculpted lips to hers once more. A wild shaking engulfed her. Her knees melted and she had to force herself to stand firmly away from the bed. The smooth expanse of the quilt spread across her mattress seemed to call to her. All she'd have to do would be to step back two tiny steps and they could sink into the comfort it offered. His thorough search of her, the sweetness of him against her mouth made her want to forget everything, welcome him, let him do as he willed... but she couldn't. Not now. Not here. Tonight, when everyone had gone would be time enough.

"Tonight," she whispered. "Tonight will be better, won't it?"

He shook his head as if trying to clear it. "Tonight? Where? I'm going to hold you to that, Annie."

"Miss Annie. Are you in here?" Henry Trent's voice boomed from the kitchen door.

"Uh, Henry." Uncle George's voice sounded as if he were struggling up from sleep. "Naw. Annie Lee ain't here. Has the dancing started?" Annie could hear her Uncle shuffling to the outer door, talking as he went.

"Aye God, Henry Trent, I'm right glad you wakened me 'cause..." The door closed on his words.

Annie put her hand across John's lips.

"Tonight," she whispered. "You stay here a few minutes. Do me up, first." He had already lifted her dress top and was fumbling with the buttons at the back of her bodice. "I'll go on out and you can join us later. Probably no one will notice in this crowd." She turned and looked at his shadowed face once again. "Sweet John." He pulled her into his arms for a long, lingering last kiss. "I saw you nipping up at the barn this morning." She smiled into his mysterious eyes. "You sure you aren't still a little drunk, John Wesley Matlock?"

"I'm intoxicated with platinum and ivory, Annie girl. I'm full of you."

It was hard to leave him.

John waited until he heard the twirling notes from George's fiddle before he stepped out onto the doorstep and across to the roofed open area.

"Where the hell have you been?" Henry Trent growled the words from behind Matlock. He tried to ignore the older man but a heavy hand fell on his shoulder and whirled him to face the gray suited rancher. His automatic reaction was to clench his fists and swing but he controlled himself. This man was a lot older than him... besides, this was Annie's party.

Trent's right fist swung from his hip to crash into Matlock's face. John let his own best uppercut swing upward in answer and the fight was on. Bystanders shouted and Buell and Sharky and another of Trent's ranch hands waded into the fray. Men who'd just been watching with interest took a stand at the unfair odds against Matlock and in seconds the fight had spread like prairie fire across most of the males in the congregation. Women pulled children off to the side of the floor. The boys laughed and shouted. Little girls screamed and cried.

George let his fiddle lower to a safe space under the wooden floor and he pulled out his jug from the same space. He took a long drink then raised the crockery weapon to crash it against the temple of the cowboy who had picked up one of the Broughton's chairs. The cowpoke had seemed set to break the wooden piece of furniture against John Wesley Matlock's shoulders. The cowboy went down silently. Uncle George crowed his victory.

"Stop." Annie shouted. "Stop this." The men were too involved in the melee to hear or heed her command. Some of the younger fighters were laughing. John Matlock wore a grim smile on his face.

Annie bounced into the kitchen and out again. She leaped up onto the bench again and raised George's long gun then pulled the trigger. The blast tore a hole in the new roof and the rioting fighters and the screaming women froze in place. Statues for just a second.

"That's it." Annie let her voice pour out all her pent up scorn and anger. "You men go on home now. You rotten bastards. I'm ashamed of all of you."

Within minutes she saw the backs of wagons and buggies and single horses disappearing over the ridge and into the distance.

She stepped off the bench and crumpled into sobs over the long gun. When the pair of shiny black boots shimmered into her vision she screamed the words that she couldn't control.

"You done ruined our Sunday School dance." She sniffed back a deep sob. "You and George is both drunken louts. You ain't no different than all them other trashy old men."

"Oh, Annie. I'm sorry. Trent hit me and I guess I..."

"Go away. I ain't never going to talk to you again. Get on out of my sight." There was silence for a moment and then the boots moved away.

Chapter 17

"Well, I've done everything but wring myself inside out for you, Annie. I don't know what else I can do." John shifted from foot to foot before sitting down at the table. "It's been almost a week now. I've apologized for the ruckus. I've begged your pardon for ruining the dance for you. I've promised to behave in the future. What else do you want me to do?"

"Nothing." Annie didn't look up at him as she slammed the pan of hot biscuits onto the platter in the middle of the table. "Sit down and eat your breakfast. You gotta finish that line of fence up past the cedar breaks."

"All right. I get it." John leaned forward to look into her face. "I guess you want me to leave Circle Twig? Is that it?" He clenched his teeth to keep from saying more. *If I do leave Annie Twig,* he wanted to add, *I'll be forced to take you with me.*

He watched the color rise in her face, saw her mouth tighten and her hand clutch at the kettle of herbal tea she held. He waited coolly for her answer. Her fingers left the teapot handle to touch something beneath her cast off shirt. *That blasted platinum heart,* he told himself, *a lot of good that hunk of Jewelry did me!*

"What do you say, Annie?" He looked into the glorious cobalt blue of her eyes. Something flickered there. A smile, perhaps?

Uncle George took his usual stool at the head of the table.

"Yeah, Annie Lee. You done punished ussens enough. We didn't mean to get into no fight but Aye God, girl, old man Trent started it all, anyways." Her uncle held out his cup for hot herbal tea as he sputtered his indignation at his niece's continuing punishing behavior.

Annie nodded. John felt cheated when her gold tipped lashes lowered to cover the glorious blue. "I know. I know. It's just that I wanted our Sunday School and dancing to go so well." She rubbed her forehead with the back of her hand. "I reckon I have been tramping around a bit much on you old boys these last few days."

"You have that." John reached for a hot biscuit.

He broke the biscuit and lathered it with butter. "I've been feeling a lot like a well used road."

Her uncle nodded agreement and so did Aramantha.

"Yeah, Annie. I don't like it when you're mean to John Wesley or Uncle George. Junior told me he was afraid to come over 'cause of you being so hateful."

Uncle George nodded agreement. Aramantha continued.

"I think you even scared old Lucifer, sister." Aramantha used the flat wooden scoop that John Matlock had whittled out of a piece of blackjack wood. She shoved a mound of fried potatoes right from the iron skillet onto each person's tin pan. "That mule has been real quiet. And Mrs. Gulliver hasn't been in the house for two or three days 'cept to sleep."

Annie felt a flash of panic. She couldn't let this man leave. Not while they still had so much to do to prove up the place. And that wasn't even the important reason. Even if he had made her lose her temper she still felt something special for him. Well. All right. She loved him. She probably hadn't been fair. Not that any woman had to worry about that where any man was concerned. No man was fair and most of them were bastards anyway, and deserved whatever they got, didn't they?

All right. So maybe old Henry Trent had started the fight. Maybe Matlock hadn't struck the first blow but even if he had, Matlock had probably had enough punishment... unless she could think of something to do that would pay him back just a little bit more but wouldn't drive him completely away from her and the Circle Twig.

She looked him straight in the eye for the second time that morning. She hadn't really looked at him in more than a week. His tanned face was still the handsomest thing she'd ever seen... the sensual lips busy with hot biscuits... black brows drawn together in a frown. All right, maybe she wasn't quite through punishing him yet, but she too had had about all she wanted of the anger that had eaten at her. She could do something else to pay him back, something he wouldn't even realize she was doing. Anyway, the air needed clearing around here and maybe now was as good a time as any to do it.

"John, Uncle George, maybe I oughta accept youall's apology. I know you're both sorry."

She smiled at her uncle and then at the hired man. "Likely I went too far because I was setting such store by our first Sunday School and dance." She smiled then at Aramantha sitting at the table in her old petticoat, shirt, apron getup. She watched her sister lift Wesley Ann from Uncle George's arms.

"I been kinda sulky with you too, sister. I'm sorry. I was just trying so hard to start Wesley Ann off along the right track that I let my ambitions for her get in the way of my family feelings for the rest of you." She nodded and let her gaze fall toward the biscuits and fried potatoes on her tin dish. "You just tell Junior Trent to come on over, if you've a mind to. I'll let him know I'm not mad any more."

"Funny you say that, Annie," Aramantha jiggled Wesley Ann and grinned widely. "It just so happens that Mr. Junior Trent is a calling on me this very evening. Now I can invite him to come on into the house." She let

Scoundrels' Bargain

Wesley Ann have a small piece of cooled biscuit crust. "He'll be glad to hear you ain't mad no more."

"You two are getting pretty serious, aren't you, little sister?"

Now it was time for the younger woman to lower her gaze. She nodded, smiled, and color rose pink in her cheeks. She didn't speak.

"All right." Annie waited for her sister to look up. "I'll say something nice to the young Mr. Trent." She wagged her finger at her sister. "And I'll be expecting him to make his bows to Uncle George pretty soon."

Uncle George widened his eyes in a surprised manner but said nothing. Aramantha stopped jiggling the baby to question Annie.

"What do you mean... make his bows to Uncle George?" she asked.

"Well, Uncle George is the head of our family, isn't he, girl?" Annie gestured toward the end of the table where their uncle sat. She waited for Ary's dubious nod. "Uncle George'll sure be wanting to know about his intentions and if that boy don't come up to the mark, little sister, we sure don't want him hanging around over here all the time. And we *sure* aren't gonna be having us no more babies by ourselves. Babies need daddies."

She felt pleased at John Matlock's silent applause at the ultimatum. She could see it in the warm copper glance he gave her, the skin around his eyes crinkling at the edges. She was glad he felt the same way she did. Wesley Ann needed a daddy and even more, Ary needed a husband.

Uncle George straightened his shoulders and puffed out his chest.

"Aye God. Your sister's right. Yes indeedy, Aramantha. I want to know what that there young man has in mind." He tweaked Wesley Ann's cheek to cause her to gum a biscuit smile up at him. "Is he an honorable man or not? You tell Junior Trent I asked you that, girl. You hear?"

Ary nodded and flushed again. "I'll tell him what youall said." she murmured

Later that night after her long talk with Junior, Annie made her decision. When she rode away in the buggy with Junior Trent, Lucifer tied onto the back, Annie felt real guilt at leaving her family again. And she felt even more guilt for lying to them.

She'd whispered a part of the truth to Ary but the younger girl was so thrilled she had sworn she wouldn't let the cat out of the bag. So far as John and Uncle George knew, Annie was going to a distant neighbor's house to do some healing. She'd had to bring her medical supplies to make it look real but she didn't have much of anything else to carry anyway. She was wearing mama's dress and her ragged shirt and trousers were in her yarb... her *herb* sack, for the ride home on her mule.

Anyway, the Widow Stanfield really might need some doctoring for all she knew, Annie told herself. Living alone in that little white house a few miles out of Guthrie the widow probably didn't take real good care of herself. Always bent over a dress or a waist or a coat she was making for one lady or another. Annie clutched her bag to her chest in a ripple of fear and a prickle of excitement.

She was going to a ball. In Guthrie. In a new dress. Everybody who was anyone at all in the Territory would be there. It was part of the deal she'd made with Junior.

Of course, there was just one little drawback. She'd have to go as Mr. Henry Trent's guest. Junior had explained it all to her. His daddy was probably already making arrangements for her to stay with the Widow Stanfield the night before the ball and the night of the ball. For his part Junior had promised to help his daddy get a chance to talk to Annie without her family around if his daddy would give *him* permission to visit openly with Aramantha. Annie had looked at the deal from every angle and she couldn't see anything wrong with it. 'Course Henry was a bastard but she wouldn't ever be alone with him, so why not?

He explained that his father was also arranging for a dress for her. A dress made by the Widow Stanfield. The seamstress had several made up dresses on hand and Annie got to choose the one she wanted.

"Naturally, I'll give the dress to Aramantha after the ball is over," she told Junior. "I don't have no real use for a dress." She put her hand down on the outside of the buggy seat so Junior Trent wouldn't see that she'd crossed her fingers at her lie. Junior grinned at her words.

"She'll have four dresses then, Annie. I'm getting her some pretty material for a real special dress after I leave you off at the Widow's house." He clicked at the two high stepping horses. "I'll bring the stuff back by on my way back home."

"Aren't you going to the ball, Junior?"

Well, it looked like it was raining dresses on her little sister. Fine. It was about time the child wore something decent. She couldn't feel jealous of all these nice things promised for Ary. After all, *she* had a platinum heart that she could wear out to work or anyplace at all, without worrying. That heart wouldn't tear or get dirty. Ary would have to be careful of all the new dresses.

"I thought maybe you and me could have a dance, Junior." Annie's heart sank when he shook his head. She wouldn't even know one person in the whole ballroom, probably, except old Henry.

"Naw. I'd like to dance with you Annie but I'd kinda promised I'd go on back and see Ary."

Annie had shrugged and agreed. Partly to do a little something else to repay John and George for breaking up the Sunday School dance and partly because she had never been to a dance, not a real one, and now, *now*, she was going to a ball! Annie hugged herself with secret joy.

After she'd arrived and settled in at the plump little widow's house Annie was almost overwhelmed by the number of dresses she had to choose from. Seven pretty things, at least. Finally Annie narrowed the field down to a mustard colored woolen crepe with satin stripes, a gun metal gray silk and a black velvet and lace concoction. All were pretty close to a fit on her. Taking in at the waistline was about all that any of them needed.

The widow led her to the cheval glass in the corner of her bedroom to make her decision. Annie held the mustard crepe close to her face. It didn't do a thing for her but she knew the deep golden shade would really complement Ary's coloring. The black velvet was not a really good choice because it was too... something. Maybe too fast looking? Annie thought.

She held the gun metal crepe up to her chin. It seemed to make her eyes bluer, her hair brighten to the color of the platinum heart. She pulled out the necklace and let it fall against the soft silk. Beautiful.

"That's the one, Miss Twig." The widow's voice held admiration. "Mr. Trent can't help but adore seeing you in that dress even if I do say so myself." She lifted a strand of Annie's hair. "You do have such glorious hair. Such an unusual color. You're about the only woman in the Territory who *would* look so lovely in that bluish gray. That's why I still have it on hand." She lifted the dress up to let Annie try it on. "The woman who ordered it had kinda reddish hair. She hadn't realized it but this particular color of gray just made her look sick. She refused the dress." The seamstress took the garment from Annie and smiled as she shook her head. "And here I thought I'd never sell it." The widow helped Annie pull the silken frock over her blonde head. The gown made faint whispers of sound as it settled about her body. Annie loved the rich sound.

Annie nodded and fought back the guilt. The dress probably wouldn't do anything for Ary's complexion either... but Annie wanted it, even for only one evening. Ary was so young and so pretty that any old color would look all right on her. This dress just had to be Annie's own dress for at least this one night.

"I'll take this one." She smoothed the silken pleats on one leg o' mutton sleeve. "Keep the skirt a little bit long, Mrs. Stanfield. Maybe no one will notice my work shoes." Annie looked at the ruffled hem.

"Oh, no. You're going to be much too beautiful to wear those things." The widow dug into a trunk that sat under the one window in the room. "Here. Wear these."

Annie could smell the faint scent of cedar shavings when the bosomy little woman held up a pair of black leather hightop dress shoes decorated with gray suede spats. "These were my wedding slippers, dear. They're a bit old fashioned now but they are certainly prettier than your work shoes."

"Oh, ma'am. I couldn't take your wedding shoes."

"You certainly can." The plump little widow gestured toward the trunk. "I'll loan them to you. I haven't had them on in years. I wouldn't even allow you to wear that dress out of this house with those ugly old things of yours on your feet." She lifted the silken skirt and swished it through the air. "You'll be dancing, my dear!"

Annie heard the soft hush-hush of the silk skirts and she nodded in happy resignation. She back up to sit on the trunk. With Mrs. Stanfield's help and the use of a buttonhook, she fastened the soft leather, delicately pointed shoes. She put her feet straight out in front of herself. The wedding shoes stood neatly buttoned up around each of her slim ankles.

"A little loose, ma'am, but I can walk in them." Annie wobbled just a bit in her trip back to the mirror. "Not used to them there heels," she explained.

The beautifully sophisticated stranger in the mirror looked back at Annie and smiled. She felt tall. She lifted her hemline to better see the fancy shoes, let the silken material drop, then turned first to one side, then to the other, to look at her bustled profile. She twirled and turned her back to the glass so she could peek over her shoulder to see the reflected woman's bustled bottom wag flirtatiously. Annie put her doubled hand to her mouth to keep from laughing aloud.

"Wonder what John Matlock would say should he see Miss Annie Twig a looking like this?" she asked her dressed up image. The prickle of guilt touched her once more but she went on making pictures in her head. Pictures of herself and John Matlock waltzing in a brilliantly candlelit room.

"You'll have all of Guthrie on its ear, Miss Twig." Annie heard the older woman's voice through the wispy fabric of a daydream in which she, enclosed in the strong arms of John Wesley Matlock, swept round and round the ballroom floor. Mrs. Stanfield's next comment brought Annie right back to the reality of the widow's bedroom. "You're a very lucky young woman." The seamstress smiled and sighed. "It's more than likely Mr. Henry Trent will offer for your hand after he sees how gorgeous you are in that dress."

Sleeping in the widow's store-bought bed that night was just a little icing on the cake of her dreams of dancing in the new dress.

Next evening in the buggy riding toward the Territorial Ball, Annie kept as far away from Henry Trent as she could. He smelled like some kind of strong cigar. For a moment she wondered how a woman would like kissing a mouth that smelled like cigars. She shivered with distaste. Nothing to do with her, anyway. She was never going to be tasting the old bastard.

Before she'd stepped up into the buggy she'd reminded him of their deal. No use making the old man think this was anything more than a friendly three way bargain they'd made. She would go to the ball with him if he would let Junior come openly to visit Aramantha. A little voice inside her crowed one of the other reasons.

"And what about the dress? And what about the dancing? Reckon neither of them things persuaded you to come to Guthrie, Annie Lee Twig." She tried to ignore the inner voice as she made polite conversation with the man who had made the trip possible. "This would really get John Wesley's goat iffen he knew." the voice continued, "And isn't that part of it? Didn't you want to make him pay just a little bit more?"

Annie straightened the borrowed shawl that lay across her skirt and stared straight ahead. She could feel old Trent's gray gaze taking in every part of her.

"Since I'm your host, it's very nice to see you chose a gown of my favorite color, Miss Twig."

"Call me Annie." The words were automatic. Oh my God. She'd forgotten that everything about this man was gray... including his disposition. *He thinks this pretty thing was chosen in his honor!*

"Oh, this here gray silk was just about the only thing Widow Stanfield had that would fit me, Henry." She lifted a pinch of the blue gray silk between her thumb and her forefinger. "I'm afraid it didn't have anything to do with you." She risked a quick look at the man. With a few words the old bastard had almost ruined some of her good feeling about the evening.

"Anyway, I do thank you, Henry. I appreciate the dress and the chance to go to the ball. If it wasn't for you I reckon I never would a known what a real ball was like." She couldn't help the little nip of joy that returned to jump up and down within her. "And now, I'm going to get to find out all about a fancy party and fancy dancing whilst wearing a fancy party dress."

The man was silent for a moment. He slowed the horses.

"You certainly do the dress justice, my dear. I expect we will be the center of attention, tonight." He gave her another chilly smile. "Your looks and my money will put the two of us well above the rest of the hoi polloi." His reached to pat her hand. "That's one of the reasons I believe that Henry Trent and Annie Twig are destined for each other. Tonight I want you to remember that you are just to smile and look beautiful and I'll do all the talking for both of us at this affair."

"You old bastard. You're just spoiling for a fight, aren't you? Are you saying my talking isn't good enough for the folks at this here ball?" Annie kept her voice low but the words burned their way through the noises of the prancing horse and the moving vehicle.

"Well, certainly you know your English grammar ain't none too good, Miss Annie. But that's not important, is it? For a woman, I mean. All a woman needs to do is to be decorative, anyway, ain't it, my dear."

"Well, I *certainly* know enough about English grammar to know that 'ain't' isn't good English." She clamped her lips together and faced forward again. What had gotten into her? She was already roped into this agreement and she'd almost forgotten how much she despised this old fool until he brought it to mind.

"Come now, Miss Annie. If we're going to be close we can't always be arguing about small matters. Just do as I say and all will be well." He prinked up the horses again.

"Henry... onliest way you and me is ever going to be close is when we're dancing them three dances I promised you." Annie spoke without looking at him. "Aramantha might be your daughter-in-law but you and me... we're not even going to be related."

"Daughter-in-law," He slowed the horses again. "Whatever gave you such an insane idea?"

"Henry," She felt compelled to turn and look at him. "I think Junior and my Ary are thinking about getting married. Didn't you know that?" She again straightened the dark blue shawl that Mrs. Stanfield had insisted she carry against the late night chill. "I thought that was a part of our bargain, part of why you asked to take me to the ball."

"Get this, Miss Twig. We've been over this before. My son will never marry your ragged hoyden of a younger sister. I have much better things in mind for my son."

Annie gritted her teeth. The buggy was rolling too fast to jump out. Better just act as though they were simply conversing in a genteel way.

"You may not like it, Henry, but I'm pretty sure Henry Junior has got his mind set on my little ragged hoyden of a younger sister."

"My Junior is a good and obedient son. I'll arrange for him to go somewhere, off to school maybe." He smiled a grim lipped smile at her. "He ain't going to marry your sister, who is nothing more than another man's leftover, anyway. He will not marry your sister. You can count on that."

Annie clenched her fists and lifted her chin but then let herself relax. No use arguing with this rotten old duffer. The two young people would do whatsoever they wanted to do, she was pretty sure of that.

"Now, Miss Annie, let us get ready to enjoy an evening in the finest society that Oklahoma Territory has to offer. Remember, keep a smile on your face and keep your mouth closed, madam." He whipped up the animals and they both kept silence for the few miles they had to travel.

Scoundrels' Bargain

"I don't want to talk to you, anyways, Henry." Annie whispered the words so he wouldn't hear them over the noise of the buggy wheels. No use spoiling the whole evening. She let her gaze pass over the new town, pleased to see that most of the tents had been replaced with half wood, half canvas buildings. Some two story wooden buildings had also sprung up. The two new brick and stone buildings were real wonders to her.

When they drove into the stableyard where the guests' wagons and buggies were parked, Annie smiled and glanced at the gray profile beside her before she made a vow to herself. She looked up at the windows that blazed light, probably candles *and* oil lamps from the look of it. No matter what came afterward she was going to enjoy herself. No. Not just enjoy. She promised herself to wring every last drop of pleasure she could out of this evening. She was bound and determined to more than make up for the fun she'd missed at her own Sunday School dance.

Since they weren't moving the odor of old cigars came strongly on the wind. She twisted her lips with distaste and turned her face away from him.

Nothing was going to spoil her evening. This had to last her whole life. She was pretty sure she'd never be asked to such an affair again. Not to mention that she'd probably never again in her whole life get to wear a silk dress, nor tippy toe around in high heeled shoes, nor dance at a real ball ever again, with real musicians playing. She *would* have a good time, she was determined on that point. No matter what happened, she *would* have a good time.

She hoped she would never be sorry about taking Junior Trent up on his proposition. She hoped her lies to her family wouldn't somehow come back to haunt her. She clenched her fists with determination. She *would* have a good time!

Chapter 18

The ball was more than Annie had ever dreamed it would be. She whirled and danced and laughed and drank punch and laughed and talked. She talked a lot, no matter what Henry Trent had said on the way in. She knew she should probably feel guilty for letting John and her Uncle George think she was working but she pushed the thought away. She was determined to have an evening to remember so she talked and laughed and danced and nibbled on the party food that sat on a buffet table set to one side of the dance floor. Once she sang along with the music and her partner liked her singing.

All of her partners seemed to like whatever she was saying, as well. They listened and they asked questions. They smiled and they kept coming back for more.

During the evening it became very clear to her that Henry was not the only man who found her attractive. More than once during the evening, several of the single men almost fought for the privilege of dancing the waltz with her. Annie smiled and tried to be fair. She used her own special system of deciding whom to partner.

When she'd given each man one dance she started down the list a second time. She would have died rather than tell the men that she danced with them by size. She chose the shortest suitor for the first dance then worked her way up to the town's tall lanky undertaker, Mr. Farqhuar.

Mr. Farqhuar was taller than Matlock, she realized. For a second she closed her eyes and dreamed she was twirling about the floor with her hired man. Her closed eyes and her secret smile went right to the undertaker's head and he tried to pull her closer to himself on their second turn around the hall. She pulled away gently but she did it in such a way that she didn't hurt the man's feelings. He asked her for the very next dance but she had to decline. Henry Trent came to where she was standing, determined to have his turn.

"Are you having a good time?" He smiled his gray cigar smelling smile down into her face.

"Wonderful, Henry. Thank you for inviting me. This is an elegant party."

"This is our last dance, my dear. We will speak to the hostesses then we must leave." He dipped and whirled and held her the regulation eighteen inches away from himself. "We would not want to wait until the very last moment to leave, now would we?"

"Oh, why not wait a little while, Henry? I'm having such a good time. When will the party be over? Are you sure we have to leave?"

"Of course. The dance will go on for an hour or two more, but we don't want to be caught in the melee of the general exodus from the hall, do we?" He nodded in satisfaction and answered his own question. "Now is the most correct time for our departure."

Their goodbyes took only moments and before she knew it, the wonderland of the ball was a thing of the past. Their walk down the stairway and out to the buggy was very subdued. Annie felt like a child who has had a brightly painted toy torn from her hands. All she had left of the fairytale evening was the movement of the soft skirt of her silk dress and her high heeled walk in her borrowed wedding shoes. She smoothed the front of her dress. Even though the orchestra music from the hall grew softer and softer and the lights grew dimmer and dimmer as they neared their vehicle, Annie's attention remained inwardly fixed upon the people and the lights and the music and the dancing that she had left behind.

She never saw the tall Pinkerton man who quieted his horse within a shadowed corner of the yard, the better to watch Henry Trent help Annie up into his buggy. When they left the stableyard the detective followed at an easy pace.

"That was a wonderful party, Henry. Thanks for giving me a chance to see what a ball was like." She stretched and yawned. "All them people were really nice to me." She stretched again. "They even talked to me, Henry and I talked back to them. No one fainted dead away with shock at my grammar." She yawned again.

"Sleepy, Miss Annie?"

"Yep. The widow's little old trundle bed with that store-bought mattress is going to look real good to me tonight."

They rode in silence for a few minutes.

"Shall I come back for you at midday, Miss Annie?" Henry Trent turned and smiled. Annie realized that while she had been dancing he must have been stepping out to nip at the bottle. He smelled like moonshine and old cigars now. She knew that the men always kept a jug somewhere away from the bright light of parties and from the eyes of their wives. The skin of Trent's face looked mottled and dark in the bright moonlight.

He also seemed relaxed in a way that she had never seen him before. He even slumped a little in the leather buggy seat. The gray eyes seemed to devour her as if she were something good to eat.

"No thanks, Henry. I'll just go ahead and take my old mule the way we planned. The family will be looking for me to come back that way." She waved toward the road stretching ahead of them and yawned again. "The moonlight's so clear tonight you got a nice lighted drive. You can make it on home to your place real easy."

"I expected you to ride with me." His voice sharpened a bit. "We'll just stop by the widow's place so you can gather your belongings."

"Me riding on home with you in your buggy wasn't part of our agreement, Henry." She let the timbre of her own voice rise. "I'll stay the night with Mrs. Stanfield."

"No, no, my dear."

"Yes, yes, Henry. And I'm not your 'dear.'"

"I have everything arranged, little girl. I'm taking you home with me, Annie Twig." His almost silent laughter made Annie's scalp crawl. "Right to my ranch." Did he think he could force her to spend the night with him? Annie tried to think about what to do. They were getting fairly close to the Widow Stanfield's little house.

"You're not taking me anywhere but the widow lady's house, Henry. Get that through your thick skull." As she talked she began loosening the shoe buttons on the widow's pretty wedding slippers.

"No need to be coy with me, dear girl. I know what sort of family you come from." He turned his head to smile at her. "An overnight stay at my place will be no problem to anyone even if they should learn of it." To Annie the moonlight shining on his face turned his features and his smile into the very image of a death's-head, just like the skull and crossbones she drew on her dangerous medicines. Her fingers struggled and finished the right shoe then moved to the left.

"Henry, I've tried to tell you as nice as I could. I am never going to stay with you at your place... not even for one night." Her hand forced one more recalcitrant button through a loop. "I don't call that being coy. I call that being plain spoken. And you leave my family out of our discussion."

"Widow Stanfield's place is right ahead. I'll just go inside with you, my dear."

"You aren't going into the widow's house with me and I'm not going home with you." She slipped the left boot off, then the right. "Slow this danged contraption down, Henry."

"No need. We'll come for your other things later... maybe tomorrow. You'll feel happier about all this tomorrow." He raised the reins as if to whip up the horses.

"Stop this buggy, damn you."

"Now, now. We'll just go right on, Miss Annie." He spoke as if he were soothing a willful child.

Without another word, Annie lifted the boots, the soft leather uppers held in both her hands as she slapped them across Trent's face. He leaned forward, one hand moving under his nose. She could see the dark glint of blood on his hand. She drew the wedding shoes back and crashed the heels into the back of his head. He shouted and hunched his shoulders and the reins dropped from his hand. The horses stopped.

Scoundrels' Bargain

Annie threw the borrowed boots over the side then jumped from the buggy. Her bare feet landed in deep sand.

"Thank God for Territory dirt," she murmured and reached for a handful of the pinkish soil. When Trent crouched and moved to the side of the buggy as if to jump down also, she threw the handful of dust into his eyes.

"You bitch." He screamed and fell back onto the seat.

"Now, do you understand me, Henry? I'm not going home with you, now or ever. The Twigs may be poor but we ain't trash. Now leave me alone." She turned to begin her solitary trek to the house of the seamstress.

Both Annie and Henry Trent were shocked to hear a deep male voice call from the shadows of the road behind them.

"Miss Annie Twig, may I give you a ride to your ladyfriend's house?"

"John? John Wesley, is that you?"

"You get out of here, cowpoke." The older man sat rubbing his sleeve across his eyes. "This dispute is between Miss Annie and me."

"Yeah, I could see that. And one of you was losing the fight, I noticed." John Matlock's deep laughter was velvet in Annie's ear. She couldn't help it. She laughed too.

Henry Trent whipped up his horses with a curse, then over his shoulder he trailed a threat.

"You better watch your back, Matlock."

"Did you sleep well last night, Annie?"

John's question was accompanied by a smiling twinkle from his brown eyes. He was teasing her.

"The widow's place was nice but I missed all of you. I think old Lucifer felt the same way. He kept trying to run when we was coming home this morning."

Annie spread a bolt of blue checked gingham across the cleared and scrubbed kitchen table. She looked first at Ary, then John, Uncle George and Wesley Ann, in turn. She glanced over at Mrs. Gulliver who stretched, grunted, blinked and turned over to make herself more comfortable.

"Sure is good to be home." She smiled at John holding the baby.

"Junior bought this for me?" Aramantha picked up an edge of the new cloth.

"He sure did." Annie smoothed the cloth to ready it for cutting. "He left it at Widow Stanfield's for you and then me and Lucifer brought it on down to the Circle Twig just for you. I thought I'd start cutting it out this evening if you want, little sister."

"He's coming over to see me this evening, Annie."

"Remember what I said." Annie pointed her mother's scissors at the younger girl. "That boy's going to have to talk to your Uncle and right soon."

Ary nodded her understanding and let her gaze wander down to the waiting checked cloth.

"I love this here color." Ary held the edge of the blue and white printed cloth up under her chin and posed for the others. "Junior says it will look perfect on me."

"That shade of blue is just right for you, Aramantha." John nodded and bounced Wesley Ann on one knee. "It makes your eyes look even bluer."

"John Wesley," Aramantha smoothed the cloth flat again then clasped her hands atop the gingham covered table. "Would you tell us again about how our Annie fought with Junior's silly old papa."

John laughed and tossed Wesley up into the air.

Annie felt her cheeks warm.

"John... you surely haven't told them...?"

"That you were at a ball with old Henry Trent? Didn't need to. Ary did the telling for all of us."

"Well, Annie, I was just worried that you might not be all right with that old bird." Ary tried to defend her tale bearing. "Come on John. Tell us what was going on between our Annie and old Henry."

John grinned across at her.

"Now John..."

"Yes sir, John Wesley," Uncle George pounded the cloth covered table, "Tell us again how our girl got the better of old Mr. High-and-Mighty Henry Trent."

"Well," John cleared his throat and narrowed his eyes. "Miss Annie was very polite at first. She started out by thanking him for making it possible for her to go to a ball."

"Now, John Wesley..."

The detective continued to tell the tale as if she hadn't spoken at all.

"When the old man told Annie he was taking her to his house all hell broke loose."

"John Wesley Matlock..." Annie knew she'd turned a bright red but it didn't matter. No one was noticing her. They were all entranced by John's repetition of the story.

"I'll stay with the widow, thank you very much." John raised his voice to a girlish falsetto.

"No, no, Miss Annie." The reported rejoinder was made in an uncanny mimicry of the deep grating voice of the rancher.

"I'm never going to go to your stupid house." Falsetto again.

Scoundrels' Bargain

Ary and Uncle George laughed. Annie couldn't help it. She had to laugh also.

"Aye God, what did he think of that?" Uncle George's old blue eyes glinted with merriment.

"He didn't like her answers much. Nor her shoes across his face, either. Our Annie let Mr. Trent know in no uncertain terms that she wasn't going home with him."

"What'd she say, John? Exactly." Ary grinned at Annie. Wesley Ann crowed and waved her fists in the air. "Wesley Ann wants to hear the whole thing, too."

John cleared his throat. "You're not taking me anywhere but the widow's house, Henry." It was the falsetto again. "Get that through your thick skull." John let his voice deepen to his own normal voice again. "Then after a few more well chosen words on both sides, our Annie just whipped off her shoes and whacked old Henry across the nose with both of them." He jounced Wesley Ann from one knee to the other.

"Aye God, our girl drew blood." George cackled and reached for the baby.

"She did that. When he leaned forward to keep from getting a spot on that fancy gray suit of his, she whacked him again across the back of his head."

"What's he say?"

"He yelled. Guess he couldn't believe he'd been whipped about the head and shoulders by a little blonde girl."

"Go on, John Wesley. What happened next?" Ary's eyes danced and her grin widened.

"Annie threw the shoes over the side and then jumped out of the buggy herself. She landed barefoot in the road. Before you could shake a stick at her she'd scooped up a handful of red dust. When old Henry looked as if he were going to come down out of that buggy she threw dirt square in the man's eye."

Even Miss Gulliver oinked, passed wind and joined in the cheers and laughter. Annie was still protesting.

"Oh, John... for heaven's sake."

George, still holding the baby, stepped to the door and fanned the foul air out of the room without missing a word of the story.

"When I butted into their disagreement he said their fight was private. I said I could see that but that I thought he might need a little help seeing as how he was the one who was losing."

"Oh, John, John, John." Annie had to laugh with them. "You're sure making a lot out of this. I bet youall haven't done nothing but talk about this while I was trying so hard to get home to you. How many times today have you told this silly story already?"

"Let me have that little darling." The Pinkerton man took the baby away from her uncle.

"We hope our Wesley learns something from this." Uncle George laughed at his remembrance of Annie's fight with their rancher neighbor. "Sometimes little girls has to take care of themselves." He shook the baby's hand.

"Your aunt is a real fire eater, little one." John tossed Wesley Ann into the air again. The man and the baby both chuckled. "Remember what I told you little girl." He kissed the red curls on the top of the infant's head. "You just better not fool with your Aunt Annie."

Later John listened to the two sisters talking about what Aramantha should wear for her visitor.

"I'll just pull your hair up real quick after you dress, Ary."

"What should I wear tonight, Annie? Should I wear the gray silk you brung me?"

"Well, aren't you the fine lady? You got so much choice now you can't even decide what to wear? You gonna be just like one of those ladies who has to *decide* each morning what she's gonna wear that day? Or maybe you're going to have the maid chose your outfit?"

"I want to look nice." Ary stood in the doorway, twisting the stained apron she wore over her shirt. "I think Junior's going to talk to Uncle George tonight."

"You look real nice in mama's brown dress that I fixed for you." Annie looked up from the new cloth. "Why don't you just wear that and save your two silk dresses for church... or for your wedding?"

"Wedding? You mean I'm going to have a wedding, Annie?"

"Well, what did you think Junior was going to talk to Uncle George about?" Annie cut through the checked gingham without looking up. "This here will make you your fourth dress." She nodded at the cloth. "My, my. Four dresses... two for everyday and two for Sunday. Not many girls got all that, honey. You can save your old shirt and apron getup for working in the field or spring housecleaning or something."

"I know. I'm awful lucky, Annie Lee."

"We both are." Annie nodded solemn agreement.

John peered closely at each of the sisters. They were perfectly serious. Both thought Ary, the almost naked, fourteen year old, orphaned mother of an illegitimate baby was *lucky*. These two young women were made of strong stuff, he thought. Instead of crying about how bad things were, these two thought they were lucky if they had a cup to drink from and some water to put into it.

Scoundrels' Bargain 133

Ary ducked into the dugout bedroom at the knock on the door. George passed the baby back to Matlock and opened the door to allow Junior Trent to enter.

"I was just waiting on you, boy. Aye God, Ary's got so many dresses now she couldn't decide which one to wear. Likely she'll be out in a minute, I reckon." He motioned toward the path that led to the barn. "Whilst you're awaiting her let's you and me just step out to the barn. Do a little talking man-to-man."

Junior solemnly nodded at Annie then turned to follow the oldster.

John watched the sturdy overall clad boy get in step with the fragile older man.

"You been a coming to see our Ary for a good long time now and we..." George continued to talk and Junior listened with a serious expression on his face.

John knew he should probably go up to the barn with them but he didn't want to leave Annie. He wanted to watch her, to talk to her. He had a lot of questions to ask her.

He sat in silent contentment watching her work. The questions could wait. This girl had magic fingers when it came to making things. He wanted to see the new dress take shape. *Oh Hell. Admit it,* he told himself, *It's just that you want to be close to Annie no matter what she might be doing.*

"John, would you mind going up to the barn with them?" Annie straightened from her cutting chore. "I don't want George getting that boy drunk before he even asks our Ary to marry him."

Ary stepped into the kitchen and giggled.

"He's done asked me, Annie. We had a long talk. I told him all about Pap and cousin Fleury. I told him everything. Was that all right?"

"Oh." Annie stiffened and stood silently staring into space for a moment, then nodded. "That's good." She glanced quickly at John then back at the cloth. "But I'd still like John to go and keep a watch, if he would. After all, he's the one who'll be doing the marrying."

"What?" John choked on the word. "I'll do what?"

"The wedding. You're our preacher, aren't you? Someone's got to preach the vows."

"By Heaven Annie, you're made of brass. You are not, repeat, not, going to get me to officiate at a wedding." John shook his head and stared a long moment at the bent head of tousled platinum hair. "I am not a real preacher and you know it, Miss Twig."

"Why not? Mama's brother Cornish get the 'calling' one day right out in the middle of the corn field and he went to preaching right away, Mama said. All you have to do, John, is 'get the calling' and find yourself a church. We done got the church, right here." She giggled a little. "And I'm giving you the calling."

"I think the 'calling' you're talking about, has to be from God, Annie, for God's sake."

"Well, how do you know he isn't calling you through me?" She pointed her needle at him and grinned. "God doesn't always do things the way we expect. My mama told me that when I was just a little tad."

John grunted but he grinned back at her.

Annie motioned to the younger girl. "Get the comb and your rat and I'll comb your do up in about two shakes of a lamb's tail." She made a gesture toward the barn and then blue sapphire sparkles and an upturned smile turned his way. "Ary'll be mighty pleased to have you be the preacher who hitches her up with Junior. You do that kind of Bible speaking better than any other preacher I ever seen... Baptist or Methodist." She bent to the table again. "And much as I'd like to talk to you, I gotta get this here dress done so I can't talk about either the ball or the wedding with you right now, John Wesley."

The next dress Annie works on is going to be her very own, John vowed as he left the room, still shaking his head. *And I'm going to be the first person to see her in it... or maybe I'll be the one to help her out of it.*

He had to shake his head again and laugh as he headed for the barn.

She's doing it to you again, boy, he told himself. Pretty soon now, she and I are going to have to have a long talk about me pretending to be a preacher again... and then I'm going to get down to the truth about her attending that ball and, after all that, we're going to talk about old Cousin Addison Fleury. It's way past time I got to the bottom of all her Arkansas family secrets.

Chapter 19

Annie smiled at John and Aramantha when they came laughing into the house. Mrs. Gulliver grunted her way in with the two of them, trying desperately to stay between John Matlock's long legs as he walked. John kicked at the pig in a half hearted way but he leaned down to give a friendly tug to her right ear when she flopped against the wall and slid down into her favorite napping place.

Annie felt pleased to see him smiling at the little fat hog. A man who'd treat a pig that nice would probably treat his woman real nice, too. He had the best everyday manners she'd ever seen on a man, and his public manners was fit for a visit with the Queen, or at the very least with the President.

"Sky looks strange. Green almost." John took off his hat and slapped it against his thigh before he hung it on the peg beside the door. "Kind of a greasy pea soup color."

"Yeah." Aramantha nodded her red gold upsweep. "It looks real strange out, Annie." She stepped toward the stove. "But I guess it's nothing." She ran the palm of her hand from her neck up to the pouf on top. "It ain't raining or nothing. It's real quiet. Did you see? I didn't even get my hair messed up. It surely feels funny with no wind blowing. I thought the wind always blew in the Territory." She stretched to lift a bowl of herbs from the shelf. "How about iffen I brew us up some tea?"

"Where's Uncle George? And Junior? And the baby?" Green sky? Greasy pea green sky? Annie squelched the quick stab of panic that tore through her.

"Oh, they're a coming down in a few minutes. Junior wanted to show Uncle George that pretty piece of land old Henry Trent gave him as a birthday present when he was sixteen years old." The younger girl shifted the grate to work up a small fire. "Junior has the papers for the land and everything." She crinkled some dried leaves from the starter box. "John, hand me a piece of wood and some kindling." She raised the smallest front stove lid with the metal lifter so she could drop in the kindling and the short stick of wood the detective had handed her. She smiled her thanks at him.

"Tea would taste good." The tall man stretched and smiled back and settled himself in his usual place at the table.

"Was we to get married Junior said we might fix us up a house on that little piece of land." Aramantha continued. "I sure don't want to try to live with Junior's daddy." She shook the grate again. "And it would be a mite crowded for us here, don't you think, Annie Lee?" She turned to her sister for confirmation.

Annie nodded before she gathered the scissors and the pieces of cut up gingham to her bosom.

"Did Junior talk to Uncle George about you and him getting married?" Annie's question was almost absent minded. No use getting Ary all scared about the baby. "We might could get the summer kitchen boarded in for you." She felt a prickle of anxiety pierce her somewhere in her chest just behind the wad of blue and white cloth she was clutching. "The wedding's on I guess, John. You'll have to get some kind of ceremony ready."

The hired man gave her a look that said, *Don't start with me, Annie.*

"Uh huh," Ary answered without looking up. "We kinda set a date, Annie. First Sunday in December."

Annie walked around the lounging cowboy and swung the door open. Mrs. Gulliver squealed disapproval and plunged through the low door into the dugout bedroom.

"Wesley Ann's with George and Junior?" Annie tried to smooth the anxiety from her voice. Before she'd finished her question she felt the tall man standing close behind her.

"Something wrong, Annie?" His question was barely a sound in her ear. He put his right hand at her waist and she had to compel herself to keep her back turned to him.

"Might be some weather brewing." Annie searched the sky again. Heavy clouds moved to make a cliff of darkness in the distance. The sky right above the Circle Twig still bore the ugly yellow green tinge John had spoken about. "Where was them old boys when you come down the path, John?"

"Why, they were out in the pasture behind the pole barn. Way over at the far edge near that low place. They were looking across at Junior's land." He stepped out onto the stone lintel and turned back to look into her eyes. "You worried about something?" he whispered.

"Cyclone." She let the word slip soundlessly out of her mouth. "Was George drunk?" She asked the question in her normal tone. Her sister answered.

"He'd had a little to drink. And Junior, too. But neither one of them was what you'd call drunk, sister." Ary joined them at the door. "Something wrong? I wouldn't have left Wesley Ann with them iffen they was wobbly. You know that." Annie was able to look down at a new crease which had formed between her young sister's eyebrows.

"Now don't you go to worrying, baby sister. Let me do that. You know how I am. I always think I'm the one who has to worry about everything." She grinned at her sister and looked back at the stove. "I know those two old boys will take good care of our baby. Why don't you pour us out some tea, honey?"

Scoundrels' Bargain 137

"You want me to go after them?" Again his voice was for her ears alone.

"Might be too late," she whispered back and pointed to the black funnel that was forming at the tail of the dark cloud formation. "Sure as hell that's a cyclone."

"Heading this way. You and Ary get into the bedroom and I'll go get the baby." He raced up the path. Annie closed the door on his last words and dropped the bundle of cut cloth on the table. Her mother's scissors clattered and slid to the bench on the far side.

"Come on, sis. Let's take our tea and get ourselves into the bedroom." Annie's words were almost drowned by a deep roaring sound, something like the rhythmic clatter of an approaching train. She dropped the latch on the outside door and grabbed up a dishrag to lift the boiling teakettle from the stove. Tea might just calm Ary's nerves. She swept up two tin cups in the other hand and pushed the younger girl ahead of her toward the dugout.

"Quit pushing me, Annie." Aramantha tried to twist against Annie's urging. "What's wrong with you?"

"Cyclone coming, honey. We need to get ourselves into the dugout." Annie shoved the smaller girl through the bedroom door.

"I ain't going nowhere without my baby." Ary's words were a scream against the sound of the approaching storm. "Wesley Ann!"

Annie barred the way with her body then put the hot pot on the ground under the bed. She forced Ary to sit on the bed, pressing one hand down on each of her sister's shoulders. She couldn't let the distraught young mother kill herself in a futile attempt to save the child. John was bigger, faster and stronger. If Wesley Ann and George and Junior could be saved, John Wesley Matlock would do it.

"John's gone after her, sister. Ain't nothing you can do right now. We done seen a funnel coming." She patted her sister's cheek. "You can't do the baby no good iffen you're carried off to Kansas or knocked cold outside somewheres." God. Let him and the baby be all right. If she could just see him or touch him one more time. If she could only kiss those perfect lips once again.

Aramantha went limp and fell back against the bed. Sobs shook her.

"Our baby. Our baby. We done lost our baby, sister."

Annie lifted the pot from the floor and poured a cup of the warm herb tea. She lifted Ary to a sitting position and put the cup of tea into her hand.

"Drink you some tea, girl. We ain't lost nobody yet. You got to keep your spirits up." Annie had to shout against the sounds from outside. "You can trust John Wesley to take care of our little girl." She sat on the bed beside her sister. Mrs. Gulliver put both front hooves on the edge of the bed and Annie hoisted her up to the shuck mattress behind them. The little sow pressed herself as close to the young women's backsides as she could.

She and Ary both stared through the door and into the kitchen. The roar from outside increased. Something thumped loudly, as if it had been thrown against the wall next to the door. Metal jangled above their heads. The storm's tumult now seemed to surround the little house on all sides. Annie half expected to see the kitchen room and everything in it disappear as they watched but the only movement was from the tin cup she'd left behind. It tilted and rattled against the table then rolled in two circular arcs to fall to the dirt floor.

John had run only a few steps out of the back of the pole barn before he was engulfed in the swirling blackness of the debris laden wind. He tried to walk upright but couldn't.

He was thrown to his knees but he forced himself forward, clutching at the pasture grass with each hand as he pulled himself in what he hoped was the direction of his last glimpse of George, Junior and the baby. When he felt both of his feet being lifted with the force of the wind he froze in place and tried to become one with the ground. He could see nothing ahead nor to either side, nothing other than soaring masses of broken limbs and flying pieces of leather harness. A bale of hay sideswiped him and rose into the air ahead of him as if floated up by magic. He moved another inch and his shoulder struck something hard. One of the cottonwood trees. John circled the base of the trunk with both arms. He put his face down between his two arms.

He was fairly sure he was going to be swept up like that bale of hay or be hit in the head by one of the tin roofing sheets as several came scudding by. He couldn't move. He couldn't stand. He was probably going to die right here on the Circle Twig with the winds of hell beating against his eardrums while he and the slim tree were levitated into the angry maelstrom. He couldn't hear or see or think.

Annie. He only wanted to see her one last time. Wanted to see the blue of her eyes once again. Wanted to kiss her and hold her and never let her go. He wanted...

Red dust swept across him and almost buried him, then huge drops of water pelted the dirt to mud on his face and his body. The keening noise of the swirling winds seemed to have died down a little. He pulled himself to his knees, never letting go of the tree, his tree.

For long minutes the air was still harsh on his skin but he somehow understood that he could withstand it. To wash the dirt and debris from him he turned his face into the pounding deluge of water and stood upright. His tears mixed with the pelting raindrops and he stood rooted to the place where he'd almost taken flight. He stood firm on his own two feet for just another second and then relaxed his hold on the tree.

Scoundrels' Bargain

First one arm, then the other. He patted the young cottonwood. He was alive. His tree was still standing. The devil's own funnel had gone on to suck up other things or other beings into the grinding maw of a cyclone's hunger. He took two tentative steps. What was he doing here? Why had he come out here, anyway? His mind seemed to be whirling as much as had the wind which had passed over him.

Oh God the baby. Uncle George. Junior.

John staggered drunkenly toward the far edge of the pasture. In seconds he could see the place where the two men had been standing earlier but he saw no one and nothing there now, no one and nothing at all.

John lurched back to the top of the hill to stare down at the house. He passed his palm across his eyes to try to clear his vision against the pouring rain. Down below he watched the backdoor slam open and then he saw Annie burst out and push her way up the path, her silvery blond head bent against the strong wind and the heavy rain. Aramantha stumbled up the path just behind her sister, her red gold hair plastered across her face. Both were already soaked to the skin by the driving rain.

He had to find George and Junior and the baby. He had to. He turned back to the pasture. He had to find them before the two sisters arrived. If he could just pull himself together. He had to think. Where might they be? He would just keep walking until he found them. He turned again to stumble toward the place where he'd last seen the three of them.

He wanted that irritating shrieking sound to get out of his ears. He lifted his hands. If he could just clear his ears he could put his mind to the search. He put his hands over his ears for a second but he never stopped walking. Even with his hands covering his ears he could still hear the nerve racking screams of the wind. He let his hands drop. In fact the sound was growing louder.

That wasn't the wind. The shrieking was the sound of a baby crying. Wesley Ann! He broke into a run to reach the side of the bowl shaped indentation in the land. Below him, Uncle George lay face down, arms spread wide across Junior Trent, who lay on his side.

Oh, God, the baby must be under one of them. John skidded down the brushy slope toward the sound of a very angry infant. His boots mired in the red mud and slowed his descent. It was as if all the wet arms of the scrub bushes were reaching out simply to delay him. He shouted as he shoved his way down the slope.

"The cyclone's passed, George. You can get up now." John sent his voice into the wind even before he reached them. "Everything's all right." He could see Junior's arms, then his legs, moving. George didn't move at all. The old man continued to lie face down in the mud with his arm laid out across their neighbor's son. "Get up George. Wesley Ann's crying. Are youall smashing her?" He swerved around a man-sized boulder that had not been there earlier. He could see the crushed bushes where it lay. "Are you drunk, George. Answer me, man."

"I don't think he can, John." That was Junior's voice from below. "I think he's hurt or something."

Wesley Ann's shrill cries lowered somewhat as Junior lifted her muddy form from under her uncle's silent place on the ground. She held her arms out toward John.

John wrapped her in a one armed embrace and tried to shield the baby from the rain with his chin stretched across her red curls.

He lifted one of the old man's wrists with his other hand. After a second he looked up at Junior and shook his head.

"No pulse. I think he's dead. Was he hit by something?" John let his eyes search the old man's body. "Let's turn him over." He and the younger man gently turned the old man so his sightless blue eyes stared up at them. The rain washed the red clay from his face. It bothered John that water pounded against the old man's unseeing eyes. With his thumb, John closed each lid over the milky blue gaze. "He doesn't look as though he was in pain."

Junior pointed at the two women who were climbing down inside the depression. Both men stood silently waiting for the two sisters. Wesley Ann sniffled a bit and then she quieted, also, her face against John's chest.

"What is it? What's wrong?" Annie struggled through the muddy brush to stare down at her uncle. "Is he sick? Or drunk?"

Ary grabbed Wesley Ann into a tight embrace. "Mama." The word slipped into the air.

"Annie. Did you hear that? She said 'mama' plain as day."

"I heard, honey. Our Wesley is a real smart baby."

"I think your Uncle George done saved our lives, Miss Annie." Junior reached to draw Ary and the smiling baby to his side. "We didn't hardly make it down here before stuff was just flying around our heads. George, he yelled to me to get down on the ground and I did and he put Wesley Ann down against me and then he put himself down on top of us." Junior's voice was a shout against the wind. "And we all stayed there until just now."

"Is he dead, Annie?" Ary tightened her grip on her child until the little one grunted in protest.

"I don't know, sister." Annie bent to touch the back of her hand to her uncle's wet face. John saw her face whiten as if the blood had drained from her. She knelt in the puddled mud next to the old man's body.

"He's dead, Annie," John lifted Annie's hand from the old man's forehead then raised her to her feet. "I'll carry him." John bent and lifted

George from the mire. Surprise at George's lack of weight made John overbalance and shuffle back a step. He straightened to begin the climb, able to carry the skinny old man as easily as he would have carried a sleeping infant.

"He was a right good old man." Junior muttered and only Ary indicated that he'd been heard.

John looked to Annie for permission and she nodded. He promised himself to take her into his arms as soon as he could. She stood up straight, shoulders back in her usual take-charge stance but her face wore the look of a shocked and stricken child. She would try to comfort the others, he knew, but he also knew she would need a lot of comforting herself. He dug his boots into the sliding red earth to began the difficult climb through the muck and the brush.

"I think he saved our lives." Junior repeated his words into the wind as he and the grief stricken Twig sisters struggled up through the mud and brambles of the sloping side of the depression, Annie dry eyed, Aramantha sobbing, Wesley Ann, also, was weeping in sympathy with her mother's tears. When they reached the top they could see John Wesley Matlock with his burden cradled across his chest. He was well ahead of them striding toward the path that would lead them to the house below.

With Annie alone in the lead, Ary, Wesley and Junior entwined in a little family group, the sodden procession silently followed the big detective. John Matlock was fetching their Uncle George on his last trip home.

Chapter 20

John had already placed Uncle George's body down on the old man's own bedroll by the time Annie and the others reached home.

"He doesn't have a suit." Annie stared down at the thin old man. "Nor no clothes any better than what he's got on." She felt suddenly tired. The bench seemed to welcome her. She sat down, then leaned, elbows on the table. She stared into the darkness behind her cupped hands. "And we sure don't have no box to bury him in."

"No problem about that, Miss Annie." Junior Trent jiggled Wesley Ann against his right shoulder. "I'll go on over to my dad's place and get some boards."

Preparing to leave, Junior handed the baby to her mother and nodded reassurance to Annie who let her hands drop and her hopeful gaze turn to the redheaded youngster. Maybe with Junior's help they *could* bury Uncle George with some honor.

"I'll help you get that coffin made, Trent." Junior looked surprised at the lawman's use of his last name. His shoulders straightened and he smiled at Aramantha, then stepped briskly out the door, bound upon a grown man's mission.

"It'll be awful big on your uncle but I can let you have a suit," John looked quickly at Annie, "If you and Ary want to use it."

"Oh, John, no need to do that." Annie felt as if her eyelids were weighted down but she forced herself to attend to what was needed. Now, she really was an orphan. Now she was the head of the family. The oldest member of the Twig family in this house. She wondered if losing their Uncle George was somehow her fault. Maybe she should have watched him a little closer? Checked his jug more often? Fed him up a little better? Maybe all those things. She sighed. Anyway, it was too late now.

"But I want him to have my suit, Annie. Your Uncle George is a hero." He looked down at the fragile old man's body. "We need to do this right." He reached for his saddle bags.

"How come he died, sister?" Ary swayed back and forth on the bench to quiet Wesley Ann. "Did something hit him?"

"I figure his heart just give out, Honey." Annie looked at John for his nod of confirmation. "Neither one of us could find any bruise or cut on him."

John shook his head. "Ary, I learned today that a cyclone's scary enough to kill anyone. I thought I was dead and I'm strong and healthy." He drew his shoulders forward and shivered at the too recent memory.

"Yeah." Annie nodded. "Anyone who's not scared by a cyclone is a fool." She looked down at her uncle's body once more. "Letting us use

Scoundrels' Bargain

your suit'd be awful good of you, John. I guess we better get him ready soon as we can."

John nodded.

She looked across at the tear filled blue eyes of her little sister. "We'll put him up there in that line of cottonwoods. Right near his old still. That all right with you, sister?" She reached to put her hand on Ary's. "Probably tomorrow afternoon." She stood and ran her shirt sleeve across her eyes before she touched her sister's arm. "We better get our old uncle cleaned up, girl." John dug into his saddle bag and the tossed a black woolen coat and trousers across the table. "If you'll bring us in some water, John, we'll get on with it."

On the following afternoon after the funeral, Junior Trent put his arm across Aramantha's shoulders as he made their announcement.

"We ain't a gonna wait, Miss Annie. Ary and me want to get married up right away if that's all right with you."

"What's your daddy gonna think about that, Junior? He's gonna be pretty mad."

"I'll be twenty years old in a couple of months. Plenty old enough to be married." Junior clutched Aramantha just a bit closer. "And there ain't nobody gonna part me and my Ary, not even my old man." He kissed Aramantha's temple. "Life's too short."

Ary nodded. She ran her hand down the skirt of her gunmetal silk dress the same way she'd done when she was wearing the apron over the shirt. Her blue eyes held fright.

"Yeah. People can die anytime." She murmured the words and looked up into Junior's face for reassurance. "Look at what done happened."

"Well, I guess that's true. I'll leave old Henry Trent to you two kids to handle. I sure don't want anything else to do with him." Annie fingered her platinum earbob. It felt strange to wear things hanging from her ears but she'd liked the way they'd looked in her mama's mirror. "When did youall want to get married, hon?"

"Right now, iffen John Wesley'll do it." Ary smoothed the blue gray silk of the Widow Stanfield's dress that Annie had shortened for her, "I got on one of my good dresses and Junior's got on his good trousers. He could go bring back some of the Broughtons for witnesses." She picked up one of the doughnuts Grandma Broughton had left on the table. "If John is marrying us I guess he couldn't be no witness. Anyway, they probably ain't even clear home yet from the funeral."

"Now wait a minute, Ary, Annie, Junior." John raised both hands palms out. "I could be in some real trouble impersonating a preacher, maybe legal trouble."

"We sure liked what you said about Uncle George." Ary's voice was a whisper. "You always sound like a real good preacher to us, don't he Annie?"

The emptiness inside Annie grew. Now she was going to lose her little sister and the baby, too.

"But... but... what about the license?" John's voice was a sputter of denial that he could be once again pressed into the role of preacher.

"I reckon I could ride into Guthrie someday soon and get that license, couldn't I, Matlock?" The red haired young man asked his question man-to-man.

"Well, I guess you might as well do it for them, John." She looked into her little sister's eyes. "If you're sure that's what you two want." Annie pressed the platinum heart against the breast of her blue and white cotton dress. "Iffen youall are determined to do this. I guess little Wesley Ann is sure enough going to need herself a daddy, now."

"Hey! I thought George and I were doing a pretty good job of fathering that little girl." John's voice held a petulant note.

"Oh, you two been real good with her." Annie had to keep herself from smiling. He didn't want to lose the little darling any more than she did. "I bet Ary and Junior'll let us keep her any time we want her, won't you sister?"

"You don't need to worry none, Matlock." The younger man left Ary's side long enough to move toward John with the child. "I love that there little girl as much as I love Ary. I'll be a real good daddy to her." The younger man lifted Wesley Ann to place her in John's arms. "Right at first we was hoping you and Miss Annie would keep her here for us. We got a lot to do getting ourselves a house fixed up and all."

"We got us a little place, Junior says." Ary nodded. "He's gonna skid that old shed out in back of his pa's place. It's where the cook used to live." She grinned. "The one Henry Trent fired for burning his breakfast. You remember that, Annie?"

Annie chuckled. "You two are feeling mighty brave, I see. You can use the mule, Junior, and the wagon too, if you need it. I don't think Lucifer would be much use to you." Annie thought for a moment. "In fact I'll up and *give* you that old mule. Help you get your garden in and cart stuff for you. My wedding present."

"Oh, Annie," Ary squealed her gratitude. "I told Junior you'd help us if you could."

"Come on, dance for Uncle John." John dandled Wesley Ann on his right knee. "I'll sure miss this little girl... and you too, little Aramantha, but if you're determined to do it I'll help Junior get the house pulled over to his land."

Scoundrels' Bargain

"We already talked about this, John. Junior and me, we know you're gonna be there for our Wesley Ann. Why, she's your namesake. If our next one is a boy we're gonna name him George, if that's all right with youall?" She looked first at John then at Annie.

They're talking to us as if we were a couple. As if John Matlock is always going to be here. Like we're an old married couple, too. Annie knew it wasn't so, couldn't ever be so, but it felt nice being harnessed up with John, even for the moment. Annie reached for the baby.

"Better get yourself ready to hitch up these two kids, Reverend John Wesley Matlock." She smiled into John's protesting glare. "There isn't anyone else around here that can do that job today, except you."

By God she's doing it again and I'm letting her met away with it. John stared into the laughing blue eyes. He realized he'd do almost anything to make her happy if he could. He shook his head slightly. Had the storm broken something loose inside his brain? He was actually planning to preach a wedding ceremony for these two innocents. *Wanted* to do it, actually! He could hardly believe the words coming out of his own mouth.

"Well, if you're sure Ary... Ju... uh... Trent. Just let me get out my Bible and see what I can come up with."

Oh, well, what the hell? Maybe Pinkerton detectives were authorized to preach funerals and weddings. No one had ever told him otherwise. The two kids sure believed he was a preacher and the neighbors 'round about had started calling him "Brother" Matlock. Annie was the only one in the whole area who knew he was a religious ringer and she constantly egged all the others on in their delusions. She thought the whole thing was mighty damned amusing, so far as he could tell.

John raised one eyebrow and leveled a dark gaze on her that silently asked, "Is this forever-mimicking-a-preacher-thing a part of our scoundrels' bargain?" The sapphire glimmer of laughter from across the table, told him the answer to his unspoken question was, "Yes."

"You have a ring for your bride, Trent?" He tried his damnedest to look the soul of preacherly zeal and piety.

"Not now, Matlock, uh, Brother Matlock, but I'm going to get one soon as I go to town for that there license."

John just couldn't look at her. If he did they'd both burst out in hysterical giggles and now was not the time to do something like that. Laughter at a time like this just might make a kid like Junior doubt his newly found manhood. John looked down, frowned and nodded, instead.

"You better do that soon as possible, Trent. Rings are real important to new wives."

"Yes sir. I know that. I'll ride into town soon as we get the cabin skidded over and get some things set up for Ary to go to keeping house."

"I'm going to have a ring?" Ary whispered to her big sister.

"Looks like." Annie whispered back.

"I ain't never had me no ring."

"Honey, lots of things you never had but you got them now. A baby, a husband, a house, a mule. You got more things than most women ever get and you're going to have a lot of other things too, starting with a wedding ring." From her seat on the bench, Annie reached to twitch the silken drape of Ary's bustle. "I don't reckon you ever thought you'd be wearing a silk dress with a bustle either, did you? But look at you."

"Oh, Annie, I'm so happy." Ary leaned to put her head on her sister's shoulder. "This is just about the best thing that ever happened to me in my life. I could just cry."

"Here, girl. Don't you go and get snot on my clean dress." Annie pushed Ary upright. "I gotta keep myself looking decent. Guests gonna be here any minute to see you married."

Junior swept out the door, calling over his shoulder.

"I'll be right back with the Broughtons and whoever else I can bring. We're going to have us a wedding."

Before the sun set the Broughtons and the older Smith brother sat with Annie and Wesley Ann under the shake roof of what had first been planned for a summer kitchen. John's deep voice rolled out into the storm washed air of the Oklahoma prairie.

"Dearly beloved, we are gathered together today in the sight of God and man and this present company to join these two young people in holy wedded matrimony..."

"He's a hell of a preacher, ain't he?" Grandma Broughton whispered her comment to Annie from behind her hand. "Talks awful good, he does. Good looker, too."

"He sure is." Annie answered.

She never let her gaze wander from the sculptured lips that always seemed to know the correct words to lips that always seemed to know the correct words to say and the best way to say them to make things right for some member of the Twig family.

Chapter 21

"It's getting kinda late so we'll skid that shed over to our place in the morning, Annie." The young man's neck flushed brick red. "We was thinking... uh... tonight... uh... meantime, I guess me and my Ary... uh... needs to stay here, maybe." Annie, surprised at such a long speech from Junior Trent, merely nodded and waited.

"Yeah, Annie," Ary's voice fluttered slightly with her embarrassment, "Do you think we could have... Her voice softened to a whisper, "...the good bed?"

Annie nodded again. What else could the two kids do?

"Of course you can stay here. This is your honeymoon night, little sister." Again she looked at John for confirmation. "You'll have your own house tomorrow. Tonight you can stay right here."

Oh God that will put me to sleeping in here with John. Annie looked at the detective again but she couldn't force any words past her lips. *Alone. Together. All night.* She swallowed and straightened. *What the hell! Maybe he won't even notice me.*

She flicked a quick look in his direction. His golden glance seemed filled with amused knowledge. He *knew* what she was thinking. His slow smile shared her realization. They'd be sleeping together. They'd be sleeping together in this room. Annie couldn't control the heat that rose in her face. *Yeah. He knew exactly what was in her mind.*

"Still too wet for the barn. John and me will do just fine here in the kitchen, little sister. You and Junior take the good bed. I'll use Uncle George's bedroll." She smiled and tried to look unconcerned. "Before youall go in there let me make a quick change into my trousers and shirt. I'll be right out." When she returned in her worn shirt and pants the two youngsters were waiting.

Junior cupped Aramantha's shoulders and grinned proudly as he guided her toward her wedding bed. Aramantha's face was drained of color but she was going willingly it seemed to Annie.

"I'll take the baby." Annie lifted Wesley Ann from Ary's arms. "She can sleep with her auntie tonight." She raised the child and bounced her in the air. John stepped close and took the infant from Annie.

"Wesley Ann can stay with her Uncle John." He kissed the baby's cheeks.

The proud honeymoon couple ducked into the dugout bedroom and in a moment the canvas door covering had been lowered to give the two youngsters the privacy a wedding night deserves.

Annie and John faced each other. Wesley Ann relaxed back onto John's shoulder. She peered up into his smile and said, "Hi."

"Annie. Did you hear? She said 'hi' plain as day." Annie tickled the baby's chin. "Hi, Wesley Ann."

The baby grinned and blew a bubble but she didn't answer.

"I do think she's awful smart, John. Ary says she said, 'Mama' when we found Uncle George." Annie blinked to clear tears that were all too quick to fill her eyes these days at the mention of the old man's name. "Now she's saying 'hi.'" She chucked the baby's chin again. "Hi honey." She gulped back the lump in her throat. "Most babies don't talk so early, she must be awful smart."

Wesley Ann gurgled and ducked her face to hide herself against John's shoulder.

"For sure five months is pretty early for saying words. She's smart as her Aunt Annie, probably." John pulled the peach basket toward himself. "She's almost too big to sleep in this thing anymore." His level gaze asked a question but Annie turned to pick up the bundle of cut out pieces of cloth at the end of the bench. *Talk about something. Say anything*, she told herself.

"I been making a coverlet for them two kids." Annie held up the crazy quilt she'd started days before. She pointed out special pieces. "Here's some of your shirt and here's some of pappy's shirt." Her hand moved to point to several pieces of brown flowered calico. "And these here bits are what I cut off mama's dress when I fixed it for Ary. I been thinking of cutting up mama's blue striped dress, too." She glanced upward. He was staring fixedly at her as if her were trying to get some meaning out of what she was saying. She knew she was babbling. "That was the one I was wearing for the funeral and the wedding. I think it'd make a cute little dress for Wesley Ann. She's getting so big she's about to grow out of them little things I cut out of your fancy shirt."

"Annie, that blue dress is the only dress you own!"

"I know. I don't mind. I don't much need a dress, anyway."

"Not even for church?" He looked down at her and winked. "With a make believe preacher?"

She flushed again and began stitching a piece cut from one of Uncle George's tobacco sacks into the finished portion of the quilt top.

"Are we having church again, John?" She didn't meet his eyes until she said his name.

John felt the flash of blue fire tear through him as she asked the question. This woman could somehow always touch his soul. They had to talk. Tonight.

* * *

Scoundrels' Bargain

Mrs. Gulliver complained loudly when Annie tried to uproot her from her regular sleeping spot. As if she were still asleep, the enraged animal kept her eyes closed as she kicked and squealed in protest.

"Selfish pig." Annie muttered and let the little sow collapse back into her place against the wall. Annie glanced at the canvas covered opening into the bedroom but there was no sound from there. She felt a twinge of worry. Did the two youngsters know what to do? Was Aramantha frightened? She glanced at John. He was staring at her. He winked again and grinned.

"It's okay. They're probably still getting acquainted." He whispered and pointed to the bench across from him. "Quit worrying at Mrs. Gulliver and harassing yourself. Come on and sit down for a minute. We need to talk."

Annie put herbs into the pot to let the mixture steep in the boiling water and placed tin cups on the table.

"Yeah. I reckon we do." She kept her voice down so she wouldn't disturb the newly married young lovers. Better to *talk* than try to *sleep* rolled up next to this guy, she told herself. Anyways, now Uncle George is dead it don't matter. I can tell Mr. Detective any old thing he wants to know.

After she'd poured the steaming herb tea, she stepped over the bench and sat facing him. *Hell. Looking into John Wesley's eyes is almost as bad as trying to sleep next to him would be.* She let her glance drop toward the snoring pig.

"It's for sure Mrs. Gulliver isn't going to let me have her place." Of course the man wanted to take advantage of the situation. What man wouldn't? It was not as if he was crazy in love with her or anything.

"Looks like you'll just have to put George's bedroll next to mine, just the way he did." His low voice caressed her. She could feel her cheeks warming but still she didn't look at him.

"I may try sleeping on the table." She moved the baby's basket toward the dark end of the wooden surface. She ran her hand the length of the scrubbed wooden table and pushed the lamp further toward the other end. "It's almost as long as me."

"You do like to tease, don't you?" He reached for one of her hands. His hand felt large and warm and protective. "Annie," His voice dropped lower. "I expect you've figured out the fact that I came to your place on orders." She nodded and tried to pull her hand from his but he held on. "I came to the Circle Twig for a specific reason, Annie Lee." He kept his voice to a low rumble.

He let his other hand join the first to gently massage her fingers. He turned her hand over and bent to touch his lips to her palm. His kiss sent bolts of lightning-like pleasure through her arm and into her chest. She told herself to draw her hand away but she couldn't. Her innermost life seemed to pulse in the spot where his sculpted lips had touched her and her whole attention was mesmerized by his golden glance. Her whole being longed to lie down close to this man. She remembered her promise to herself.

"Oh, all right." She murmured. "Go ahead and ask your damned questions. I already knew you was, uh, were trying to pry all our family secrets out of George and Ary." He allowed her to pull her hand free and she felt a surge of disappointment that he had given up so easily. She sighed and waited for his words.

"First, I'd better tell you why I'm here and who sent me."

"Do we really need to go into all of this right now?" Annie whispered and looked anxiously at the bedroom opening. "We might be disturbing them kids."

"You prefer that we lay out our beds now?"

"Yeah, I reckon I do. We can always talk when we ain't, aren't going to wake up the baby nor disturb anybody's honeymoon."

John's smile turned brilliant, his teeth gleamed white in the nearly dark room.

"I agree, ma'am. We need to get right to bed." He threw both legs over the bench. "I'll turn out the bedrolls, Annie. You damp down the stove." He stood and stretched. "I am feeling like I need a little sleep." He turned sharply and bent to busy himself with the bedding. Annie glanced at the baby. Sound asleep. She looked at the man again.

She watched him stretch and put his palms against the highest point of the rafters as did nearly every morning and almost every night. The muscles in his chest and arms stood clearly defined against the cloth of the shirt. Her knees weakened at the sight. She would not, could not, allow her gaze to move any lower.

No way getting around it now. She and John Wesley were bound to finish what they'd started in the barn so many weeks ago. When she saw him flapping out George's blankets on top of his own bedroll she felt her mouth go dry. She turned to the stove and shook down the ashes, then turned the damper. She felt the platinum heart lying warm between her breasts. She touched its rich smoothness, then with her fingertips she stroked the shape of the sapphire heart set into the locket.

He straightened and they stared at each other across the table. Nothing to do now but blow out the lamp and crawl into the nest he'd made. She wasn't sure she could move around the table under her own power. Maybe she'd just stand here all night, a metal statue of herself, frozen in place, wanting the man but unable to do what was necessary to have him.

If he didn't say something she knew she was going to die, or faint, or cry, or something. If she did go to the pallet there'd be no turning back this time. If she chose to go to bed with him and they went to sleep she just hoped Mary Broughton wouldn't walk in on them.

Sometimes the girl came early for her weekly learning time with Annie. The girl was coming along right well. Annie tried to keep her thoughts on her apprentice and not on the man on the pallet. But she couldn't. All she could think about was the man, the man with the amber eyes.

Annie bent and blew out the lamp.

She'd made her choice.

Chapter 22

When she straightened it was as if there were a slowing down of time and motion. She waited what she knew could have been only a moment or two but the moments seemed like days. She waited until she could see John's tall figure through the darkness of the room. She used the edge of the wooden table to help inch herself around to the waiting man. When her foot struck the barrier of the piled bedrolls she froze.

John's strong hands reached to steady her. He bent his head to brush her mouth with his, lightly, lightly. Still she couldn't move. His hands slipped from her shoulders and moved to unbutton the top button and the second button on her shirt. Annie let her eyelids drift closed. Nothing more she could do. She'd let it happen, let him do whatever he wanted to do. She couldn't stop what the strange circumstances of this day had set in motion. No use lying to myself, she thought, I want this more than I've ever wanted anything.

His hand pulled the shirt from the trousers. He fumbled with the third button, the fourth was missing, then the last button and the shirt was open. His fingers gently lifted the left shoulder of the shirt to cause it to slide down her arm, the same on the right shoulder. The room was cooling quickly. Annie shivered.

"Come on, beauty," His murmuring voice warmed the side of her face. "Let me try to make you snug." She nodded mutely and went to her knees on the bedroll. "Sit down. Let me take off these boots and these old trousers for you." She nodded again and sat back on the pallet. As he worked to remove her heavy work shoes she could not control the trembling which seized her body.

In moments he'd tucked her into the softness of the combined bedrolls. Uncle George's heavy woolen quilt scratched almost like cockleburs against the tender places on her bare skin. For a second she thought she heard the sound of the old man's words, the echo of his laughter. "Ain't nothing finer than loving a woman who loves you back." She smelled the quick fragrance of tobacco, moonshine and of clean overalls. She smiled into the darkness. In the only way he could, George was letting her know he approved... even if it wasn't a real wedding night honeymoon for her. She guessed that he'd probably visited with Aramantha, also.

The detective still loomed above her, and she watched his swift movements as he removed his own shirt and trousers. Then his boots landed under the table and he was beside her under the heavy quilt which her uncle has said was made by her grandmother. He warmed their pallet

Scoundrels' Bargain

and the feel of his long body stretched beside her slowed her thoughts to nothing but pure emotion. Still she couldn't say anything.

He pulled her onto her side so they lay facing one another. His hand was like a brand on her bare hip. Her breasts, nipples hardened with desire, yearned to touch his broad chest.

"Miss Annie Lee Twig." He whispered.

"Just call me Annie." She breathed.

Laughter rose between them and Annie pulled the quilt up over their giggles to keep from disturbing the others.

"Ah, Annie girl, I love you." His voice was filled with laughter as he pulled her into his arms and kissed her. He doesn't really mean that, she warned herself. You can't take his words serious. He's just funning now, girl. But his words warmed her as much as did his embrace.

"I love you, too, John." There was no laughter in her voice. He kissed her again and rolled onto his back, lifting her on top of him, her silvery hair the only light in the dark room.

"I haven't lost my place in our lovemaking since that damned mule bit me." She could feel his chest heave with laughter. "I've just put you on top this time so if little old lady Gulliver does any biting she'll be nipping at her mistress and not at me."

Their muted laughter trailed into the darkness and died leaving both dark eyes and blue sobered and staring, gleaming through the darkness each at the other as if they were truly strangers newly met. Once again a tremor railed through Annie's frame.

A tremor also shuddered through John's body. He was doing the very thing he'd promised himself not to do. He couldn't help himself. This game little woman called to him both physically and spiritually. She made him laugh, she made him crazy, she was all that he wanted in a woman.

He groaned and pulled her against him in a long and searching kiss. Her sweetness opened to him with her quivering mouth and questing tongue.

"Annie, Annie, Annie." She lay sprawled across his body, her mouth only inches from his. He pressed her against himself with one arm around her shoulders, the other circling the lower part of her body. "I've been crazy for this moment." He whispered.

"Me too." Her words were only a wisp of sound.

"I want you, girl."

"And I want you, John Wesley."

Was she lying to him? He was aware of a small stiffening in her body. She held herself slightly away from him as if she were expecting to be hurt or as if she were afraid of something. As always, this beautiful young woman was withholding something, keeping something back from him. Could she ever let down her guard, allow him to know the real Annie?

She could feel his heart beat. As if the organ were sending her a message. What was it saying? Get what you want from this woman and then get away from this poor imitation of a ranch. Go on back to where people don't sleep on the ground inside their houses. Was that it?

Or was it telling her he loved her the same way she loved him? Shut up, she told herself, shut up, "...just shut up" the last three words were spoken aloud against his chest.

"What'd you say, darling?" He lifted her chin so she was looking at him.

"I've got to get up," She raised herself from the cozy place against his broad chest. "Better put the baby under the table. She might fall off iffen she got to moving around in the night."

Oh, the baby. Of course. He couldn't believe he'd forgotten the child. Such was the power of Miss Annie Lee Twig. Her presence sent all other thoughts straight out of his mind.

He rose. "I'll get her. We can put her basket on the floor at the end of the table, close to Mrs. Gulliver." He stood and reached across her, hand outstretched for the cane bale of the baby's sleeping basket.

The tiny amount of available light seemed to flicker and dance against his white skin, darkening and shading his paleness to a golden bronze. Annie could see the maleness of him standing proud in the cool air. She sighed. She wanted to see more, to feel him against her once again. Why lie to herself? She wanted him inside her. This was not like the angry interlude with Cousin Fleury. Nothing at all like that several moments of ugliness. This was a magnificent male, a man she wanted. A man she could live with for the rest of her life. She sighed again. Nothing for it. She was going to have to tell him everything or at least a part of the story before she could relax and let him love her.

Maybe he wouldn't want to go ahead after she told him?

He lifted the basket and gently placed the child's makeshift cradle on the floor, sheltered from harm. Wesley Ann didn't move. He smiled an unconscious benediction down upon the mite. He had to have Annie but he had to have his little namesake too. After he learned what he had come to learn he'd go on back to Arkansas and get everything all straightened out with the Fleurys.

"I've decided we better talk before we... uh, go to sleep or ... anything." Annie clutched Uncle George's quilt up to her chin as she pushed herself back to sit with her back to the wall. "Would you light the

Scoundrels' Bargain

lamp again, John? Please?" Her hair, loosened from her usual braid, slipped forward to cover her shoulders.

She heard the match strike against the underside of the table. The light of the match blazed against the dark. John felt himself blinded for a moment by the brilliance of the flame. He fumbled for the lamp and lighted it then turned the oil soaked wick to its lowest level. When the light was securely tended he held the lamp high and looked at Annie crouched against the wall, her body still covered with the old man's quilt.

"Do you call that fair, Annie? Here I stand, naked as a jaybird and there you sit bundled up with only your blue eyes showing."

Annie couldn't speak, she could only stare. He was like a classic figure carved from white marble, a glorious display of 'the perfect man.' The dim lantern light swirled over every inch of his sculpted perfection. Her mouth felt dry. She tried to swallow. The magnificent male animal stepped around the table and knelt at her feet. It was somehow frightening, almost as if the statue in Ft. Smith had shed his clothing and now knelt at her feet.

"Well? You did want to talk, didn't you?"

"How can I? Talk, I mean? With you showing yourself like a pagan statue?" She let down one side of the quilt just a little. "You must be freezing. Get in under the quilt and we can speak quietly together like civilized folks."

John took his time returning to the pallet. He checked on the bedroom door opening, on Mrs. Gulliver and finally he tucked the tiny quilt more tightly around the sleeping baby. *I don't know if I really want to hear what she has to say,* his cautious inner voice cried out but he gave in and slumped against the wall. Annie covered him with a quick flap of the old quilt.

"Well?" He waited for what was coming next.

Annie clenched her hands together in an almost prayerful attitude although it was only meant to hold the quilt against her chest. With eyelids still lowered she spoke very softly.

"I know you been looking to see what you could find out about us Twigs." She took a deep breath and stole a glance at her hired man before she looked back down at her hands. "Reckon it's time you learned whatever it is you been wanting to know about us."

"Well?" His dark gaze burned the side of her face, tried to force her to look directly into his eyes. She tightened her clasped hands and stubbornly kept her eyes down.

"Well... what?" she whispered as if asking the question of her own fingers.

"Well hell, Annie," he almost groaned the words, "You can be the most exasperating of women. You're the one who said she wanted to talk. My mind was set on something else entirely."

She allowed her vision to turn to meet his. She had said she wanted to talk, now it didn't seem so important. Maybe they could just turn the light off again and go back to bed. When she opened her mouth ready to suggest this, John interrupted.

"No, Miss Twig, I am not going to turn the lamp down again. Let's get the talk out of the way." He reached for one of her hands and he sat stroking the back of it as he peered into her eyes. "I'll go first if you want."

She nodded agreement.

"Well, we agreed early on that we wouldn't question each other, I know. I'll just tell you why I'm here and what I already know." He lifted her hand and let his lips brush against the angle of her bent fingers. "I'm here to investigate your family. I'm sure you know that already."

She nodded and tugged at her hand as if to remove it from his grasp. With a smile the detective held on. She didn't try very hard to free herself. She let her gaze drop again as he continued.

"Some of Addison Fleury's distant cousins from Little Rock, distant cousins of yours too, perhaps, sent me here to find out exactly what happened to Mr. Fleury."

"He's dead." She muttered the words.

"We figured that. What I need to find out is where and how and why he died."

"Guess there's no harm in telling now, seeing as how he's dead. It was Uncle George did it."

"George? George couldn't have killed anyone." His hold on her hand tightened to a painful degree. "Why are you saying George did it?"

"I'm telling the truth. Uncle George killed him."

"Oh God. George?"

"Yeah. Him or Pap. I figure George did it 'cause Pap died in the fracas, too. He was more of a drunk than old George was. I think all the excitement was too much for his heart."

"I can't tell you what a relief that news is, Annie." He lifted her hand again and kissed the tip of each of her fingers. "That's the revelation I wanted." His sigh sounded heartfelt to her ears.

"Why are you so pleased about it being George?" She studied his face. "Oh. Oh no. You thought it was maybe me who killed Cousin Addy?" She laughed. He could hear the bitterness in the sound. "So, you thought I was a killer? I notice it didn't keep you out of my bed!" She yanked her hand away from him.

"I just didn't know, Annie. I had to consider everything."

Scoundrels' Bargain 157

She nodded. "Plenty of times I wanted to kill Addison. He was a bastard and a brute. But no. I didn't do it." She smiled up at him. "I buried him. Ary and George and me. We buried Pap first, then on down the road we buried Addison so no one would ever find him. I was so scared someone was going to clap Uncle George into the jailhouse before we could get ourselves our own place in the Territory. None of us ever did talk about it after we buried them."

Pity for the two sisters coursed through him.

"And then I came along. I guess when you learned I was a Pinkerton Detective that was pretty frightening?"

"Naw. I knew you weren't going to find out anything." She slid further down under the quilt. "Anyway, I feel better getting this stuff out in the open."

"Well, there are some other things I need to ask you." He turned and patted the pillows in invitation. "Why don't we just burrow down into this warm bed and go on with our talk? What do you say, Miss Annie?" He nodded meaningfully toward the bedroom door. "We could be a lot quieter in our discussion."

"I *am* cold." She moved to the spot she had lain in previously. He stretched out beside her... one of his arms slid under her head and neck and the other grasped her hip and pulled her nude body close to himself.

"Why did you hate Addison Fleury so much?"

"Well, they was plenty of reasons but worming his way into making Pap let him have little Ary goes to the top of the list. I guess old Addy is Wesley Ann's father. But maybe you already knew that?"

"Yes. Poor little girl. Raped, or at the very least taken too early by her rich cousin. May his soul rest in hell."

"Amen to that."

"Annie, little Wesley Ann is going to have a good daddy in Junior and of course, she'll have a real good uncle right here."

"Uncle? Are you forgetting he's dead?"

"I know that honey. I was talking about myself."

He was callinq himself "Uncle" to Wesley! Exultation raced through her veins. She inched a tiny bit closer to John Matlock.

As they had talked Annie had felt herself relaxing into the warmth that John radiated. She ran her hand up his side and felt him draw a quick breath that was almost a groan.

"That Addison is a father won't be good news to my employers." He nuzzled the blonde curls that lay just at the level of his chin. "But it may be great for you two Twigs."

* * *

Annie raised her face for his kiss. His firm lips opened against hers and she let his mouth take her. She felt as if he were sinking into her, his taste sweet and velvety in her mouth. Her own tongue moved and clung to his. It was as if her soul were being wrapped within the soul of this tall man. No question. She loved him. She was lost to him and she didn't care. Tonight was for loving. Tomorrow could take care of itself.

She almost cried out with joy when his hand found her breast. He cupped it, his thumb circling around her hardened nipple, sending lightning bolts through her chest.

He pulled his lips from hers and murmured something.

"What?"

"I said you taste like flowers."

"I expect it's the herb tea," Annie whispered. "You taste really good, too."

He leaned forward to let his tongue trace the outline of her lips. Annie shuddered. He was doing to her what she'd wanted to do to him ever since she'd first seen him. When he lifted his head the lamp light flared and the flame seemed to dance in his eyes.

She felt him shift against her, his thumb still circling her nipple. Another kiss and she arched to meet his every move. He moved to straddle her body. His gaze was searching.

"Are you sure, darling?"

"I'm sure John. Please. Don't make me wait anymore." She lifted her hands to pull him into herself but he resisted and remained poised and gazing down at her. He whispered the words and they burned into her mind.

"What you and I are doing... is .. it means a lot to me."

"Me too, John."

"Everything that happened in the past is just that... past."

She nodded. What did he mean? Was there something awful in his life that he didn't want her to know? She longed to feel his body against her once again, his mouth on hers, his manhood inside her. If this was all she was to have she wanted it now. No speeches. No more waiting.

In a way he was pleased that she had had sexual experience. No worry about pain, no holding back necessary. And she did want him. No mistaking that. Gorgeous woman, all heart. And good right down to her bones. He knew if he did this thing he'd be lost. He could never leave her.

He kissed her in a series of short kisses, drinking sips of love from her lips. His body ached and throbbed to consummate the urgent need he felt within himself. His entire being screamed his desire for fulfillment. He kissed her again.

"I love you, my sweet Annie," he groaned, then plunged himself into her.

It wasn't until he had thrust deeply within her that he realized that she was a virgin. Her body arched and stiffened as she gave a smothered cry. He couldn't believe he'd been so mistaken. Had he misunderstood what she had told him about Addison Fleury?

His need still pounded within him but he started to pull away. Her hands gripped his buttocks to keep him from withdrawing.

"Don't leave me," she said and arched herself against him. "You can't take yourself away from me now." She moved her hips as if drawing pleasure from the feel of him. "Don't stop." Her plea was a breathy whisper.

Her movements and her words drove all thought from his mind. He couldn't stop now. "No. I won't stop," he whispered before he claimed her lips again. His hips moved rhythmically against her and she lifted herself to meet his need, each thrust more deeply penetrating than the last.

Much, much later he asked her the question.
"Why didn't you tell me you were still a virgin?"
"I ain't...wasn't... no virgin."
"You were. I felt your maidenhead tear."
"What?"
"I could tell that you'd never had a man inside of you before."
"Nobody but that bastard, Addy."
"But Annie... if he'd ever been inside you he would have been the one to break the soft barrier."
"Oh, he was inside me, all right. It was when I was about fifteen. He put his finger in me and then he whispered something dirty in my ear."
"Is that all he did?"
"Just about. And wasn't that enough? I sure thought so. I grabbed a handful of that yellow hair of his and I said iffen he ever again even *tried* to put his finger or anything else up inside me I was gonna tear off his balls."

Annie felt the detective's chest heave with silent laughter.
"And he must have believed you, sweetheart."
"Good thing too. I meant what I said."
"Oh, I love you, Annie Twig."
"And I love you, too, John Wesley. I'm real glad you aren't upset because I wasn't no virgin. Old Addy got hold of me before I knew what was happening. I expect that's the way it went with Aramantha and him too."

John closed his eyes and nodded against her cheek. "I expect so, Annie. That and a whole lot more." he murmured and pulled her even closer. "Good night, sweet girl. I think all that preaching today just about wore me out."

Chapter 23

After the hard labor of helping skid the tiny shed from the Trent place to Junior's acreage, Annie threw herself down in the meadow just outside the place they'd chosen for Ary's new home. Annie made it a point to check Ary's face. Was she happy? Aramantha held the baby and jounced it in her aproned lap. The baby was laughing and so was Ary. Annie decided that the wedding night had been a good experience for her little sister.

There was no question as to how Junior Trent felt. He'd been strutting around like a turkey cock since early morning, full of juice and his own importance. At every opportunity he'd shown off for Ary's benefit and she had always been properly admiring.

Annie smiled. It looked like their new little family was going to take root and flourish.

"All right now. Let's go on home and have a bite to eat." Annie couldn't wait to give Ary the tied quilt she'd made for their little "stolen" house. As they made their way back to the Circle Twig, John bouncing Wesley Ann on his shoulders, Annie made some decisions. Ary could have either the coffee pot or the crockery bowl. Both had belonged to mama. She'd give her the mirror, too or the comb... whichever little sister wanted. It was only fair to give her half of their mama's pretties, Annie told herself.

And Uncle George's bedroll would do the little Trent family for a bed until Junior could get a bedframe made for them. They could each have a tin plate and a tin cup. When she told Aramantha what she'd been thinking the younger girl gasped.

"Oh, Annie. I just can't believe I got me my own place and stuff to keep house with." She giggled behind her hand. "Did you notice we got us a wood floor?"

"You're pretty high society, all right, little sister. You think you're gonna be happy there with Junior?"

Aramantha nodded.

"Junior says he's gonna build us a little room on back for a kitchen. It'll probably have a dirt floor but he's gonna build us a chimney place too... where I can cook. I told him you'd let us haul water from the Circle Twig. We could carry it on the mule until we could get us a well dug." She pointed at John galloping in circles as he neighed and bucked like a horse for the baby's benefit. Both sisters watched the man with the infant for a moment. Both laughed at the antics of the pair.

"Everything'll be right cozy here. Junior says we three'll be snug as bugs in a rug." Aramantha gestured around them at the low growing bushes and the few blackjack trees. "I'm going to have me a garden. We're going to be happy." She stood and Annie stood with her. They both ambled through the meadow toward the path that led to the Circle Twig house. "I'm going to fix up my house real nice just like you fixed up our place, Annie." She took a deep breath. "Junior is going to be a real good husband and father."

"Sounds like it, little sis. I hope that old Henry Trent don't get on your case. He can be a bad one if he's riled."

"Junior says he ain't afeered of his daddy, Annie. He's gonna sneak the wood for the lean-to right out of Mr. Trent's lumber pile." Ary giggled again and almost danced down the path to the house. Annie followed, pleased that all was well with her sister. She wouldn't allow herself to think about her own honeymoon... only it hadn't been a real honeymoon, she reminded herself. She would let herself think about her night with John later, when she had some privacy.

Just sneaking a small peak at the memory of last night's time in bed with John made her stomach lurch with excitement. They'd be alone together again tonight. *Quit it,* she told herself, *think about something else.*

When Annie and Ary put the dinner on the table the two men took a minute to appreciate the look and the smell of the cornbread, the fried potatoes and the pinto beans. A cup filled with fresh green winter onions stood bravely in the center of the table as centerpiece as well as a side dish for the beans and potatoes. The work they'd done all morning had given all of them strong appetites.

After they'd eaten, Annie threw a glance at John then looked at Junior. John nodded then straightened as if coming to attention.

"Little sister," She leaned toward Aramantha. "Have you told Junior Trent all about yourself?"

"I've told him a lot, Annie." She looked quizzically at Annie. "Just about everything, I guess." She looked quickly at her new husband before she asked her question. "Junior knows Addy was having relations with me. He thought that was bad for me but it was something I couldn't help. I told Junior I didn't like it with Addy but I like it with Junior. I told him so." She glanced at John. "Is it okay to talk about our family now, sister?"

"I guess so, honey. I've told John most of what I could about why we left Van Buren. He wants to know what happened with Cousin Addison Fleury." Annie reached to touch Aramantha's hand. "Do you feel like talking about all that?"

"I don't mind telling, I guess." Aramantha bowed her head and looked down at her tin plate. "I done told Junior almost all of it. What was you wanting to know, John?"

"Just where and how and why he died and where he's buried and things like that, Ary. You tell it any way you want to."

Scoundrels' Bargain

"Well, I didn't much like what Pap was making me do them days." She looked an apology at her young husband and he nodded understanding as if giving her permission to tell everything. "Nearly every Saturday Addy would give Pap some money for moonshine and that night Pap would make me lay down for Addy." She looked again at Junior. "I never did like any of the things Cousin Addy did, Junior. He was mean, not good and kind like you."

Junior nodded once more, his lids lowered as if he were wishing he didn't have to hear this story again.

"Pap was taking money for you?" Annie gasped the words. "From Addy?"

"Uh huh. He told me not to tell you, sister."

"I'm not surprised at that. He knew I'd likely put a stop to his little scheme. But Ary, what about Uncle George? Why didn't he do something?"

"I don't know." Ary shook her head. "Too drunk, I reckon. Anyway, Annie, I just want to forget the whole thing."

"I know, honey. Just tell John what happened that last Saturday night. Okay?" Annie sat back on the bench and sighed. "I've already told him about burying Pap and Cousin Addison outside of Van Buren on our way to the run."

Wesley Ann made a demanding sound so Junior Trent lifted her to hold her a moment before passing her on to her mother.

"Well, Uncle George told me not to never tell anyone what happened but I guess it wouldn't matter now he's gone. I'm going to tell how it went so we don't always have to keep secrets from John, now he's family." She bounced the baby and smiled into the little one's eyes. "Both Pap and Addy was real drunk and George was passed out so I thought they wouldn't even know what I was doing. I decided I wasn't going to lay down for Cousin Addy any more anyway."

Annie felt as if something had suddenly clutched at her heart. Foreboding filled her. Somehow she knew Ary was going to tell them something Annie didn't want John to hear.

"I told him I wasn't going to let him do nothing and he said he'd already give Pap his money. I told him I didn't care, he could just take his money back for all I cared." She nodded solemnly. "I told him and told him and he wouldn't pay me no mind."

"You weren't there, Annie?" John's voice was hoarse.

"No. I had me a little job washing dishes in a boarding house on Saturday night and Sunday mornings. I got 20 cents and carrying privileges."

"Carrying privileges?"

"They let me take home all the food that was left over from supper." She stared across at John's angry face and shook her head. "I didn't ask either of them any questions." She shrugged. "I thought for sure it was Uncle George."

Ary glanced from the hired man to her sister.

"No John. Annie wasn't there. It was me and Pap and Uncle George and Addy. We was all over at Addy's place."

"Can you tell us what happened that night, Aramantha?" John's question was very careful.

"Well, none of us was feeling any pain. Pap always made me take a drink or two afore we went to Addison's house and then he always made me take one after I got there. But that wasn't nothing to what he and George drank." She held the baby with one arm and wiped her eyes with her other hand.

"I didn't want to worry you, sister. I knew you was working and getting food for our family and doing the best you could for us." She swiped at her eyes again. "'Sides, at first, I kinda thought our trips to Addison Fleury's house was fun. You know, like a party? Me and Uncle George used to sing some pretty songs."

"Oh God, John." Annie reached for the baby. "I don't think I want to hear this."

"Let's get it all sorted out, Annie, once and for all. Let Ary tell her story." John's voice held a warning note.

Ary nodded and went ahead with her story.

"Sometimes Addison would let me wear one of his grandmother's pretty colored, fancy party dresses. I guess his grandma was kind of little like me. That night I was wearing the one that was a funny kind of green that changed colors when you moved." She smiled, remembering the dress. "Changeable Taffety, was what Addy called it."

"She was *your* grandmother, too, Aramantha." Annie extended one hand toward her sister. "You had as much right to her dresses as old Addison did."

"She was my grandma, too?"

"She was *our* grandmother, child, your's and mine. Our mama's mama."

"Oh, I didn't know that, sister." Ary was silent for a moment. "Well, anyways I was sick and tired of him a messing around with me. The whole week I was feeling kind of sick anyways, throwing up most of the time."

"Pregnant." John breathed the word to no one in particular, his jaw set, his face hard.

"Uh huh. I guess so. Anyways, I wasn't having any of him and Addison decided he was going to *make* me do what he wanted." Ary

Scoundrels' Bargain 165

turned on the bench so she was facing Junior. "You remember what I told you?"

"Yeah. That you was trying to keep out of his reach." Junior's face and neck reddened with anger. "But he wouldn't leave you alone."

She turned back to look at John. "He wouldn't listen, John. He even tore his grandmother's pretty dress." Tears welled in her eyes. "I didn't think I could hurt him, him being such a big man and all. 'Course he was pretty drunk. Maybe that's why it happened."

"What happened?" John's whisper reverberated in Annie's head.

"I kept backing away and he kept coming after me. I shoved him real hard and he stumbled and kind of run backwards a ways and fell and hit his head on the edge of the mantle." Ary rubbed her hand across her eyes. "He was real quiet and I thought he had passed out like Pap and George so I went upstairs and went to sleep in his bed." She sniffed and reached for Junior's hand. "I guess I slept most of the next morning." Junior put a soothing husbandly arm about her shoulders.

Annie picked up the story. She felt as if she'd been suddenly thrown back to that nightmare tine.

"When I got home from the boarding house it was afternoon. George came in and told me he thought Pap and Addison was both dead. I drove Lucifer and the wagon over there and we gathered up Pap and Cousin Addison and whatever else we could get together that night and headed for the Territory. Them two was dead and I was afraid George would have to go to jail. He'd always lived in our little shack and he was the only decent acting man in our family and me and Aramantha loved him."

Ary nodded all through Annie's speech.

"Yeah. We wanted to get away from them there damned Fleury's so we just headed for the Territory." Ary cried openly now. "We was afraid they might take us all to jail."

"I told you where we buried Pap and Addy." Annie's words were dry. "I guess you don't need to hear nothing else, do you?"

"No. Nothing else. I can make a full report now." John stood. "I better ride on in to Guthrie this afternoon. I may not be back until tomorrow morning." He dug in his saddle bag for his dark woolen suit jacket. He shrugged it on and turned to Junior. "I'll try to get over to help you with your new place Trent, soon as I return."

"But what's going to happen to Aramantha?" Annie stood and grasped his arm. She felt chilled by the hard line of his jaw. His face looked as if it had been carved from angry stone. "What are you going to tell them?"

"The truth," he said and walked out the door.

* * *

Annie watched the tall rider astride the big horse, moving up over the ridge to lope down the trail that led to the house. John Wesley already. Her heart twirled with happiness. He'd only been gone a few hours. Maybe he'd decided to wait until morning to ride into Guthrie? Maybe he too had wished for a time alone with her as she had wished for time with him?

But the horse didn't look right. It didn't have the right gait. This horse was a plodder. The man didn't look right either. He was tall like John. He wore a black suitcoat like John's. He had broad shoulders like John's. But he wasn't John. She could just tell. The man was thinner than John. He didn't ride like John. She felt a tiny quiver of fear.

"I'll just be on the safe side," she said aloud. She stepped back into the kitchen and lifted Uncle George's long gun from the wooden pegs where it hung on the wall.

She stepped back outside and stared at the approaching rider on the slow horse. There was something familiar about the man.

When the visitor rode into the dooryard and doffed his black Stetson she recognized him. Her dancing partner! The one who had stood in for John while she was dreaming of dancing with the hired man. What was the man's name. Oh yes, he was the local undertaker, Farqhuar.

"Mr. Farqhuar. Howdy. Get on down off that horse and come inside. What brings you out so far into the country? Annie gestured hospitably toward the open kitchen door.

The pale quality of the man's skin made Annie peer at him more intently. He did look a little sick. Maybe he'd heard about her skill with herbs. As she watched he brushed his black coat and trousers with the black hat. His hand betrayed nervousness. Maybe a secret illness. He was awful skinny. His big stand-out ears were rimmed with pink.

Annie kept the smile on her face and gestured again toward the door. She stepped in ahead of him and rushed to hand the gun in its regular place.

"You come on in here, Mr. Farqhuar. I didn't recognize you for a minute there. Sit down." She turned to smile at him again.

He nodded without speaking.

"We had a few unwelcome intruders a few days ago so that's the reason for the gun. I sure wouldn't want you to think that you wasn't welcome on the Circle Twig."

Silently, the man ducked to enter the door and glanced around the room before taking the stool that had always been Uncle George's special place. He barely flinched at the sight of Mrs. Gulliver flopped in her usual place in the corner of the room then he looked away.

"How about a cup of tea, Mr. Farqhuar?" Annie darted to the stove. Well, hell, this man dealt with dead bodies all the time, a sleeping pig shouldn't overset him. Annie smiled at the snoring hog.

Scoundrels' Bargain

"Leroy." The man's voice had a strangely rasping quality, as if he didn't use words very often.

"What's that?"

"Leroy. That there's my first name, Miss Twig."

"Oh, call me Annie, Leroy, everybody does." She poised the tin pot above a tin cup. "Tea?" She looked to him for an answer. "This here is herb tea, not the regular store bought kind of tea. We like it right well on a hot day." He nodded. She poured. She set the cup on the table in front of him, then poured a cup for herself. "How's everything in the city of Guthrie?"

He made a slight sound that Annie thought might mean, "Everything was fine in Guthrie."

"What can I do for you, Mr. Far... Leroy?" She sat down on the bench at an angle across from him. He kept his gaze down as if he were afraid to look at her. He took a drink and raised the cup in a complimentary way.

"Mighty nice," he rasped. He cleared his throat and set his cup down on the table before he placed both his hands flat on the wooden table top, palm down, each motion deliberate and careful.

"Thanks." Annie drank and waited. "Was you maybe wanting some herbs or some help with a sickness or something?" If she didn't get this man talking they might be here 'til next winter, drinking and grunting at each other.

"Well, I was hoping to find Brother Matlock here. I understand he works hired hand for youall."

"Brother Matlock?" Annie had to forcibly squelch the giggles which tried to rise at his use of the term, "Brother," which John hated so much. "No, I'm real sorry. He's not here now. Could I give him a message for you?"

"You know I'm in the undertaking business in town?"

Annie nodded.

"Well, sometimes I'm in bad need of a preacher. I ain't so good at talking, myself." He stared down at the tin cup.

The silence grew long. Annie tried to jog him into speaking once more by saying, "Yes, Leroy?"

He started as if awakening from sleep. "And sometimes there is some of my customer's families don't go to church or don't know no preacher or there ain't no preacher available at that time. I was hoping I could get Brother Matlock to preach a funeral for me now and again." He allowed his gaze to rise to meet Annie's. "'Course, I'd pay him. Cash money. I hear he's a mighty good preacherman."

"The very best." Annie permitted herself to smile. "Well, Leroy, Brother Matlock is in Guthrie at this minute where he's tending to some business. Was you there, you could talk to him yourself about this." She expected the undertaker to rise and hurry back to town to try to find John Wesley, but the man continued to sit in silence. She laughed inwardly. She'd give a pretty penny to hear the undertaker's conversation with the big Pinkerton man.

"Was they something else you needed?"

"We danced pretty good together, Miss Annie."

"Oh, yes. We did. Wasn't that party nice? You're a real good dancer, Leroy."

"Well," He nodded. "Since then I been thinking I would come out and ask for permission to pay court to you, Miss Annie."

"Because we danced so well together?"

"Well, yes, that and other things, anyways, dancing nice together is as good a reason for hitching up as any other, I reckon." He closed his mouth and cleared his throat again as if he had said more than he was used to saying.

Bless this old boy's heart, Annie thought. He'd be a pretty good catch for any girl. He had a good business, he looked pretty strong and he sure wouldn't wear you out chattering all the time. She thought of Mary Broughton. Not many young single men ever came way out here. The girl was of an age to marry. Why not Mr. Farqhuar?

"You're thinking serious on marriage, are you, Leroy?"

"I am. I need me a wife and I was thinking your kind of business might fit in right well with mine, you with your midwifery skills and all." The red suffused his ears completely now and even began to venture onto his bony cheeks. "Excuse me for being so blunt, Miss Annie, but I done made up my mind to marry this year."

Annie rose and looked down at the man.

"I can't oblige you, Leroy. I ain't, that is, I'm not looking to marry, but I can do something even better for you. I ain't never going to leave the Circle Twig for marriage or anything else, but I can introduce you to the prettiest, nicest, sweetest young lady you would ever be likely to meet."

The man stood and looked at her with hope.

"Yes sir, Leroy, just let me get my mule and I'll take you on over to my neighbor's house. That'd be the Broughtons. Their oldest daughter, Mary, is apprenticing herself to me. Now there's your midwife for you, Leroy, and maybe your wife, too. In a few months she'll know as much about healing as I can teach her."

At the Broughton house, Annie was soon able to take her leave, as she saw the tall silent undertaker being drawn into the room by the friendly, talkative, Broughton family members. Grandma Broughton was patting the man's long skinny hand as Mary let Annie out the door to return home.

"Mary, you pay attention now. This man is worth thinking on. I believe he's a good man and for sure he's a good businessman... *and* he

Scoundrels' Bargain

needs a wife. He told me so himself." Annie touched Mary's cheek and then marched herself toward the still saddled Lucifer. Her mule greeted her with a clacking yellow smile.

Annie swung up into the saddle.

"I think I done right, Lucifer." Still, she couldn't help the twinge of self pity that rose within her. Every woman or girl she knew was falling in love and getting married. Everyone except herself.

At home she ate a lonesome supper and tried to read her mama's Bible a little before she turned in. She had always heard that the word of God was solacing and when she closed the book she felt at ease, but she still intuited loneliness sitting somewhere down there inside herself. When she replaced the book on the high shelf she touched the pig gently with the toe of her boot. Gulliver was pleasant company but she wasn't quite enough.

If only John were here.

Annie went to her own bed with only Wesley Ann to comfort her. After the baby slept Annie let the tears slide down her cheeks. Now nothing was the way she'd thought it would be. Nothing at all.

Here she was, alone except for the baby, and on the good bed and John was in Guthrie... probably making big plans on the telegraph line with his boss in Little Rock. Probably making plans to get himself and his rotten tin shield on back to Arkansas. Probably going on to other jobs without so much as a by-your-leave. Losing John was going to be almost as bad as old Calvin up and dying on her. She sniffed and patted the baby. At least he hadn't taken little Ary off to the jail.

The house seemed so empty, everything so quiet. Shocked at herself, Annie realized she was lonely. She'd never been lonely in her life... until now. She threw back the quilt, stood and padded into the kitchen. She picked up Mrs. Gulliver, who simply grunted from a deep sleep, and placed the little sow at the foot of the bed. That hog was a great consolation to her even if she couldn't fill all the empty places in Annie's heart. The pig turned over happily and burrowed into the covers.

Before she went back to sleep, the baby girl cuddled closer to Annie. With Mrs. Gulliver snoring at their feet, Annie patted Wesley Ann's back and tried to put her own mind on the far fence corner that needed to be shored up. She decided to spend the next morning there. Maybe the whole day if she needed to. She been just a child when she'd learned a valuable lesson. She'd found out that work was the best answer to scaring away all your troubles.

She thought of John's muscular arms. With him to help her she could probably have gotten that sagging fence corner right back up to snuff in a couple of hours. But he wasn't here. She didn't know if he'd ever be back on the Circle Twig again.

She let a tear slide down her cheek before she fell into restless sleep.

Chapter 24

In her dreams John floated above her and smiled down into Annie's face. He reached for her hand.

"Sure you don't need my help on that fence repair, darling?" He seemed to be pulling himself back to the ground using her hand as an anchoring post. Somehow it seemed bad manners to pay attention to his vague attempts to become earthbound so Annie kept her eyes slightly averted and she talked loudly so he would have something to hang on to.

"I can finish it up in about half an hour, then Lucifer and I'll scat on home." She nodded. "I'll whip us up a good supper before the young Trents go on to their new house."

She pulled her hand from his and felt her cheeks warming. She could feel him staring at her now that he was standing on the ground. Tonight. One more night with him. They'd have the bed, and no one but Mrs. Gulliver and the baby would be in the house with them. No use even thinking about the future. They'd have this one more night. In her dream she told herself that that was as far ahead as she could allow herself to look.

Still dreaming she pushed the enticing thoughts from her and turned quickly to climb on the mule.

"I'll see you at home later, John Wesley."

He moved closer to the animal. Lucifer's ears rolled backward but the animal didn't bare his teeth.

"See. Old Lucifer's getting used to you."

"Well, let's not test him." John moved back a step and raised his hand. "I'll see you at home." His amber eyes seemed to hold laughter and an unspoken promise.

Annie kicked Lucifer into a trot and her dream ride on the back of her mule seemed to last for the rest of her restless night.

When morning came Annie took the baby to its mother. At Aramantha's invitation, Annie looked the new little home over more carefully, inside and out, then after admiring the wooden floor and seeing what Ary had done to scrub down and fix up her little love nest she explained where she would be working on the fence line in case they needed her.

"I'll probably have to spend the whole morning over there. Why don't you kids come on over to the Circle Twig for dinner? We'll rustle up something until you've had a chance to lay in some supplies."

She swung up onto her mule, then just as she'd done in her dream, she rode Lucifer hard to the far back corner of the Circle Twig. When she swung down she patted his nose then let the animal wander without hobbles. He munched contently, untethered amongst the cottonwood trees while she strode to the fence line to begin work on the collapsing fence corner.

After a quick survey of the line she bent to study the main problem, a leaning, perhaps a rotten post at the corner. As she straightened from her survey she heard a small crack, the breaking of a twig under a heavy boot. She whirled and found herself encased in solid gray arms.

"Now Miss Twig," Henry Trent murmured, "I'm taking you home with me." He tightened his hold and motioned to his helper with his head. "Come on boy, and get her legs lashed up. She's a hellion and I want to see to it she ain't getting away from me this time."

The cowboy named Buell, moved forward hesitantly. "But boss. Hadn't you better...?"

Trent cut him off.

"Get over here and do what I say if you want to keep your job, compadre!"

Annie stood paralyzed within the clutches of the rancher. She smelled stale cigar each time he breathed. What was she going to do? She forced herself to stand silently, eyes closed. She had to think of a plan, a way to get away from this man. There was no one within miles, no one to hear her if she screamed. She had to come up with some sort of a plan.

She opened her eyes and looked directly into the triumphant gray gaze of the rancher.

"You don't need to bind me. I'll go quietly, Henry."

He smiled and nodded. "Reckon you realize there ain't nobody to hear you if you did scream your head off."

She nodded and lowered her lids again. She tried to look submissive even though her heart was pounding and wild rage tore at her insides. *This old bastard. She'd fix him.* She let her lashes sweep down over her eyes so he could not read her intent.

"Henry, you can let me go. I'll not make any trouble for you." She said the words in a soft girlish treble.

"Oh, no, Missy. I have your number now and I will keep a tight rein on you." Annie could feel his cold gray gaze on her face. "I'll have your legs bound and you'll ride up on my horse without creating a disturbance."

Annie nodded as if she were conquered.

"Could I ride my own mule?"

"No indeed, little lady. You'll be riding with me on Big Gray." Trent once again gestured to his hired hand and the man twisted a short piece of rope around Annie's ankles. She closed her eyes and pretended nothing

Scoundrels' Bargain 173

was happening to her. Somewhere along the way, or later in the old man's house, she'd have her turn. She'd just have to be ready for the opportunity.

"Well, iffen I'm going to be staying at your place could your man here lead my mule? I hate to just leave him out here all by himself."

She glanced up at Henry's face. She could see that he thought the idea reasonable but he seemed to be turning her request over in his mind.

"Once you're on my horse you'll ride peaceably with me?"

"What else can I do?" She nodded again.

"Where is your animal?"

She motioned with her head toward the copse of trees nearby.

"Is he hobbled?"

"No. He'll come iffen I call him."

Trent was silent for another moment.

"Very well then, Miss Annie. Call your mule and let us be off. You've wasted too much of my time already."

Annie turned her head, thankful for a reason to be breathing out of the line of the man's stale cigar emanations.

"Hoo, Boy. Lucifer. Come on, boy. Hoo boy, hoo." She made her voice as loud and harsh as she was able. She picked up the sound of an answering bray and tried to relax. Now. There was nothing else she could do but stay ready and see what she could do later.

When Lucifer had come within a few yards of where Annie and Henry Trent and the cowboy were standing, the mule stopped and surveyed them. It was as if the animal were deciding what to do next.

Henry glanced at Lucifer and shouted at his helper.

"Well, Buell, what are you waiting for? Go get the stupid animal and let's get on with it."

The man stepped toward Lucifer and the mule rotated his ears backward. The man stopped.

"What's wrong, now?"

"Mr. Trent, that mule is a putting his ears back."

"So?"

"I ain't going near no mule what's putting his ears back."

"Well, never mind the mule. Help me get Miss Twig up on the horse." Trent released Annie to the arms of the waiting cowpoke then swung himself up onto the big gray animal. He nodded to the man who lifted Annie to the front of his saddle. Again Annie was besieged with the used smoke of his breath. His right arm crushed her into his solid body. He gave a grunt of satisfaction.

"My mule, Henry..." Annie made her voice a plaint.

"We'll have no more discussion of the mule. If he will follow, fine. If not, fine. Mules are far down on the list of my current interests, Miss

Annie. Let us not trouble ourselves with this poor man's excuse for a horse."

"Well, he's a good mule. You got no call to insult him."

Trent grunted and set the big gray horse into motion. Annie tried to keep herself apart from the man but his determined embrace allowed not even a tiny space between them.

Finally she allowed herself to slump against his fierce hold on her... but she let neither her mind nor her searching gaze relax. She was aware that Lucifer was following at a distance because she heard him making the noises he always made when he was irritated. Somehow that fact comforted her.

At the Trent place Henry had the jug eared cowpoke help him carry her into the house through the front door. He really did have wood floors. She tried to see as much as she could. Everything looked new and expensive. She could hear their heels tap and their spurs jingle against the shiny floor.

Henry and his helper took her into another room and laid her on her back on the fancy feather bed then the old man walked to stand at the tall footboard to look her over. He dismissed the hired man. She glanced from side to side. She was lying on a fancy, embroidered silk and velvet crazy quilt. The high bed was against the east wall of a square room with several pieces of heavy, dark wooden furniture in it. One wall held a window covered with off white lace curtains. Or maybe they were that "ecru" color John had told them about, like Ary's pale, creamy silk dress.

"What are you going to do to me, Henry?"

"What I've been wanting to do since I first met you, Miss Annie." He nodded and ran his tongue across his thin lips. "You are a very pleasant challenge, my dear. I plan to savor the experience." He cleared his throat. "I think that after you've experienced what I have to offer you'll be willing to stay here of your own volition."

Own volition. That must mean I'll stay here because I want to., Annie explained to herself and she silently gave her answer, *I'll stay iffen I have to. Henry Trent, but I'm never going to want to.*

"Henry what's that stuff covering up the boards on all your walls? That gray stuff?"

"That's paper, my dear. Builder's paper. The best and heaviest to be had in Guthrie." He stepped to the right a few feet and ran his hand down the gray clad walls. "Not exactly European wallpaper, but more civilized than bare boards, don't you think?"

"It looks like the stuff that wasps spit up to make their nests out of, Henry, if you can call that civilized."

Scoundrels' Bargain

His florid face reddened a touch more.

"I'll have to teach you to keep a civil tongue in your head, my girl." He stepped closer to look directly down at her.

"Henry, it's going to be a shock to you when you get some of that European wallpaper and you find out it don't come in *gray*." She stared up at him. "Say, could you untie me now? I got to go outside. I need to relieve myself."

"I ain't listening to none of that. You're here to stay, girlie." He walked to stand close to the footboard again. He smiled coldly down at her. "I'm going to see that you learn to love this house and everything in it."

Annie turned away from him and onto her side then curled herself into a circle that bespoke pain. She groaned softly and looked back at him.

"Henry, I got to go."

"You little wildcat." She could see the thin smile appear. "You'd try any trick to get your way, wouldn't you?"

"Well, I don't know about you Henry, but I can't do nothing when my guts are telling me that they have the call of nature." She tightened the circle of her body and groaned again. "I couldn't enjoy *anything* right now, not feeling the way I do."

"Oh, very well, girl." Annie could hear the annoyance in his tone. "I have been led to understand that females have less control over such things." He stayed silent a second. "The outhouse is several yards from the back of the house."

"I'll just be a minute." Annie straightened and turned so her bonds could be loosened. "I'll be right back."

"Now, now, Miss Annie," His chuckle sounded as gray and filmy as cigar smoke. "You needn't think me such a fool. I will, of course, go with you on your journey toward relief." The almost silent laughter again drifted about the room. "Who knows? Perhaps the whole thing will turn out to be somewhat titillating."

What did he mean by that? Something to do with her tits? She knew whatever it was wasn't good. Annie let the air out of her chest in a long sigh of resignation.

"Well, you'll have to help me get up and then take these ropes off me."

He reached to pull her to a sitting position.

"I'll take the rope from your legs and then at the outhouse I'll remove your arm restraints." Again he chuckled with almost no sound. "You see, I ain't taking no chances with you, Miss."

What am I going to do now? She asked herself the question but no answers came. *Gotta think of something.* She sat, limp and helpless, in the possession of this crazy old gray devil and there was nothing she could do.

Might as well go on out to his old privy. Better than staying on his old bed, she told herself.

During the walk to the outhouse, Annie's head was filled with thoughts bumping into each other, twisting, turning, but no answer, no plan came. Ary and Junior knew where she'd been working but they wouldn't worry about her, not for a long time. And John was gone.

She felt an instant flare of anger at the thought of his absence. If he hadn't been gone she wouldn't have been out in the field at all or she wouldn't have been alone at any rate. She shook her head and let the anger slip from her. Nah. It wasn't his fault. He'd sure warned her about old Henry. Now, everything was up to her. She'd have to figure out a way to help herself, somehow. She had to get away from here.

From the corner of her eyes she glimpsed a dark figure standing under the blackjacks. Lucifer. One of the ranch hands appeared as if curious as to what his boss was doing. Suddenly, she knew what she had to do.

Just at the open door of the small building she turned dutifully, head bowed in submission, waiting to feel the rope slip away. As soon as her hands were freed she raised her head and shouted. Immediately Henry Trent grasped her again in a tight embrace. She screamed defiance.

"Hoo Lucifer." Annie roared the words. "Get 'em boy. Come on, Baby. Help me, boy." Henry snarled and fumbled with the rope to try to hold her with one hand and tie her with the other. She could hear the pounding of the mule's hooves, his teeth clashing in warning. she twisted in Henry's arms to see what the mule was doing. "Hoo, boy."

"Shut up." Henry dropped the rope and slapped her with his free hand.

Lucifer bared his teeth and sidled up closer to where Henry Trent still held Annie.

"Help, Lucifer. Help!" Annie screamed again.

"Shut up, you little virago." Trent turned his eyes toward the nearby cowboy. "You there, kill that mule. Hurry up."

"I can't. I ain't got no gun with me."

"Run him off then."

"I ain't getting near him, boss. He looks like some kind of a devil mule."

Lucifer clacked his yellow teeth more loudly and sidled a bit closer, ears flattened back on his head. The hired hand backed several yards away from Henry and his prisoner.

"You coward. Pull my gun out of my holster and shoot that damned mule."

"I'm going to go get help, boss." With those words the cowhand turned and sprinted toward the ranch bunkhouse.

"Get him, boy!" Annie began to struggle in earnest. She kicked and twisted to break Henry Trent's grasp.

"I'll kill that damned mule." The rancher used one hand to reach toward his pistol.

Annie redoubled her efforts and her shouts. Lucifer pranced behind the struggling couple.

The animal's hard head ducked and the yellow teeth clacked once, then the man screamed. Before he could pull his gun from the leather holster, Annie drew her knee back then lifted it to connect with the rancher's private parts. Trent screamed again and bent forward cradling himself. "Oh, God. I'm killed." Annie yanked completely away from her captor and as if that were a cue, Lucifer turned his hind quarters to the suffering man and kicked him with both hooves, propelling Henry Trent forward several feet onto the ground, face down.

The rancher shouted an incoherent sound, then slumped silently into the wet grass.

Annie ran to take Lucifer's reins. She whispered and patted the animal to keep him from finishing the job by stamping his sharp hooves across the rancher's unconscious form.

Fear that the Trent hirelings would burst out of the bunkhouse at any minute made her try to drag the heavy rancher toward a nearby bush. She had to make them think they'd both gone back into the house.

She felt torn. She couldn't just go off and leave the old man like this. She was supposed to be the neighborhood's granny woman. It was her duty to help if someone was hurt.

She tugged on his arm a bit harder. If she could just hide the old man she could run and get Junior to come and take care of his father. A voice just behind her left shoulder froze her in place.

"Old Henry hasn't learned his lesson yet?" John's voice was mild. "He should know by now that he'll never be a match for Miss Annie Twig."

"Oh, John. Am I glad to see you!" She felt happiness radiating throughout her body. "I was going to go get Junior to take care of his daddy. I think he might be hurt bad."

"Only in his pride, I'd imagine, Annie Lee. I'll just take the old boy off your hands, sweetheart, but I won't take him to his son. You get on Lucifer and ride to Junior and Ary's place. Stay there. I'll be back but our Mr. Henry Trent has just bought himself a ticket to jail."

"I thought you couldn't put people in jail?"

"Well, wasn't that our bargain, darling? That you wouldn't tell the whole truth and neither would I? The truth is, I can put people in jail and so can you. It's called 'citizen's arrest.'" He chuckled. "Of course, my badge doesn't hurt." He raised his gaze to the nearby bunkhouse and rested his hand on his holster.

The men stepping out of the building behind Buell seemed more curious than angry.

"Annie, toss me that rope that that bastard was using on you." He spoke without looking at her, his line of vision never turned away from the ranch hands. The cowpoke who had helped Trent kidnap her seemed to speak for all of them.

"None of us ain't in favor of stealing no women, mister. You go ahead and do whatever it was you was of a mind to do. We won't try to stop you."

"Good." John kept his hand on his holster. "If one of you would be so good as to bring Mr. Trent's gray out here and if someone else would boost Mr. Trent up on the horse's back before tying his hands, I'd be very much obliged." He turned the brown gaze on her and it warmed with promise for later. "Will you be all right?"

Annie nodded and clambered up onto Lucifer. John was here. He was taking Henry to town. *Oh hell!* She felt a stab of disappointment. He probably wouldn't be home tonight again neither, but just the same, everything would be all right. She set the prancing animal onto the road toward home and she didn't look back.

She patted and praised the strutting mule every step of their way toward the Circle Twig.

Chapter 25

"Well, now I know the truth, ma'am. When I'm not here this crazy pig is the one who keeps you company in your bed?"

Annie sat up straight amongst the bedclothes. Mrs. Gulliver raised her head, snorted herself awake, then struggled to her feet to trot across the quilts so she could jump down to speak to her favorite person.

"Ouch. Watch them sharp hooves, girl. You just stepped on my ankle." Annie raised her foot to sooth the injured part. She stared up at the tall handsome man in the doorway. She knew how Mrs. Gulliver felt. She was so glad to see him that she wanted to run and rub against him, too.

"Her babies are well beyond their due date, I believe." John smiled as he bent to scratch behind the happy pig's ear.

Annie's heart leaped in her chest. He was here! She wasn't dreaming.

"I think the little sow was faking, or the Broughtons were mistaken." Annie pulled the quilt up to her neckline. "What time is it? It's awful early, isn't it?"

"It's not early enough for me, Miss Annie. I've ridden like the very devil to get back to you." He smiled again. His eyes were molten bronze. "You're beautiful even when you've just been awakened."

"You want some tea?" Annie ran her fingers through her hair. She pushed past the smiling man to hurry to the water bucket. She poured water into the tin hand basin and tossed cold water in her face. With a tin cup of water in hand she stepped to the back door to use her twig to clean her teeth. She stepped back inside and dried her face and hands on the flour sack towel before turning back to the waiting man. She took a hesitant step toward him.

"John Wesley. I'm so glad to see you. What happened to...? Did he...? Is everything all right?"

"Oh, yes. Old Henry Trent is sitting in a cell in Guthrie. Says he's not talking... which is fine with me. I'll let the local law take care of the bastard."

"He wasn't hurt really bad, was he?" Annie felt torn in two ways... she wanted the old man to be all right but she wanted him to feel punished. Maybe John had the right of it. Let the law take care of the rancher. He'd asked for everything he'd received! She put Henry Trent out of her mind.

"You want breakfast?" She opened the stove ready to start the fire. She stared at John. He had such a strange look on his face. His amber eyes seemed to be asking her something or telling her something. He opened his lips as if ready to make an important announcement but he closed them again and nodded. Strange, she thought, strange how brown eyes can look so different all the time.

"Yes. Tea would be nice."

"I'll start the fire then I'll get dressed and get us some breakfast."

"Honey, never mind the fire or the tea." He rose to his toes then rocked back on his heels. "Why don't you go put on the blue striped thing. Your mother's dress. And the necklace and earbobs." He nodded to emphasize his words.

"My dress? How come?" She searched his face for more information.

"I want you to go into town with me."

"Into town?" Anxiety raised the timbre of her voice. "Do I have to go make a complaint or something?"

"Well, yes. You'll have to file against Henry Trent."

"File?"

"Yes. At the jail." He made a scatting motion with his hands. "Go get dressed. We'll stop by and get the Junior Trents and then we'll all head toward town."

On the way out Annie pulled the rope on the school bell that had been donated to the Sunday School by Mr. Smith. She raised her chin and listened as the last of the sound died away.

"We have to get serious about our Sunday School, John. We have to start up again. We haven't heard any lessons from you lately and everyone thinks you're the best preacher they ever heard."

"Annie, Annie." John shook his head and laughed.

"It's true, John Wesley." She pulled on the rope once more to wait until the clanging was over. "You weren't here when Mr. Farqhuar, the undertaker, rode through last week. He was looking for you to help him with a funeral."

"Now Annie. What was Farqhuar really doing way out here?"

"He said he wanted you to preach a funeral..."

"And..."

"And..." She giggled. "He said he wanted to ask for permission to court me."

"Who was he going to ask? Me?"

"I don't know. I guess so." She smiled and shoved Mrs. Gulliver out onto the path toward the pole barn. "I told him I reckoned not."

"Hmph." He kept his horse as close to Lucifer as possible on their ride toward the Junior Trent family's little house.

On the road toward town all four kept silent. Soon Ary and Junior and Wesley Ann, riding in the mule driven wagon had lagged far behind Annie and John.

Scoundrels' Bargain

John stopped his horse and gestured to Annie to pull Lucifer up, too. He pointed.

"Up ahead a few miles is the Widow Stanfield's charming cottage. We'll stop there."

"What's going on, John Wesley Matlock?"

"Mrs. Stanfield has some things for you. We'll get married there and she's going to let us stay several nights in her bedroom. She will go on to Guthrie with Junior and Ary for a visit with her daughter there."

"What did you say?"

"I said Mrs. Stanfield has something for you."

"No, no. That other thing."

"She's going to Guthrie with Ary and Junior so she can visit with her family?"

"John!"

"Will you marry me, Miss Annie?" He smiled widely. "At the Widow's house? Legally? No fly-by-night preachers for us. We'll be married by a real judge from Guthrie. I made sure of his credentials."

"You want to marry me?"

"I do."

"You really want to marry me?"

"I think I'd better get you into harness as Mrs. Matlock before some other old boy spirits you away from me."

"Do Ary and Junior know what's happening?"

"Yes. I suggested to Junior that he and Ary could also get their vows made a bit more legal today, as well. Get their papers, so to speak."

"I thought you'd be going back to Little Rock, as soon as you could, John."

"I suppose I must go back in a few days to get all the Fleury family business settled. Do you want to go with me?"

"I ain't... am not, ever going back to Arkansas."

"I thought you'd say that but I wanted us well and truly married before I ever leave you again."

John clicked at his mount and Annie kicked her spotted mule into motion. They rode in silence for a few more miles.

"Annie, there is something you need to know. Little Wesley Ann is undoubtedly going to come into a bit of money and I'm going to suggest that you should be the one to administer her estate. Nothing against Ju...uh, Trent and Aramantha, but they are almost children themselves. I don't think Ary would mind, do you?"

Annie shook her head.

"All of Fleury's material goods will be going to Wesley Ann as Addison Fleury's heir."

"None of us is ever going back to that house."

"I understand, but we want Wesley to have a good start in life, don't we?"

Annie nodded, her eyes lowered, her head bowed in thought.

"If you want, John, you can ship her all the things that they tell you was our grandma's and just let the Fleury's have the house and the land and the rest of Addison's stuff. If there is any money, I'll take that and keep it in the bank in Guthrie for her until she grows up." She smiled almost shyly at him. "I reckon if we get married you'll have to help me take care of all Wesley Ann's business, won't you?"

John nodded and stretched his hand toward hers.

"I'm not sure you should give away the baby's heritage so easily, Annie."

"I don't want none... any, of his stuff."

"We're talking about an inheritance for the baby, not for you, darling."

Annie nodded.

"I hope you'll trust me to do the right thing, sweetheart. I love the little girl, too, you know." He clicked at his horse. "We'll talk more about what we should do about Wesley's inheritance a little later, okay? After we're married. Right now marriage... to you, is what I have on my mind."

The widow greeted John before she embraced Annie. Almost at once she drew Annie into the bedroom for a private talk.

"I'm so glad you didn't marry that Henry Trent, Annie. He might be the richest rancher around but he seems poor in spirit to me." She pulled Annie close to her motherly bosom then stepped back to look into Annie's face. "Now, this John, this lawman, he will never be dull but he will never be cruel, either. You made the right choice."

"Thanks Mrs. Stanfield."

"I'm *giving* you my wedding slippers this time, my girl." She held up one hand to forestall Annie's protest. "And you may take your choice of whichever dress you want to wear for your wedding, my dear."

When Annie appeared in the doorway wearing the black velvet and lace dress she'd tried on weeks earlier, on the day before she'd gone to the ball, John gasped, rose from his chair and stood staring. The official from town stood also, his mouth dropped open.

Her hair curled about her face and the longer strands in back were twisted into a figure eight knot, what the widow called a "Psyche knot," on top. To John her hair looked like moonlight itself, silvery gold and platinum fire. The platinum necklace had been woven around the top knot with the heart gleaming against the bright edifice of her hair. The earbobs and the necklace sent out a blue fire that matched the blue fire of her eyes. Her pale shoulders rose like those of a creamy marble statue from the low cut black velvet folds of the dress.

"Oh, Annie." He felt rooted to the spot. She was the most entrancing sight he'd ever beheld. "My very own Annie." His whispered words were heard by everyone in the room.

Junior's and Aramantha's knock broke the tension in the parlor and Annie hurried to welcome them and to hug her little sister, to tell her she was marrying John, to explain that now John would truly be Wesley Ann's uncle, to introduce them to the Widow Stanfield.

Within minutes, the two couples and the child, sound asleep in the widow's arms, were all standing before the official from Guthrie.

Annie never was able to remember exactly what the judge had said to them other than the last part. "By the powers vested in me by the United States Government and the Territory of Oklahoma, I now pronounce each of you man and wife. You young men may kiss your brides."

John's kiss was light and sweet, a quick warm brush of those beautifully sculpted lips against her own. A promise for later, she knew. The most thrilling moment of all came when she signed the marriage certificate, "Annie Lee Twig Matlock."

After signing, she and Ary turned to look at each other. They each understood what the other was thinking. Now they'd have some legal papers of their own to put in the box with their mama's wedding certificate and her wedding ring. After they'd congratulated each other, the Widow handed the sleeping baby to Aramantha so she could hurry into the kitchen to see to the wedding refreshments.

The sisters held out their hands, side by side to compare their wedding rings. Annie's silvery looking, like the metal in her necklace, Aramantha's a circle of gold.

"Junior told me that John was bringing a ring from town just for me. I guess he told John what kind of wedding ring he wanted me to have." Ary switched Wesley Ann to her other arm. "Ain't it pretty, Annie? Look at the little rosebuds all along the edges."

"It is beautiful, Aramantha." She held up her own hand so the twisted circlet of platinum gleamed in the light from the window. For a moment a flash of memory of their days in Van Buren rose behind her eyes. Their lives were so much better now... a thousand times better than they ever would have been had they stayed there in Arkansas.

Yes. She'd done the right thing. "I think we're two lucky Twig girls, don't you?"

"Yeah, we are." The younger girl lowered her voice to almost a whisper. "Say, sister, do you suppose Uncle George and maybe Mama knows what we all did here today?"

"Aye God, as Uncle George would say, I think they're *both* smiling down on us from heaven, honey, and now he's got sober, maybe old Pap, too." Blue eyes met blue eyes as they mutually banished the apparition of Addison Fleurey to his own hell.

After light-bread sandwiches and homemade dill pickles and cake and real coffee in the widow's kitchen, John and Junior helped the Widow Stanfield and her large carpet bag portmanteau into the Trent's wagon and the younger couple with their passenger, set out for their last few miles toward Guthrie. The judge rode along with the Trents in his own buggy, "Just to be sociable." he'd explained.

"I think that old judge has eyes for the Widow." Annie whispered.

"I agree." She loved hearing the deep rich chuckle and knowing that it came from her very own husband.

In another few minutes Annie and John had waved everyone out of sight and John had gently closed the front door. In the Widow Stanfield's parlor they faced each other at last.

John stretched and yawned and let his amber gaze move over every inch of his smiling new bride.

"I know it's just barely noon, yet, Mrs. Matlock, but I feel a powerful need to find that featherbed that the widow so very kindly gave us permission to use." He gestured toward the bedroom. "Aren't you feeling a bit sleepy, too, sweetheart?"

Color rose in her cheeks and she nodded. He swept her up in his arms and carried her into their borrowed honeymoon home.

John placed Annie in the center of the plump white sheeted bed as if she were a precious breakable. He looked down at her and she raised her arms to welcome him. He removed his coat and tie and the high collar and tossed them onto the low chest by the window before he lay down beside her. He faced her and stared into the blue of her eyes, the blue of a stormy Oklahoma Territorial sky.

"I can't believe I'm married." Annie whispered.

"I never thought I'd take on the double harness, either." He lifted his hand to smooth the platinum curls back from her face.

"Are you sorry?"

"Not now. I doubt I ever will be, Annie Lee." He moved just a bit closer to her. "I've never been bored when I've been with you."

Annie put her hand on John's chest.

Scoundrels' Bargain 185

"What should I do, now? I mean, should I take off my dress or something?" She twisted her fingers in the placket of his white shirt. "Or should I undress you first?" She grinned. "What do married people do?"

"Either would be very nice, wife."

"Just think. We got our whole lives ahead of us. We don't need to hurry what we're doing, nor hide out, nor sneak around nor anything like that." She twisted to her side to sit up and get a better look at her new husband, her smart, new, *educated* husband. On that very moment, Annie resolved to learn to match him, in both speech and demeanor. She'd listen and she'd learn from this man, all during the time she was enjoying him. She'd use him as her model of all that was right and proper and educated.

"Yes, darling, I believe we're going to see that marriage does have its advantages." He pushed her back onto the featherbed again and settled on his side next to her, face to face.

Dark eyes stared into blue.

Annie felt as if she were drowning in his gaze. She knew that if it were night she might see flecks of golden fire within the dark shimmering, flecks stolen from a lamp or a hearth fire. Now, in this lambent afternoon light his eyes' darkness displayed compelling velvety pools of sensuality. He pulled her close and his mouth took hers. Their first real married kiss was deep and sweet and unhurried. *They had all the time in the world.*

John pushed the black velvet from her shoulder and bent to kiss the rounded angle of white smoothness.

"You are stunningly beautiful in this black velvet thing. Your skin is silken alabaster." His hand caressed the black velvet covering her breasts. Annie felt her nipples harden, her breasts swell. The strange, new sensations aroused by his slow stroking set her heart pounding in her throat. Her gasps of pleasure seemed to drive him to farther explorations. She wanted to keep her eyes open so she wouldn't miss a precious moment but in spite of herself her eyes closed. She allowed herself to sink into the heated darkness of being loved by her new husband.

He pressed and fondled her, stroking first one breast, then the other. His fingers seemed to seek out, to know all her secret places. They moved from her breast to trace the line of her waist then outlined the curve of her hip. He grasped her buttocks and pulled her close.

"I'll just unbutton this quite lovely wedding dress," he whispered in her ear, then turned her gently onto her stomach. "Let me do all the work." She let her eyes stay closed so she could enjoy the delicate touch of her new husband's hands as he undressed her.

This man belonged to her now and she belonged to him. Dreams she'd never known she had had were now being fulfilled by the moment. At the release of the last tiny jet button, his lips kissed her bare skin at that very spot. Annie groaned with pleasure. He made a slow ladder of kisses from the bottom of the opened placket straight up her backbone to the skin just below her hair, then around to her ear.

"I'm going to slide this sweet frock off you now." He whispered the words before he turned her again. He slowly, slowly turned the black dress down from her shoulders. Soon both breasts stood forth revealed. He bent and kissed each rosy peak. Annie gasped and reached to hold him but he kept himself just out of reach.

"More," she breathed.

He smiled down at her.

"Not just yet, my darling. I'm enjoying looking my fill at my ivory lady." He continued the rolling down of the dress and tugged it over her hips and off completely. "Oh, my God, exactly nothing underneath. You naughty girl... you're wearing not even a scrap of underclothing." He chuckled and kissed her navel, then trailed kisses down the front of her to the blonde bush between her legs.

Annie felt a warming flush creep from her head down to her toes.

"I didn't *have* a corset or a corset cover or a petticoat or nothing. The Widow said I looked better naked in the dress than lots of other women could with fancy underclothes."

"She was so right." John kneed his way back onto the featherbed until he was once again crouched above her.

"What about you? You're still covered up." She put her hand into the waistband of his trouser and yanked. "Here I am... naked as a baby jaybird and you're still wearing enough clothing to go out in polite society."

John smiled down at her as he silently unbuttoned his own shirt and tossed it aside. Annie loved her first real daytime look at the muscular chest and the broad shoulders of her own live statue. She placed her palms flat against his chest muscles and smoothed easy circles. She observed his reactions through half closed lashes. He had thrown his head back, eyes closed, sculptured lips open. He panted as if he could not get enough oxygen.

"Trousers, John." She let the words drift into the air. "Boots, too, please."

He nodded and stood again. At the bedside he hurriedly tore off his boots and socks and then the black woolen suit trousers. Last he unbuttoned his fashionable thin cotton BVD's and stepped out of them. Once more he stared down at her and Annie let her startled gaze roam over every inch of him. His upright member was larger than she remembered. Rigid, it dipped and twirled toward her as if greeting her. Oh. He was a magnificent animal... her magnificent animal. She opened her arms again.

He joined her on the bed and slid one arm beneath her and put the other around her to pull her close. His lips again claimed hers, his mouth loving and demanding. The taste of him thrilled her, set her on fire as she allowed her own lips and tongue to explore his. So good. Almost fainting with desire, she felt such a powerful hunger to feel him inside her that she groaned aloud.

"Yes, my love," his husky voice matched her need. "Let's not wait." He moved his hands under her buttocks and lifted her to meet his thrust. She cried out as she arched greedily to meet him. His weight sank them deep into the Widow's billowing white featherbed. Annie felt as if she were pressed into a soft white cloud.

"We're in Heaven on a cloud." Annie murmured as pure pleasure radiated throughout her body.

"You're my Heaven, darling." John lifted himself for yet another assault. "So good. So good."

She clung to him and writhed against the heated sweetness of him buried within her. She trembled with the quick, hard explosion of the almost painful sweetness of her climax. The world tipped and fell, and she with it. So, this was lovemaking with her husband! She now had her own glorious living statue, her magnificent man. She clutched him close with hands, lips and body, all still trembling from the glorious upheaval he'd caused within her.

He surrendered to her importuning moan and in the same instant of her cry of pleasure he spilled the seed of his manhood into her. He fell to one side, without allowing a separation between their bodies.

"Marriage is going to agree with me, Miss Annie." He breathed heavily and in the next instant his eyes closed. "Miss Annie Lee Twig," he murmured and he was asleep. Annie smiled and nestled against his shoulder.

"Just call me Annie... Annie Matlock," she answered.

EPILOG
November 1907

"Papa's going to be preaching today, boys. I want both of you to be on your very best behavior." Annie Lee Twig Matlock smoothed the silky blond curls of her oldest boy. "You hear me, Johnny Wesley?" She smiled into the eight-year-old's brown eyes. So like his father. She wanted to hug him to her but she knew he would be embarrassed by such a motherly display. He was the most dignified of the two.

The last time she'd hugged him he'd grunted and said, "Why do girls always want to hug you?"

"And just who are these girls who always want to hug you? Are those youngest Broughton girls sweet on you?" He'd looked at her as if to say, "How'd you know?"

She turned to the seven-year-old. His black curls tumbled down onto his forehead just the way his father's curls always did.

"Now Georgie Twig," She looked into replicas of her own blue eyes. Mischief danced in their depths. "This is a really important occasion, dear. Mind now." She pulled both boys into a quick embrace. Even Johnny would put up with a three person hug if it weren't too long.

"How come papa's preaching again today, mama?" Johnny unbuttoned the top button of his shirt which she had just finished buttoning.

"Our regular preacher can't come because he's going to be part of the assembly for the declaration of statehood. Our very own preacher will be standing right on the steps of the capitol building."

"I hate it when everybody calls Papa, 'Brother Matlock.'" George ran his shirt sleeve under his nose.

"And Papa don't like it neither!" Johnny declared.

"Doesn't." Annie's correction came almost absent mindedly.

"Doesn't what?"

"Papa *doesn't* like to be called 'Brother Matlock.'"

"Yeah. That's what I said."

Annie laughed as if she had a secret. She had to keep after them with their speech. After herself, too. If she didn't they'd both grow up sounding like them Broughton kids. Both boys stared up at her waiting for her explanation.

"Maybe you'd better ask Papa about his preaching. Did you know he was our first preacher at our very first church right here on the Circle Twig?"

Solemn blue eyes and questioning brown eyes silently asked for more of the story.

In the buggy she kept them entertained with the story of that long ago fistfight at the Methodist Sunday School and Dancing Academy. She acted out the parts that both Uncle George and their Papa John Wesley Matlock, had played. Their father grunted a few times but before they got to church he was chuckling along with the three of them.

After the singing, Annie handed Johnny, on her right and George on her left, a small slate and a slate pencil before their father began his sermon. "Remember, you have to be quiet. You can draw pictures if church seems too long." When George took a quick peek at the pew behind them she dug her elbow into his side. "No looking back. No giggling."

"I was just looking at Aunt Ary."

Annie took her own quick glance at her sister's family. Wesley Ann had all five of the little redheaded Trents sitting in a well behaved, silent row. At some distance, at the very end of the pew, Ary snuggled close to Junior Trent and he had his arm around the smiling young woman as if they were a young couple just newly courting. Ary gave her big sister a tiny wave.

Grandma Broughton and the two youngest Broughton girls occupied the bench between the Trents and their growing brood. Annie turned in the other direction to smile at Mary Broughton and her two little jug-eared Farqhuars who sat in the pew across from her. Mary's husband must be preparing a body this morning, Annie thought. A certain proprietary feeling rushed through Annie. That particular marriage had worked out real well.

Annie glanced at others across the congregation. Sunday mornings were always so pleasant she thought. Everyone around her looked to be in a most agreeably combed out and starched up Sunday mood.

John stepped up to the pulpit and began his sermon with the words, "Well, folks, my wife seems to have roped me into preaching one more sermon."

Grandma Broughton tapped Annie on the shoulder and spoke loudly enough to be heard at least seven rows away. "My lands Annie, ain't he just the best talker ever? I always did say your John was the finest preacher I done ever heard."

Annie suppressed her smile as she turned forward to catch the eye of 'Brother Matlock' before he began to speak. She winked. He smiled broadly down at her from the pulpit as he launched into his sermon on the theme taken from Proverbs, *A good woman's price is far above rubies.*

Ah... how she loved that man.

Scoundrels' Bargain is dedicated to the memory of Mr. James Camp, who spent many hours talking with me about mule behavior and psychology.

Peggy Fielding

Peggy Fielding is an Oklahoman who spent several years outside the USA in Cuba, Japan and the Republic of the Philippines. She now lives in Tulsa, Oklahoma where she is a teacher and writer of both fiction and nonfiction. Many of her former students have gone on to publish short stories, articles and more than 350 books. Fielding has published hundreds of articles and short stories, several nonfiction books and has sold both contemporary and historical novels. She belongs to Romance Writers of America, The Author's Guild, Oklahoma Writers Federation, Inc., Oklahoma Mystery Writers and the Tulsa NightWriters. Visit Fielding's web site: www.peggyfielding.com